also by Nicolas Freeling

Fiction

LOVE IN AMSTERDAM

BECAUSE OF THE CATS

GUN BEFORE BUTTER

VALPARAISO

DOUBLE BARREL

CRIMINAL CONVERSATION

THE KING OF THE RAINY COUNTRY

THE DRESDEN GREEN

STRIKE OUT WHERE NOT APPLICABLE

THIS IS THE CASTLE

TSING-BOUM

OVER THE HIGH SIDE

A LONG SILENCE

DRESSING OF DIAMOND

WHAT ARE THE BUGLES BLOWING FOR?

LAKE ISLE

GADGET

THE NIGHT LORDS

THE WIDOW

CASTANG'S CITY

ONE DAMN THING AFTER ANOTHER

WOLFNIGHT

THE BACK OF THE NORTH WIND

NO PART IN YOUR DEATH

A CITY SOLITARY

COLD IRON

LADY MACBETH

NOT AS FAR AS VELMA

SAND CASTLES

Non-fiction

KITCHEN BOOK

COOKBOOK

THOSE IN PERIL

NICOLAS FREELING

THE MYSTERIOUS PRESS
New York · Tokyo · Sweden · Milan
Published by Warner Books

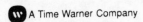 A Time Warner Company

First published in Great Britain
by Andre Deutsch Limited
105–106 Great Russell Street London WC1B 3LJ.

Mysterious Press books are published by
Warner Books, Inc., 666 Fifth Avenue, New York, NY 10103

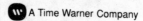 A Time Warner Company

The Mysterious Press name and logo are trademarks of Warner Books, Inc.

Printed in the United States of America
First U.S. printing: January 1991

10 9 8 7 6 5 4 3 2 1

Library of Congress Cataloging-in-Publication Data

Freeling, Nicolas.
  Those in peril / Nicolas Freeling.
    p. cm.
  ISBN 0-89296-412-X
  I. Title.
PR6056.R4T47   1990
823'.914—dc20
                                        90-50547
                                          CIP

I am forever reading books prefaced by writers praising the patience-and-forbearance of their wives, and frequently giving them credit for reading, correcting, and even rewriting every single word.

I am amazed: I had thought that the editor's job.

So that I hereby dedicate this book to Esther Whitby and Howard Davies in London, and Michele Slung in New York.

My own wife does nothing like other people, and quarrelled with me during every day of the writing.

When it was finished, she refused pointblank to read the book. But since she has been the beat of my heart for thirtyseven years I must add: 'To Renée'.

Grandfontaine, France 1990

'Shall be liable, to an imprisonment of between three months and five years, whoever may fail, wilfully or by negligence, to bring assistance to a person in peril that he could provide, without risk either to himself or to a third person, through his personal action or in promoting such aid.'

Paragraph 2, Article 63 of the Penal Code

THOSE IN PERIL

Scree, n. (Mountain slope covered with) small stones that slide down when trodden on . . .

Thus far the *Concise Oxford Dictionary*. And thus far ourselves, for the most part. A definition; a conscientious teacher might dwell briefly upon the nature of erosion, for a class of schoolchildren.

But who trod, and why? He, she? They? Slide, did they, along with the stones? Fall, perhaps? How far? One can hurt oneself; it is not at all uncommon. One can even get killed.

A journalist at that point would begin to ask questions. The weather, the time of day, the visibility. What were they doing up there? A slide area is it, known to be treacherous? Officials may have more questions: doctor, lawyer, coroner, even a police officer maybe, and to some small local embarrassment: this sort of publicity doesn't do the village any good. A patter of falling scree turns once in a while into a dangerous landslide; a line in the dictionary into this book. So too with Castang.

Definition, again: *Police Judiciaire* would read as a laconic line. 'Equivalent, in France, to Criminal Investigation Department.' Quite so, and personal 'Castang' references on, say, a Home Office computer would not take up a lot of space. High officials have minuted sometimes on the margins of a confidential dossier with – say – the Bundesnachrichten Dienst in Western Germany.

The details of this career need not delay us. Present employment: attached Regional-service Lille. Present rank Principal Commissaire PJ. The middle of the three grades of commissaire, roughly equivalent to a Superintendent CID. Consult the civil-service handbook and you'd find that the emoluments are not too bad. Basic rate, not counting perks, indemnities, something over sixteen hundred pounds a month. But what with inflation and two small children, he doesn't count himself rich. The scale runs from five to thirty but that is naturally a pyramid. He's two-thirds of the way up and won't get much further.

He would be in line for promotion to Divisionnaire; a Chief Supt. He'd get posted then to command of a district. Two thousand a month; big car. Right now, he's the chief of an 'antenna', a satellite of the big, thickly-populated Lille district. In an industrial job he'd earn a lot more, but plums of that sort – security chief to wealthy, secretive enterprises – are fairly rare and he wouldn't much like the work; a lot dirtier than anything he does now.

As with the slip or incautious step upon the scree, this tale began banally, in that moderate-sized town of northern France where he lived and worked; centre of a largish administrative area, astride the ancient provinces of Artois and Picardy.

It was late at night, and raining; the light greasy rain of anywhere in the Brest/Orkney/Hamburg triangle. Or anywhere else where one stands on the pavement and fumbles with keys, because the street lighting is wide-spaced and the locks get more and more complicated. There's a basement key, to the garage, and a front-door key (after you punch out a code), and two different apartment keys (bourgeois residence in a modern block). Wet fingers dropped them all on the deck and a voice said damn, but patiently and without emphasis. Vera, his wife, waited; a silent echo, still and quiet.

The street was empty but for the row of parked cars glistening in the wet; and silent this late in a provincial town. The patter of running feet – like scree falling – was audible. Now the PJ is rarely spontaneous: its movement is laborious by definition, called into being by bureaucratic palaver; if so happen there's been a crime, perhaps there'll need to be some investigation. But it does sometimes happen that it improvises, and Castang did so now. It isn't really his business. A young woman running, at the limit of her endurance, may be in need of police, but it's Police-Secours she needs. Not the PJ.

He didn't like the running, though; it had an irregular, hysterical sound. He held an arm out, commanding the pavement. Neither tall nor broad, he has the police trick of appearing massive.

"Easy, then." She gasped to catch breath which came out in a yell.

"Let me go!"

"Now quieten down," said authority, "and where's the fire?"

"I – I – I – I," shivering uncontrollably. Long dark hair and features in disorder.

"You need some help, I'm it. Officer of police."

An inaudible mutter; the lungs heaved. "I've been raped."

"Ah," not at all surprised. He knows this particular statistic by heart: threethousand onehundred ninetysix the last notifiable year. Known, that is; since any cop will tell you the true figure is anywhere between fifteen and thirty.

"Where?" In shock they can only answer very simple questions. She pointed vaguely – back there.

"Far?"

"I don't know." Not helpful, but sounds genuine.

"Very well. We'll walk quietly. This is my wife. Like to give her an arm? She's Vera, I'm Henri. Confidence – all right? We'll go talk to the police, that comes first."

"You are – you said you were."

"Off duty. Just a bit of help and comfort. It's not far." She nodded, and clutched at Vera, satisfied.

The desk man on night duty saluted when he saw Castang, with no enthusiasm. Dogma: the PJ is an Enemy. And the State. Police-Secours is a local, a municipal body. But a Commissaire is a chief, must be treated with respect and handled with caution.

They will no longer treat with mockery a young woman who has been the subject of sexual assault. Or says she has – this trade teaches scepticism.

"All right, miss," hitching the typewriter towards him, "let's register your deposition." The unemotional manner has calmed her.

Castang, disinclined anyhow to give orders to municipal agents, is wondering whether there's any point in sending a patrol car. Is one going to find any evidence?

"Tear your clothes, did he? Burst any buttons or, uh?"

"Better call a car in," interjecting. "It has to be verified. He can take her on up to the hospital." The transmitter is humming on standby; the cop picked up the microphone.

"Whereabouts are you, Albert? Better come in. Job for you." He went back to the typing, mentally rehearsing the next phrase of the familiar jargon used.

"He then . . . threat with knife . . . forced me to remove . . . my underclothes . . . He then . . ."

"All right, miss. Sign here please." Not difficult, but her hands were still shaking.

Albert entered, rain-spotted. An Oh-oh face at sight of Castang. Who is careful to sound polite.

"Need to verify a scene-of-crime. We've a rape here, likely." One has to say likely, because fabrications are frequent.

Vera, who hadn't said a word, intervened.

"I'll go with her to the hospital."

"Very well. We both will."

The Rue de la Loi. An archway to a courtyard. As described, which doesn't mean much. No traces remain.

"Not got your knickers, miss?" asked Albert, apologetic. "Evidence, you know."

Taken with him, thought Castang, like a trophy. She started shuddering again. No, she hadn't screamed. With a knife under her chin?

Albert knows the way to the Service des Urgences – no one better.

"You again?" said the night casualty nurse. "Another over-dose? Oh, a rape. Gynaecology, miss, tomorrow morning." Bureaucratic obstruction. Just as well Castang came himself.

"PJ, Sister. Better have the duty intern, don't you think?" Vera, with an arm round the now silently crying young woman, mouths a stony 'Leave it to me'. But the staff nurse clacks her phone down, patters briskly with a pill and water, pulls the curtain on a cubicle.

"Lie down here then – he'll be here in a minute."

Castang stands wooden. Albert has gone for a smoke in the car. An aide is cleaning a nasty-looking facial wound on a man who sits dogged while she searches for tiny fragments of glass. An overdose is going Wah Wah Wah in a corner. A quiet night, so far . . .

The intern came, gave Castang a quick glance and nodded. A young aide ducked in with her trolley behind the curtain. The staff nurse went back to writing her log; sotto voce mumbling was obscured by the yells of the girl with the overdose.

The doctor came out and jerked his chin at Castang, who followed him in to the office where he scrawled morosely on his incident pad.

"Frontally, some irritation and reddening, but no tearing or real bruising. So you've only her word for it – sorry, nothing that would count as evidence; still that's the way it is, four times out of five. No anal aggression, no fellation. Just as well – you get an aphasia sometimes; I'd one who threw all her food up, for days on end . . . Vaginal vault traces, I've a specimen for you, has to go to the lab, but a possible match if you get the chap. She's had a shot of sedative, is fairly stabilised by now. You going to take her home?"

"What the police are for," with no apparent irony. "You can say though that she was forced, unprepared?"

"Mm, yes. But no real violence, you know."

"Man puts a knife under your ear, tells you open your legs, how d'you react?"

"True. This'll be typed up in the morning, okay?"

"As long as she gets a copy, without that gook talk about its being confidential." They aren't really callous. Just overworked.

"Thank you!" she said to Vera. "The humiliation is the worst."

Castang took her hand; sat her on a grey plastic chair.

"Listen, come in and see me; here's my card. Tomorrow if you can; it may be a help. Gave you a chit, did he – day off? Good, Albert will see you home. He'll drop us off." She hasn't realised that being raped is only the first of the humiliations.

"Glad you went with her," he said to Vera, getting the keys right this time.

"It's never nice," she said gravely. "Turn over then. Knee – elbow. Spread. A woman is so vulnerable. Suppose it happened to me?"

She came, though, and she sat in his office, tidy with her hair done, collected, and said that yes, she would go through with her complaint. Yes, she realised she'd been imprudent, wandering about alone, late, but she'd never thought that right there, in the centre of the town . . . She spoke quietly and behaved modestly, and Castang thought that she'd better have the 'lecture'.

"I'm afraid it will go on being unpleasant, and you'll need courage. You can go to any of the women's help organisations and they'll tell you the same.

"You'll have to persevere. It was a stroke of luck – not meeting me, but you've got your complaint in, and you've had your medical. Things it's better to have done with. But know anything about judicial process? No, most people don't.

"All complaints go to the Procureur, but rape is a serious business. Not like a tail-light on a bicycle: this is Court of Assize. He'll name a judge of instruction, a magistrate who'll call you in to his office. Instructing means examining, questioning you; and quite sharply, on what you did or didn't and why. It might seem hostile, because you have to convince him – or her – that you're not putting on an act." Seeing her look puzzled – "That you weren't willing or even semi-acquiescent in a sexual – don't boil over; it can be quite hard to prove. That's why I say it's fortunate that you had a medical straight away. You've also a lawyer to advise you, free and a woman if you prefer it.

"The magistrate will always call for a police enquiry, which might come my way as local PJ; and quite likely a psychiatric report too. It means telling your story, in detail, again and again. A check on you at home, at work. A morality enquiry. Somebody might claim that you were a promiscuous woman.

"But this has to be, you see. If they find the man . . . good, you have a sperm test as evidence. But you'd still have to repeat it all again in court.

"Because think of this: if the man is convicted he faces several years in prison and that's a lot. His defence will fight for him and that can mean attacking you, your dignity and your privacy. So I warn you at the start, it'll be rough, and for some months."

Why go to so much trouble? He has not exaggerated, painted nothing unduly black. The young woman sitting there nods and thanks him, and says she has understood, and gets up and leaves. Why bother? Certainly it was not sentiment; he wasn't 'sorry for her'. In fact a tiresome young woman who has given him unneeded extra work, and will probably give more.

We-ell, it is a corner of his job. When he can, he warns

victims that legal procedure punishes too; and not just the malefactor. And by coincidence, with this one he'd had a personal involvement: he was 'a witness'. He smiled a little, lighting a cigarette. A really punctilious magistrate, going by the strict letter of the law, could disqualify him from any further investigation of the affair. Confide the enquiry to the Gendarmerie . . .

It is part of this tale. As in olden times, when Mr Jumble so kindly consented to give his interesting talk to the village, all about his travels in the Holy Land, and illustrated it with a Magic Lantern. Tap-tap, upon the lectern. Next slide, please.

Because his secretary came popping in. And he never saw the young woman again. A month later he dictated a short statement for her lawyer, about the circumstances in which he had found her on the street, in dishevelled state and disturbed mind. Six months later, Vera went to court for her as a witness.

"There's a man asking to see you. Been some time in the waiting room. Says it has to be you, and no one else. Business gent; oldish, respectable."

"Very well. Give me just a minute."

He is thinking, simply, how he hates rape cases. Vera is right; women are so vulnerable. Men don't get hoisted upon the 'camel' with their legs spread wide. The medical students, heading for the gynaecological block, have a repulsive way of putting it. *Gyne* is simply Greek for 'woman', but what they say is 'Got the Gyneys this week'.

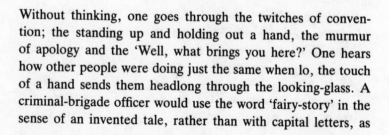

Without thinking, one goes through the twitches of convention; the standing up and holding out a hand, the murmur of apology and the 'Well, what brings you here?' One hears how other people were doing just the same when lo, the touch of a hand sends them headlong through the looking-glass. A criminal-brigade officer would use the word 'fairy-story' in the sense of an invented tale, rather than with capital letters, as in Alice's Adventures. But he must understand that to the subjects the adventure has a fairy-tale quality. This is what the wife means, when she uses the word 'surreal'.

Here were three criminal-brigade officers, and they agreed that the story was not invented. Too many little details ring out truth.

For Castang was thorough, putting on his two senior inspectors besides himself: experienced men, and hardheaded. The classic PJ technique with any tale thought to be a fabrication, the 'recoupage' whereby three stories are taken separately by three men, and then compared for consistency. He himself questioned all three, and was impressed. When Divisional Inspector Campbell, who is ten years older than Castang, and should have been a Commissaire years ago, said 'What's that American phrase? – we had better believe it' – they did.

Not without reluctance, for the story is so stagey. Luckily there is no great hurry now. We compile an impeccable dossier, send it to Lille, send it to Paris. They won't want to believe it either, complaining that it stinks of set-up.

Take the narrative first, the initial As-told-to. Between seven and eight last night (Castang was having supper, thinking about going to the cinema) a bourgeois family of Pa, Ma and youngest daughter of nineteen were getting ready for the theatre; the women at home: the man will pass by to pick them up. When the bell rings in a nice third-floor flat (much nicer than Castang's) in a quiet, expensive block, the daughter supposes simply that he has forgotten his keys. Two polite men announce themselves as police, say there's been a hold-up to which Monsieur Brun was witness, and may they come in to wait for him? The moment they are in two more appear, and in a twinkling the women are bound, gagged, blindfolded – 'they had simply reams and reams of stickingplaster' – and dumped on a bed. No violence is offered, which sounds professional. 'Are you comfortable? Would you like another pillow?'

Brun arrives, within five minutes. 'They had a driver outside on the watch.' He is tied up, pushed into a chair, and told to speak up smartly. The keys to his office and instructions how to open the safe. For Monsieur Brun is a well-known dealer in postage stamps. His father before him, in business for forty years: of course, the little shop on the corner of the Place d'Armes.

To ensure that he is compliant they show just enough brutality. A revolver barrel is jabbed into his throat, and once he is tapped with the butt. (Scalp laceration, throat bruises, entirely consistent.) He is lucid, nowise inclined to panic, and applies his common sense. Two set off to the office. City-centre, about a mile. And are soon back, cross, with the message the safe won't open. A bit of cinema, here. 'Wise up quick, mate. I've killed two men and won't hesitate.'

Brun kept his head. 'You silly clowns, the safe's open and you don't know it.' That doesn't sound very professional? No, but it's an old safe though a good one; the size of this room, the door makes a sort of suction effect, vacuum-like? So that this time he is brought to the office to show them. It is decided to take his wife's small, battered car. Some comedy, hereabout.

'They complained a good deal – almost out of petrol, tyres a bit bald – not nice that, not kind! Driver must have been on some dope, missed a big Mercedes by a hairsbreadth turning, didn't know the way, slap through a red light at ninety. I kept saying Look I don't want to get Killed, here. In the office I only had to pull the door. There are literally hundreds of albums but The Sheets, they kept saying, we want the sheets. We don't call them sheets; in the jargon we say *Planches*, but it was clear enough, they were acting under orders. They'd been told what to get, knew nothing of the subject; these sheets are where we keep the good, the collection stuff.

'But the other two back at the flat must have got bored. My wife can tell you about this but they turned the place upside-down for anything to pick up. Come on, they kept saying, you're Bourgeois, we know you, where's the gold, the dollars, the jewellery? Didn't exactly vandalise, but the most appalling mess. I still don't understand, I've nothing much and the few small pieces that are any good they didn't even recognise. They'd nothing better to do, I suppose. Not fine-art specialists. Just a break-and-enter gang. Been told to get the stamps, and take in any unconsidered trifles.'

Castang is pleased with the clarity, the selfcontrol, the coherence. It saves so much time.

"These stamps, what are they worth?"

"Hard to say, and take me a day or two to work out, there are market values, and speculative values. But they've cleaned me out. I'm totally crippled; in fact back to zero."

"Insurance?"

"The house yes, the office no. Too expensive. One can and does insure things in transit, and if good, a day's coverage might cost fifteen, twenty thousand. I couldn't begin to consider permanent cover."

When they brought him back they strapped him up and put him in a cupboard; and the two women, tied together, in the bath. Where after some hours the daughter picked some cord loose enough for her mother in turn to . . . While he – yes, he had been afraid of suffocating at first. But he could glimpse a little line of light. So where there's light there's oxygen. "So that I decided I would go to sleep. And what's more I did." He is vain of his coolheadedness. If his story is genuine he has some reason to be. And when suffering humiliation and ignominy, wouldn't one seek causes for pride?

"And this is the first alarm you've sounded?"

"There didn't seem much point in calling Police-Secours. By then the enemy were long gone. It seemed more important to get some proper sleep. Delayed shock, I suppose. I went to the office this morning. Oddly enough, there was a customer. I had to say to him Sorry, I'm not quite myself this morning; d'you mind coming back tomorrow. I shut the door and I came to see you."

"And where are your wife and daughter?"

"In the coffeeshop, across the road. I thought you'd want to see them – and the flat untouched, as the gang left it."

"We would, indeed."

And the women too had this clarity, coherence: nervous shock showing in uncontrollable giggles, but some of it genuine laughter. The experience had been 'surreal', yes, but also amazingly funny.

The PJ is not convinced. A man this coolheaded is a planner, and shows the imagination needed for a scenario. Picture him then in trouble from plunging; some speculation. Staging a robbery to cover it.

Inspector Fabre is not a specialist in fraud (they will borrow one from Lille) but he gives Monsieur Brun a foretaste. The insurance is easily enough checked. You do realise we'll want to go through your bank statements, tax declarations, all your records. Discreet? – of course. But shedding light tends to throw a glare, mm? Now these stamps, how many dealers would there be on this level? Say in France. Throw in neighbouring countries. Might know, would they, roughly what you had, or were likely to be holding? Might they know – we'll want to know! – what auctions you've been attending, whether you've made speculative buys? Private deals? A valuable collection up for sale following the owner's death, perhaps? Might there then be stuff held for longterm appreciation? Suppose an owner looked for liquid money in a hurry, you might be asking around, preferring private buyers to an auction? No no, I know nothing about stamps but you realise, there'll be a fellow down from Paris; he will. (Inspector Fabre is mistaken. It turns out that even in the Beaux-Arts section in Paris there is nobody – pictures, yes; furniture, fine china, jewellery, yes; but not stamps – and eventually an expert is located in the Customs Service, a specialist in illegal export of money.)

Now, Monsieur Uh, you wouldn't have gone pledging those valuable bits of paper, would you? As collateral say, to raise the wind for a special deal? Sure, I'm willing to accept the hypothesis as ridiculous. But Lille, you know, they'll want you to explain why.

Castang has another approach. This very controlled (too

much so?) and secretive man is of interest as a character, so that he is curious about the wife. Mr Campbell has had a fine time with her. 'Though you can't stop her talking for a single second.'

And the daughter. Nineteen, math student at the university, splendid girl, aspark with intelligence, and with simplicity and candour. Plain? Not perhaps 'pretty' by conventional standards. Ask me, and those eyes would set the forest afire after it had rained for a week. But keep silent: listen.

"I'm not the tiniest bit traumatised. I know I can't stop laughing, but really it was all straight out of a gangster movie. No, I never really worried, once I realised we weren't all going to get raped. Of course it was horrid in the bath, there's no leverage so you go round and round like a poor spider trapped in it. There we were, squirming about, must have looked hilarious, we could see nothing. Is it true that if you're blind your hearing is sharpened? I found it so, I could follow every scrap of the shuffle-fuffle, ripping the flat apart looking for gold you know, so frustrating for them because we didn't have any, and then the sound of pages being turned and I thought I don't care what else you do but if those are my math notebooks I'm going to climb out of here and Kill you, you buggers. I knew I ought to be a perfect wreck, stammering and unable to concentrate, and sorry, the thing which worries me is missing my lectures today.

"No, I always knew it was going to come out all right. I never for a second worried that they might kill my father; that was just acting, in order to impress him with being tough, and anyhow bugger those miserable old stamps, they've always been a bore. Of course my father will get a job, he's an excellent businessman and if need be I've money from my granny and that'll get me through the university. Don't get me wrong, I'm absolutely solidly behind him but I can't stop thinking how funny it all was."

The wife's name is Claudia. A tall thin woman, remarkably animated and still handsome. She is an excellent raconteuse, a good mimic. Castang has the impression that she is already rehearsing, polishing and perfecting an act, and the next time there's a bridge party she'll have the whole room in stitches at the tale.

"I do know, I can't stop talking, so if I become a bore just tell me to wrap up, but when I think, there was poor Pierre in the cupboard and us in the bath . . .

"I yelled and yapped, Do anything you like but put me with my daughter! Really they were awfully patient, I deserved a slap. My big gold earrings they took those, my ring with the sapphires – this one, they're real – I had from my mother they couldn't get it off. I said well of course you can't you've strapped my wrists so tight my hands have swollen but it's fake anyhow so don't bother, and do you know they Left It." A small but very bourgeois triumph; the 'winning a bit back'.

"But the pigs, my gold chain from Egypt, they felt inside the neck of my pullover and you know Then I felt I was getting raped. Still, I'm a nurse, there's nothing I don't know about stickyplaster so I wet all round the outside of my lips and I knew I'd be able to TALK." Yes. And already she's placing the capital letters where they'll create a comic emphasis.

"Oh, the mess, the bathroom – no, the Other bathroom, when darling Micki managed at last to chew me loose. I thought God, what I want most is a Shower, and you know they'd flung everything they'd handled in the bath, all those rolls of sticky, Fahzends of them, and then flung in litres of Oil and a whole Bottle of washup detergent, wasn't it Brilliant of them to cover their traces like that but the MESS."

It has the ring of truth. One does not invent the triumph of diddling them over Granny's sapphires, the rape of a hand on one's bare neck.

"We were dressed up, we were going to the theatre, it was *Aïda* and Pierre had trouble getting tickets and of course I was wearing Much too much jewellery so serve me right, and they put a blanket over us, we thought we'd die, it was so HOT." And the man, the lucid determination to sleep, because that would slow his metabolism and consume less oxygen. This was not faked.

In the apartment, a doubt returns. The big duplex, with the livingroom in enfilade to the southerly exposure – the entrances and exits left and centre and right so pat, the spiral stairway in the middle. So very much the stage set for a farce and this most accomplished actress now changed into a wide-swinging skirt . . .

So he will make his report: on the face of it the story is not faked. So that long and meticulous work will be called for from the Fraud Squad.

> Shown the portrait gallery, the witnesses have independently identified no. 3148, known to have adopted the same method. (Rogatory Commission Orléans, ref. attached, the old lady tied up all night and freed only by the cleaning-woman next morning.)

This report went to Paris. A copy was returned to him from Lille, minuted by the Divisional Commissaire:

> quite so, Castang, but could have done without all these Capital Letters – Sabatier, SRPJ.

What is the lesson in it all for him, in these two episodes within the same twentyfour hours? It will be apparent inside another twentyfour, when he gets the word.

He will remember then that they were simple routine. There was nothing in either to attract particular attention: nothing linked them but the timing. A young woman was raped, a simple working girl: something which happens. A bourgeois was robbed. His wife and daughter were not molested. They all showed courage. He'd had to urge it upon the first: the second had impressed him with possession of it. Each, in their way, had handled matters well.

And now it is his turn.

*

In moments of selfpity one is sustained by the courage and insolence of minor artists – clowns, cartoonists? – mourned because taken from us prematurely by something stupid, like leukemia or a road accident. While enthroned, in deep gloom, Castang noticed that somebody, probably Lydia, had pinned up the Reiser drawing of the Underdog sitting on the lavatory saying 'N'y a que là qu'on est bien' which translates roughly as 'Mankind's last refuge'. Greatly cheered, he went about his business.

He had, just the day before, been given the sack. A day after the routine events described, exciting only to Monsieur Brun and his family.

Absurd expression. Nobody gets the sack any more. Workers get laid off for economic reasons. Dismissed for serious professional misdemeanour. Many more euphemisms exist for sacking business executives, but hell, that's what they're paid for. You aren't 'handed your cards' like some drunken truck-driver. Not when you're a senior government servant 'with tenure'. They find other, politer ways of doing it, sometimes out of a blue sky.

Thus, Authority had rung up, the Sous-Chef, in an offhand uninflected voice. 'Pop in to see me, Castang, when you have a minute.'

Nothing unusual about that. The Sous-Chef, 'Deputy Director of Criminal Affairs' at headquarters in Paris, has something to say, not on the telephone which might not be discreet, and doesn't want to put it in writing. So pop in. Number Thirtysix, Quai des Orfèvres. A couple of hours in the train, for which a Commissaire gets a first-class free warrant. He had daydreamed: there wasn't any crisis he knew about. The Sous-chef is a friend. He hasn't many, but this one is high- and strategically placed. The dreams thus are pleasant. It could be 'the step' ahead of official notification.

Could be; he'd been over three years in the North, and had done well there, earning a couple of commendations. He has put down no roots, since promotion to Divisionnaire would mean a probationary passage in some other dusty corner of the Republic before getting a Regional criminal brigade. At forty-seven – by fifty one can covet a pretty good job, legitimately. The children are growing up: he'd like a university town.

The train slowed, clonking with cavernous echoes: Gare du Nord.

"Oh there you are, then. Sit down. I have here," pretending to search a crowded desk, "two reports. They both concern you. One is from RG." The acronym is for 'General Information', the euphemistic title of the political branch. Never very good news!

"They aren't pleased with you," pretending to read. "You trod upon their toes, heavily it seems to me; they complain loudly enough. Down in Bayonne."*

But good God, that is a year ago! And he hadn't thought it of Morosini. He hadn't judged the man one to carry grudges, but RG are shifting sands, like anything political.

"I would take no notice myself of their claiming you meddled in their affairs. But I do have to take official notice of stiff words from my opposite number." Alack, higher than Morosini. In fact he was guiltless of the charge: alerting a suspected terrorist to RG interest. But he realised he'd been called in to have his head washed.

"If it were only disregard of procedure . . . There's a limit to the protection I can give you. Or feel inclined to; been plenty in the past. And that's not all. I have here a service note from your superior." Commissaire Sabatier, the bland, the silver-haired, the much-respected – the wealthy, the well-connected! A pompous old ass.

"A fine administrative letter. Always was a good word-polisher, our Sabatier. But this went to the Chef. Bluntly, he asks to get rid of you."

He has guessed this one. Castang, in the car of a British

*See *Not as far as Velma*

Consul-General, had been shot at. Or the British Government was getting shot at: moot point. But he had been sarcastic with Sabatier, who always took the credit while subordinates took all the shit.

'Come Castang, let's have no dramas.'

'Oh, you mean one never gets shot at. Or well, hardly ever.'

It is an administrative necessity to show proper respect for lazy and/or incompetent superiors. Sabatier didn't like Humour. Get rid of the bugger. Worse; get rid of this Cleverbugger. At the cost of his being promoted. It would be the Haute-Loire, after all.

"There'll be no promotion," said the Sous-chef, flatly. This side of the ocean . . .

"The Chef came under pressure from the Minister, over that caper in Bayonne." Biarritz, actually, but the rose stinks by any name, at the Ministry of the Interior. "A transfer was decided upon. You'll continue in your present rank. And don't look at me; I've saved you an official censure, written into your record. And I'm bringing you to Paris where you'll get under nobody's skin. There's a vacancy in the Fraud Squad over at Fine Arts. I don't want ever to hear about you, over there – understand me?" So that even his skeletal criminal brigade was to be taken from him. This was not just to be damned with faint praise; it was stone-dead has no fellow. The Beaux Arts! He could go and track postage stamps . . .

"Now cheer up, Henri," said his kindly Friend. "Keep a clean nose over there for a year, which shouldn't, God knows, be difficult, and I'll see what I can do. If, that is, I'm still here myself. You think yourself stabbed? Nobody's job is safe – nobody's.

"Eight names were brought to the old man, for promotion to Controller. Two were turned down flat, higher up. So the Minister, foaming, was looking for china to throw, and you weren't the only piece. Sabatier will retire this year – unpromoted. If it's any consolation." It isn't any consolation. "That's all, Castang," to the squeak of a drawer opening, world-over the administrative signal that an interview is at an end. There isn't any justice either in the Palace of Justice, next door. One knows this, after twentyfive years in the trade. But the temptation is still to say 'Sod It. I Resign.' One doesn't, of course. With two hours before getting home he has stopped pitying himself by half way.

There are good material reasons; like being the wrong age, and not having clocked up enough pension-time. A professional does not sentimentalise his situation. He does not have *états d'âme*: states-of-soul the French call it: the bastards have a word for everything. He looked instead out of the window. The big smoke- and steel-grey cloudscape of Picardy on a darkening February afternoon. 'Don't be Cassius,' as Richard used to tell him. 'Don't think too much.'

Vera also thinks too much. When 'hurt' he reacts like a boxer; close the door and hang on until the bell goes. She will not show hurt either, from loyalty and out of pride. In the middle of the night, himself not sleeping, he hears her crying, struggling to make it inaudible. That has not often happened since the nights of utter weariness after a long day's fight against paralysis: she still limps a little. She calls herself a happy woman and he knows she isn't, at bottom, that she cannot help regretting Slovakia, but that like the Queen of Holland she says 'I will Maintain.'

"Paris . . ." she says at breakfast. "I'll have to learn to like it."

" 'In the destructive element immerse –' " in a guttural central-european voice.

"What?" She is not always quick at seeing jokes, but she knows stoic lessons; that the mind must make its own happiness, that our own resources sustain us. "Why don't you take the day off?"

Castang was shocked. He never takes the day off, just as he is 'never ill'. A rigidly conscientious civil servant. He leaves her in her 'studio' cluttered with drawing material, which is also her pathetic 'library' full of tatty paperbacks, and secondhand Everymans of english-classics; very Czech. Room will have to be found for all that. In Paris? He has spent his childhood there, too much of his youth. He is no longer interested in being 'Parisien'. As in London or New York, they think that outside the city limits the world comes to an end. As the gravedigger says in *Les Misérables* – 'Moi je suis parisien: vous êtes paroissien.' Make the most of it, though.

So that halfway to the office he does take the day off.

"Won't be in today, Madame Metz. Coughing rather." And goes to the 'Bains Romains' instead, exactly like a turkish-baths but instead of the oriental décor there are pillars and round arches, pictures in the floors of full-busted ladies, nereids perhaps, done in tesserae mosaic, and splendid brass nineteenth-century plumbing. After being scrubbed, slapped, massaged, this is the right place for a good sleep, nerves unjangled.

He is the prisoner in the opal. He sees the world in changing colours, vivid, fiery and cloudy. How does it change their lives, a rape or a robbery? Is it for the worse? How will one know? And myself? – is this 'for the worse'?

Vera's loyal and pathetic offer to help . . . 'I know after all a lot about pictures.' While a knowledge much greater than his own, which would go comfortably into a pint pot, hers was a painter's knowledge. Not quite that of the Fraud Squad's fine-arts division. But when inside the opal he could understand that hers would be the more valuable.

Paris has changed much since his day – nigh on twenty years ago – and in still more ways not at all. You have to be rich, as he is not, to live 'intra muros'. Even sous-les-toits the rents are absurd; nor will he accept climbing five flights of rickety stairs in the pitch dark to get to the bed-and-board. And outside the walls is the suburb, stretching today a long long way. The villages with rustic, romantic names, Ozoir la Ferrière or Boissy Saint-Léger, are today crawling hives of Levitt housing-estate. Right out to Marne la Vallée stretches the Tropic of Ruislip.

Castang is not greatly worried. So one will commute to work by the Regional Express Railway, taking one's time. The Fraud Squad is not a place for showing zeal, and a commissaire's rank has privileges.

Thus, it is through the freemasonry of senior police officers that he hears of an old lady, who has a country house, meaning a house in what used to be countryside. She is anxious to find a tenant, but it must be a most respectable man. Oh, he'll fit that bill. She is a phenomenon he understands well, because the sixteenth arrondissement of Paris does not change, and least of all old ladies living in gloomy pomp in the Rue de la Pompe.

Madame Saulnier is an excellent example. She has inherited this house from her deceased husband (who was in vegetable oils) and lives in considerable comfort upon the rents from it and other solid, gilt-edged resources. A sharp old biddy, born in this her quarter, has never moved a stone's throw from the church of Saint Honoré d'Eylau and the Lycée Janson de Sailly: wouldn't dream of it: couldn't. She receives him, by appointment, in her dark, musty, grey and gold splendours. A spry old girl with a bony, still handsome face, an expensive grey frock on a still-trim figure, grey stockings on thin and well-shaped legs, a lot of very good jewellery, and an old black shawl over her shoulders like a concierge, but concierges do not wear such smart Italian shoes with such high heels. A raking sharp eye to himself and his appearance, over which he has taken trouble. Acid voice and – he will learn – wit, some humour, and even, once every precaution has been taken, kindness.

"Mm, a commissaire of police, it appears a satisfactory reference. Where, if I may ask?"

"Beaux Arts." It goes down rather well.

"Mm. I collect too, in a small way." Indeed even in the Rue de la Pompe (a long street) you wouldn't find a flat more adequately bolted, barred and burglar-alarmed. "Mm, the house is in the Val de Marne. Quite a way. I seldom go there. I have no intention of selling it, no intention of spending money on it. I wish to keep it as it is but occupied, so that it is warmed, ventilated, and protected. In return for a tenant I find totally reliable I ask only a low rent." Castang, who was still standing up, bowed just a bit. "Mm, got a car, have you?" Certainly; parked in the Avenue Victor Hugo, meaning illegally double-parked, but what good is it being a Commissaire if one can't ignore traffic regulations? "Why don't we go and look?" Trust her! Not going to spend money on a train fare. A 280 Mercedes in the courtyard, and still cadging lifts – that's very sixteenth arrondissement too, but how d'you think they all got there in the first place?

Indeed it's a long way, right out at the terminus of the Paris railway net: a small Marne town which has still kept its cosy ingrown provincial feel despite the swarming masses now dotted about. And he gets on rather well with Madame Saulnier.

"I thought it a find, really."

"You mean you took it? Without my seeing it?" said Vera.

"Dear girl, you don't think things over in the Paris area. You say snap and if it's no good you unload it on to some other idiot at five per cent commission."

"I see," sarcastic.

"No, consider, though: ten minutes' walk to the station. Schools about the same, look okay. A quiet street with trees, five minutes from the centre. It's an old house, you see." Leading her on tactfully. "Look, I'll make a drawing." Vera makes drawings of all she sees. His are more the scene-of-crime ground plans one found in oldfashioned detective stories. This house is important; she forgets her chagrin, bends eagerly over the paper.

From the street he saw a high brick wall, and a wide double gate of bars backed with rusty iron sheeting, to keep out prying eyes. Inside is grass and neglected standard roses, and beyond a stretch of gravel the solid, ugly rectangular block of a bourgeois

villa of the eighteen-thirties. Two stories and attics. Oriented
north and south, and this is the north.

"I'm keeping the first floor," said Saulnier laconic, nipping
out with a big key, "though I'll rarely be here. The ground floor
is yours if you want it," opening the ponderous front door to
a hall in black and white marble squares, going through to the
terrace at the back. "I'll put in a door there to close off the
stairway."

To the left is a diningroom, and behind that a small morning-
room, south lit. Beyond the diningroom, at the eastern end of
the house, a big kitchen and behind that a larder and scullery,
and stone steps down to the cellars. To the right of the hallway
was the big salon, all the way through, with an admirable
parquet floor, a splendid marble fireplace; windows front
and back and still full of a grandiose French gloom. Behind,
a tiled terrace ran the whole length of the south front, linking
the rooms together; in fact a loggia, for it had been glassed in
at the turn of the century, with french-windows to a big per-
spective of overgrown garden, with some fine trees. Casually
seductive, Saulnier let fall mention of an extremely low rent.
"Since in a sense you'd be, mm, caretaker."

Castang was secretly impressed by the excellent building –
the woodwork was magnificent. And resolved not to be put in
her pocket.

"Bathrooms," he said, firmly in the plural.

"I've thought of that. I could have it built in there in
the corner of the terrace behind the larder: the waterpiping's
there."

"This huge salon – need to be partitioned – make two
good rooms."

"I told you I didn't intend to spend money. You could
curtain it off."

"And we could also compromise. If you'll put in two bathrooms, which is a good investment and the floor's tiled already,
I'll partition the big room at my expense." She looked at him
with her shrewd eyes, tapping her chin with the key.

"You've two little girls, you said, Monsieur Castang."

"Which is why I must have the rooms."

"I like children." The remark was not expected. "I'll close with you on that, on condition your carpentry does not injure the plasterwork. You'll board off the fireplace, and I'll put the big chandelier in storage. Bohemian, and valuable. My lawyer will draw up an agreement with you."

"So that's it," he told Vera. "Number five, Rue du Rocher."

"A great draughty, smelly, dusty barrack."

"Not draughty," he said. "The northwest corner will make you a fine studio." She looked at him with a Saulnier face.

"You'll have your rail pass, to Paris."

"And easy office hours."

"Where is it, the office?"

"I don't even know," with a return of sourness. "Some dilapidated palace no doubt, which the Ministry doesn't want and uses to house bits and pieces. The Department of Dead Ends. I am concentrating," in a snap, "upon looking after Number One."

Vera has Madame Saulnier's bleak direct look, and her level no-nonsense voice.

"I suppose there's no reason why it shouldn't suit us well enough. We must save money." She has saved here, the prudent housewife. To her this life is wealth: she looks at France still with her Czech eyes, over fifteen years later.

A true bourgeoise of the sixteenth district, Madame Saulnier has mysterious powers over builders and plumbers. The house in the Rue du Rocher, built by her great-grandfather, has the aura with which the French view long-established property: in the little town there are still families who have worked for her family . . . Her name has authority, which would extend if need be to mayors, even to Prefects. The alterations are done by the end of the month and they are ready to move. Silent, independent, resolute, Vera has been there for a fortnight, scrubbing at forty years of ingrained, and thus respectable French filth; making coffee for the workmen, and bribing them into doing her odd-jobs.

Castang wants to slip away quietly. It is not officially 'known' that he is leaving. The news got out anyhow over the arab-telephone. The staff say nothing: the news is neither good nor bad and they do not have 'états d'âme'. They merely wonder who they will get to take his place. The old inspectors will not get moved now: they are dug in, to cosy personal fortresses, of informers, of specialised local knowledge. Castang has been a reasonable, if eccentric, master. Only Véronique, his 'young woman' inspector – he has some fondness for this crude but straight-necked girl – has looked at him with sympathetic rather than knowing eyes; and just for once she has had tact enough to say nothing.

Only on the last day did Mr Campbell, coming in with a pile of paper, mumble, "What are you getting?"

"Sous-chef in Beaux Arts." What is the point of hiding it?

Campbell, a man over fifty, only nodded. A desk cop might like the economic brigades, but Castang had been on serious-crime squads for all of some twentyfive years. Who, in France, gives a damn about pictures? The nod is one of commiseration.

"Have a drink, shall we, this lunch-time? I hear, by the way, they're putting skids under Sabatier." Now how had he learned that? But these old cops know all about politics . . .

Varennes brought a bottle of champagne into his office that evening with one of her hot splashy kisses. He was touched by the mark of affection. It wasn't as though he'd ever slept with her; but perhaps that was why.

Vera, seeing the partition go up and the boarding nailed on, feels sanguine. She gives a damn about pictures! And now she'll be able to get into ever-closed museums (in even the ones open, dodging crowds of art-loving Japanese . . .) In this sleepy little town there is a strong heartbeat from the daily systole and diastole of the Paris-bound commuters. And this is the still-lovely Ile de France, where she has never before lived or worked. The house is weird but nice. She is ready for her man, her children, the movers' truck. She has even met

Madame Saulnier, who has flitted down to cast an eye. The two women, each of strong character, understood each other.

A story unfolds: stately word and perhaps a euphemism for deliberate, tardy. The act of recounting police enquiries follows the measured pace of the generality, and the hardy old metaphor of large solemn boots comes to mind. However, the whole of a long-standing investigation is – like art – greater than the sum of its parts. In this too like art, the enquiry has not much to do with action.

The basic fallacy in most accounts of police work is to emphasize violence, on the ground that the reader is greedy for excitement, and that a tale of this sort should be organised in a series of spectacular scenes like a comic-strip. Violence is implicit in society, as well as explicit in much of the daily newsreel, but to dramatise it overmuch blurs the picture. *Titus Andronicus* is not one of the better plays of Shakespeare. Aristotle's claim that the function of tragedy is to purge the onlooker of vulgar emotions through terror and pity – this is truer still today.

For Auctor thus to address Lector in ponderous parenthesis is ridiculous, but the Who Did It convention encapsulating most crime fiction is no less so. The police officer's task is to bring malefactors to book: a reassuring thought but the reality is bleaker. The success rate, measured in terms of suspects brought to trial, is in all European countries around sixty per cent of serious crime. This figure applies to cases known. The percentage of cases 'not known' remains unknown.

This fact can inspire us with both pity and terror.

Who raped that young woman? It will be for Castang's successor to determine. And who conceived, commanded, the robbery of

Monsieur Brun's stock of rarities? That will occupy his new department, in a leisurely, desultory way. Was it you made all that fuss about the stamps? asked Carlotta Salès as he entered the office. Yes, admitted Castang humbly. All she said was Oh, but a good deal went into that monosyllable. A man's relation to his work is also a valuable theme in fiction. But if one may without coyness address Lector, he will also find melodrama in the intimate and family lives of police officers.

It was as suspected; the Fine Arts Section of the Fraud Squad was found only with difficulty: dilapidated palaces abound in Paris. In French confusingly called Hotels; the private house in town, as opposed to the country Château, of Prince Something: since Bourbon kings had hordes of illegitimate children, obscure Princes abound.

Most of them are of beautiful seventeenth-century architecture and admirable interior design. Exquisitely civilised and in a shocking state of neglect. Façades are leprous, but the courtyard is handy for parking. Rain comes through the roof, which does not stop them housing many civil servants in obscure departments. On the top floors; the piano nobile tends to be full of art, too heavy to lug up the stairs. Museums have no space, time or energy for all this art: it got dumped here, decaying gently under a century of dirt.

A concierge, made still ruder by daily affronting fat statues of the Laocoön sort, directed Castang up dirty marble stairs of perfect beauty and simplicity. Fire buckets stood about in passages to catch drips. Notices on doors indicated dignitaries but there wasn't much personnel. An elderly secretary was found, known as the Archivist. A kind woman; effaced, intelligent and evidently efficient: Madame Morandière (why does she instantly become, and remain 'Frau Morandière'?). She welcomed him, courteously.

He enquired after his new superior.

"She isn't in, I'm afraid." So – a woman. Castang is not humiliated; hopes not, at least. "She's out a lot. You see? – we need you! She's been a bit overactive, recently. She's very nice and I'm sure you'll like her." A momentary, detestable impression that she is sorry for him.

"Oh, I'll be in again; this is just to get acquainted. I'm not here officially, as yet. But perhaps there's some homework I should be doing?"

"Learning about art?" smiling, but a nice smile. "Our big one this last ages has been the Monets, of course. Endless weeks in Japan but Madame Salès has it just about tied up, we think. But there's lots more. Active dossiers!" Humour shows, at the corners of pretty grey-blue eyes behind big shell-rim glasses.

"Perhaps I had better wait until I meet Madame Salès."

"Then why not tomorrow morning? And meanwhile I can be getting an office cleared for you. With some nice pictures!" Castang burst out laughing, and that perhaps earned him a good mark.

'Settling in' to the Rue du Rocher – there are now children's bicycles in the grey hallway, children's raincoats in the coat cupboard next the lavatory, under the broad oak stairway. When it was built, this house, the Rue du Rocher was a country road, muddy in winter, dusty in summer, smelling of wild roses. Modern houses now press in upon the row of bourgeois villas and their big gardens – valuable property, stretching to the bank of the little reedy river which joins the Marne further down. Five minutes away is the old centre of the little market town, unchanged since Monsieur Loubet was President: twisty narrow cobbled streets smelling of drains, around the parish church; buildings in the yellow freestone.

Vera could believe herself in Proust's Combray, for old women look out like Tante Léonie 'stupefied at the sight of a dog she did not know'. Tiny dark shops sell French things like seeds and fishingrods and canaries. And across the square the pharmacy is a palace of white marble, the garden centre has plants of monstrous size and vulgarity, and the butcher owns a twelve-cylinder Jaguar. It is a very French contrast. The shop of the tombstone-man, in America named a funeral parlour, is here called Funeral Pomps. There are gentle grey houses, and there are houses like giraffes, with façades in a crazed pattern of varicoloured stone and white cement joints (and one such has a puddingstone gateway too . . .) The children seem to fit effortlessly into their new schools, and Vera wonders why she should feel discontent – an unease?

Castang has achieved a near-placidity; even a balance, learning how to fit himself in between Frau Morandière who knows everything, and Commissaire Salès who knows much too much: Vera calls them Mum and Budget. Mum is unfailingly gentle, helpful, encyclopedic; Budget – what a devil for work is that girl. Capacity: voracity. She signs things 'CLS' – the C stands for Carlotta; what's the L? He asks and she blushes a bit and says 'Laurence' – henceforward Vera refers to her as 'Lorenza Lotta'. Lotta absorbs knowledge through her pores. A trained police-girl but what had gone on in that clever narrow head? Why the police?

Ambition seemed to be the answer. Terrifyingly bright, forever top of the class, at the university she had gone through art history like a dose of salts, went into the Restoration school and topped that with spells in museums (German and Swiss), became interested in fakes and (as far as he could make out) suddenly decided that there was a good career available in a specialised police world; sitting waiting for her, if she really went at it.

And she had! To this kind of scholar, schools seem effortless. Chewed up her law degree, crunched and swallowed like a digestive biscuit (she is fond of digestive-biscuits, bought from Marks & Spencer); flashed through commissaires' school at Saint-Cyr, passed out high, asked for Beaux Arts, and got it. Just like that. All by the time she was thirtytwo. The purely intellectual kind of cop. She has no use for guns; though she can be rough in her own way if need arises. Castang wonders whether this intense, concentrated woman has any emotions.

He manages to keep his balance. They have the same rank but hers is acquired, his is earned. She has her brilliant, specialised knowledge but he has experience, depth. He has seniority. And he is a man. In French police structures women are no longer a rarity but still have many handicaps. It's a traditional and conservative world. She was relieved to find that he likes women, likes working with them. It has made her a lot less edgy.

Almost at once Castang realised that no amount of work would give him the specialised knowledge. Any more than Lotta – who to her credit realises this – could acquire his, hardbought in the criminal brigades. He would have had to start at eighteen. So that they will complement one another, and do. Of course he has to learn some basics: both Mum and Budget pick him source-books from the library, and he studies them, in the train, forty minutes on the commuters' line from the florid, baroque suburban station to the Temple quarter, third district, metro 'Filles du Calvaire': the filles were an order of holy-nuns now lost to the world. The whole quarter is like this, part of the old 'Marais'.

It was a rest, at first. There was no criminal brigade to make his life a misery. No statements, interrogations ill-typed and badly spelt. No long phonecalls from Procureurs, Mayors: no abrasive spices in his dinner, from judges of instruction. He was not called upon to appear, stating at length what everyone knew already, before courts. Nor did blameless bourgeois appear with embarrassed tales about this small problem that has somehow come to light. There were no bland and lengthy instructions from the Préfecture, contradicting what they said last week, reminding him of Electoral Sensitivities: e.g. the new abortion-pill: e.g. the recent film thought to be both obscure and blasphemous (and certain to be boring). What was nicest in this new world, there was not much Politics.

Commissaire Salès was one to keep her own counsel, and did not 'confide'. She did confide a little, to Madame Morandière who was, she knew from experience, good at keeping counsel, at respecting confidence. And a civilian.

"I don't find him very easy to cope with." At the School in Lyon there was an officially-approved figure, said to be 'about right', of thirteen per cent women: one wondered who arrived at this and how. Salès had kept out of trouble by concentrating on her work. Most of the girls had been the busty toughs one saw in the commissariats, their weaponry thrown into relief by their hip measurements. The airline-stewardess syndrome tended to apply. Salès didn't care if she did get tagged Miss-Frigid-Les. But this was different; a man due to become a close colleague.

"I shouldn't worry," said Morandière, placidly. "He's wary of you, so determined to be tactful that it's making your own efforts seem stilted. And he feels humiliated. Just think, all those years in the criminal brigade, what it must do to their psyche. Over-developed capacities for concealment, evasion, and prevarication. He's nice but he's trying too hard, and so are you."

Lorenzo Lotto was a painter of the sort Castang is learning to call 'relatively painless to look at'. And so, thinks Frau Morandière, is Lotta; nice-looking young woman with dark hair cut in a trim cap, a slim figure, and remarkable eyebrows in a high flexible arch. Making an inventory, one would add her good carriage, her voice which is low and soft, and enviable legs. Pretty? One is in two minds about that; she'd be so if she gave her mind to it. Her clothes are sensible, neat; smart in the sense of well cut and chosen with taste: she doesn't think about them much. Sexually attractive but so guarded about it that men don't spend much time besieging her. Frau Morandière knows more about her, but thinks that Castang can work it out for himself, if he's any good.

Two or three days had shown him the obvious. She's demanding, but generous with her own effort. Watches everything like a hawk and especially her own step. Sensitive, vulnerable, and thus heavily armoured.

He had made a low-key start.

"We had better have it clear, between us. As you certainly know I have been stood in the corner, in some disgrace."

Lotta made a face to say that this was none of her business.

"No, but you might conclude that I'm feeling vengeful. So I am, but not towards you. I'm going to try and get back where I belong, but not by using you as the shovel." The eyebrows went up at that.

"It's been known," he said. "So that we should come to an agreement, perhaps. I'll try to learn something about art, but it'll never amount to much. So that's your territory. But come across any crime, and you might let me know: I do know something about that. Real – climbing in at the window to pinch the Corots doesn't interest me much."

"Let's think," said Lotta staring at her calendar; water-colours by Winslow Homer, painless. "You might have a shot at the duke. He lent his Velasquez," explaining, "and when it got back he said it wasn't his and wasn't a Velasquez. We're at the stage of interminable quarrels between experts." He had burst out laughing, which pleased her.

"A Spanish duke?"

"Scottish, more's the pity. The Foreign Office is being tedious about it."

"I'll study the file."

"That won't get you far. At some time fairly recently the picture has been damaged and overpainted. Now did that happen on that side – or on this? In whose custody? Roughly, who is suing who for ten million pounds? You could see if any ideas came to you . . . Now the Russian Modigliani is quite tricky. They think it a fake and it probably is. The question about that is that it wasn't done yesterday – you follow? – you can't dab your finger and say hey, Sticky. If at all, then way back, in nineteen-twenty or so. Our claim roughly is that he did it himself, in self-parody, since who bothered faking them then, when you got the original for the price of a bus-ticket?"

"And have you no dotty millionaires gloating over the

pornographic Boucher in the cellar?" She stiffened a bit at his being facetious.

"They're mostly Japanese and you agree to leave them to me."

"True."

"There's plenty of crime about," grave, "as you'd expect, with the sums of money involved. It's difficult to get the sort of proof which will satisfy a court. You could have had the lady who sold the antique coins from the Hôtel des Monnaies, but she's sub judice. You can have the damned postage-stamps!" This time they both broke out laughing. Castang's perhaps a little insincere.

There's nothing a police officer dislikes more than a criminal investigation appearing to lead towards involvement of a member of his family. Of course, the ruling is clear: find yourself in a conflict of interest and you disqualify yourself at once, turning the affair over to a colleague. In acute instances you could even ask to be suspended from duty pending impartial enquiry. The ruling is embodied in the formal questions put by every judge as a preliminary to examination. 'You have no family connection with this witness? You are not on terms of friendship? You have not nor have you had business relations such as would prejudice your views?' The formula is generally gabbled, but it is there.

It hasn't ever happened to Castang, who has little family and few friends, but if the hypothesis were raised in conversation he would be guarded in his answer. Every experienced policeman knows that the clearcut principles of legal theory are looser, vaguer, in praxis. Some officers would tell you (and some would not) that it isn't that simple, and admit (some might not) that they would look at the question as a purely family affair, and not as police business at all, until they knew better where they stood. 'If you want an aphorism, instinct is not inconsistent with integrity.'

Castang's instinct is unhesitating. The question here is to know whether the hypothesis of a criminal act can be verified. And he reaches for his telephone.

"Dr Manuel around? – still in the office, is he? Put me through would you – Castang. Denis? I've a small problem; urgent. Can I pop round?"

Dr Manuel pushed up his glasses and did a double-take.

"Castang, what have you got there?" The two men looked at the rag on the table, which was pathetic, and not very clean. "Are you in the habit of carrying young girls' underpants around in your pocket? – here, let me offer you a handkerchief."

"I think," said Castang, "it had better go down to the lab and be tested for sperm."

"Oh dear. How old is she?"

"Thirteen – fourteen – I'm not sure."

"It's not, thus . . . your child?"

"No. But in my house. A friend of my daughter's. Bad position."

"And a bad age. Bring her here."

"I suggested that. Won't come. No way I can make her. Tricky. I've no official standing."

'Look. If the test is positive that's an unsupported complaint. Any action has to come from the parents. What have you to go on?"

"Denis, the child has large angry bite marks on the breast area."

"Nasty horseplay? Adolescent hooligans? Or something worse?"

"I haven't questioned her and can't. At that age they can't express it, so they refuse to utter."

"And when they do utter, they're probably inventing."

"She should be photographed. The marks will fade to vague bruises and be unidentifiable. But I can't compel that.

No further sign of ill usage, but of course I haven't looked. There's a bit of delayed shock. I'll see what my own girl knows, and mm, conceivably have a word with the parents?"

"Short of seeing her myself there's not much I can do. You don't think there'd be a non-assistance to person in danger?"

"Hardly, on grounds this slight."

"Then my responsibility isn't in question, and neither is yours, but if this is positive," putting the rag in an envelope, "I'm your witness. I'll back you up. Parents don't thank one for bringing these things to their attention." Yes; Castang has seen other hornets' nests stirred by misplaced-zeal; is also wondering how well he knows his own daughter.

Lydia had come pattering – she doesn't sidle – in to the room where he was doing homework. She is supposed to be doing her own, in her room where they sit on the floor surrounded by litter with the radio playing as well as continual chatter in the incomprehensible jargon of French schoolchildren. They meaning Sabine, without whom Lydia finds life intolerable. Castang does not care for her much; pudding-faced child – in fact pretty, with a round vivacious face and an over-modelled mouth, eyelashes which are Lydia's despair and what the boys will shortly be calling a smashing pair of tits. There seems nothing one can do about it. Emma has also her great friend: 'that horrible Valérie' who is always so polite when she meets him. Why horrible? – long dark hair in a plait; plainly well brought up. Castang doesn't know. Too much charm, and too much pocketmoney, with which she is very generous. 'There they go, sucking sweeties in front of the television again . . .'

"Pa," in a small voice.

"What is it?" intentionally discouraging.

"Well, I think I'd like you to come and look. Sabine's in some trouble. She won't tell me what, and I better not ask." Thus alerted, Pa became professional.

Yes, the child was in a sad stew. He sat on Lydia's chair – they hate chairs, prefer the floor – made himself softspoken.

Questioning brought nothing but more tears and headshaking. Look, you know you can have confidence in me, if it's something you prefer not to tell your parents. Lydia fetched me knowing that I would help.

She sat up suddenly, eyes shut, and pulled up her sweater. No bra and no vest. How it is these children do not catch colds I cannot think.

"Have you got more of these marks? Like lower down? Well, we'll make you comfortable, you know you're safe, here. Run her a bath, Lydia. Get into bed afterwards and have a good sleep." The child was like putty and Lydia had to help her. The idea of anything said to her parents had put a flare of terror into her eyes. He might have to. We'll see. He felt hemmed in. Here he has no criminal brigade. Local police would not be impressed by him.

Some greedy boy, taking mouthfuls of a too-complacent girl? About the girls he has no judgment to pass: the liberties permitted are their affair. As for teenage boys – what can one say? That 'it wasn't like that when we were young'? No indeed (oh the agonies). Could it be possible that those bruises had been caused by an adult?

Was I a bit too casual, saying Oh, have a nice bath, nice kip? Not a very clever choice: either I'm making a fuss about something pretty banal. (Not to Lydia it isn't: why did she think it right to tell me? She puts on her lordly know-it-all act, but she was undoubtedly shocked.) Or I'm being culpably negligent.

Which is it?

I don't feel very proud, if an experienced police officer is going to have his over-casual reactions corrected by his fourteen-year-old daughter.

Castang found himself worrying about it.

Denis Manuel ... A week or so ago he had gone down

with a sharp touch of lumbago, Castang 'who is never ill', going about bent over like Groucho Marx, at which the children laughed heartily. The damp climate of the Marne valley. Psychosomatic no doubt: frustrations brought on by Art.

The place is brimful of doctors: there's nothing the French enjoy more than cossetting their health with three at a time and the charlatan for good measure: you'd think you were in California. But Dr Manuel was a lucky hit, a young forty thin on top, with gold-rimmed granny glasses and a highly-developed sense of the comic.

"Civil Servant, says the card; now what does that mean? A commissaire of police, really, parachuted in? How can I treat you, without a lot more questions? Do you sleep with the beard under or over the sheet, do you unroll the lavatory paper from the top or the bottom – I must know things about you." A spontaneous friendship occurred. They do not always last, but it is nice while they do. With himself Denis had been pleasantly unprofessional but with young girls he would change his tone at once.

Young girls: what does one know about them? Virtually nothing. At thirteen–fourteen, it's the 'fifth class' of the Lycée, a secret world of their own. Even their homework is for the most part incomprehensible; a moment now and again when one corrects their grammar or their spelling, but already one is hopelessly oldfashioned, excruciatingly out of date. One cannot follow their arcane back-slang but those clear tolerant eyes are unmistakable in the message 'don't fuss with me'. Even Emma, adorable honeybun, gentle and obstinate as Vera herself, has gone beyond his reach, but the gabby, elbowing, backchatting Lydia (so like him) is completely unrecognisable as his child. They 'come back' as everyone knows; one recovers one's affectionate and delightful daughter, but for these six years it is a total stranger, generally nasty. As for their upbringing, that is far in the past. If you have not managed to instil honesty, decency and table-manners when they were quite tiny, it is far too late now. Like all fathers Castang has got into panics about this.

Vera hardly knows more. But is placid, having been-a-ghastly-girl herself. Is reassuring about – yes, Lydia menstruates, and knows more about sex than I do, calm down, they educate one another and she's extremely modest. Vera, highly Czech, has brought them up strictly. But this is a worry.

Sabine had had an hour in bed, felt better, and Lydia had taken her home, was the report.

"Where does she live?"

"The restaurant by the river, with the big terrace. They're all right. Lavish with cake and ice-cream."

"Reasonable people?" One is trusting the judgment of a child, and will it be worse than that of most adults?

"Mm yes, a bit overfriendly, smarmy I'd call it. Sabine says in that trade they're all a bit like that."

"So they are. Now, do you know anything about this? Sabine by the look of it has been getting into bad company."

"No, I don't. She hadn't said anything to me."

"Well, if you do you had better tell me. It can be serious. Understand me, miss?" Because there was the mulish look, and the 'don't go *on* at me' look. But she knows when he's serious.

At least he hopes so, he tells Vera, who was unalarmed.

"Does the worldweary, and inside she's horrorstruck. Now please don't give me a tirade." The police, so priggish. Perhaps it is now that her years of always being there will bear fruit. Her rule is simple: we can trust them because they trust us.

"That test is positive, by the way." Denis Manuel, pouring out a drink 'after a hard day'.

"Is it? I feared it."

"You did? Being a bit intense, aren't you?"

"I suppose I am."

"These things happen. Doesn't have to be a big drama, nowadays."

"I suppose not. At the worst what would you do, assuming you're asked?"

"Abort, of course. Painless, without trauma. Why ask?"

"Finding it on my own doorstep, so to speak."

"Happens in the North too." Denis knows a bit of his history.

"Of course. Incest, child abuse; daily bread and butter."

"Perhaps I can see light. Feeling underemployed, are you? Finagling in antique shops, very dry oats after the criminal brigade?"

"Something in that."

"You should be me – steeped in crime! If it weren't for professional discretion, my delations could fill the courts for ten years. Rich old gentlemen who live too long – heirs get impatient – nothing one can do, naturally; insufficient evidence. You should meet a friend of mine – judge of instruction."

"PJ – I should say ex-PJ people, tend to get paranoiac at the bare sight of judges of instruction."

"My advice to you," said Denis dry, "is sit on it and do nothing."

Castang agreed: don't bother about what's done but what gets known.

And he still thinks he ought to say a word to the parents. In no police sense, but just being neighbourly. Two children in the same class at school.

Listen, Castang, this pretence is worthless. It is not possible to be one half the neighbourhood do-gooder and the other half cop. You'll fall down on both counts. Block off the emotional involvements.

Two people know him to be a police officer: Denis who is a

doctor and Madame Saulnier who is discreet through bourgeois habit. To everyone else he is just another ministry official, one of the thousand middle-aged men on this commuter train. And this anonymity could turn out useful.

Sabine was no more seen, and nothing surprising about that. She would feel ashamed and awkward. Teenagers have nothing to say to adults, Lydia has nothing to say to him. He decided instead upon 'a word' with her form mistress, whom he found a brisk woman, formal and guarded, polite to a dutiful parent.

Parent–teacher associations rarely make much headway in France, where a mutual distrust is often endemic: teachers think of themselves as unappreciated and put-upon, while agreeing that parents are lazy, negligent, and irresponsible: the one thing parents agree upon is that teachers have overlong holidays, while nursing suspicions about moral and political indoctrination of their young.

"Lydia? – oh yes, she came to us this term. Hasn't shaken down badly. Forthcoming – even a bit too much so." This is familiar stuff; Lydia the chatterbox, the head-in-air, un-concentrated.

"Gifted enough. She'll get through all right if she pulls her math up," consulting the daybook, "oh dear, a seven, five, four – quite a lot up." He had to drive a few chinks into these seated convictions of the imbecility of parents, at which the teacher defrosted somewhat.

"Oh good, a cosmopolitan background," said the good lady. "Even if this isn't Paris we do have a high level. Nothing racist about it but too high a proportion of arab children –" Czech apparently is a little bit better than Algerian. The word 'cosmopolitan' is highly pejorative.

"The trouble with private schools is that the little dears start regarding themselves as élite."

"Indeed, but we're quite privileged here too. By next year, if she tries, she might get into Monsieur Dampierre's group."

What?

"Come come," ice re-forming a bit, "Académie Française, a most distinguished man and gives his services free out of idealism. The most wonderful literature classes."

"Really – we'll have to see. Incidentally, what's the feeling like, in the class? – tja, the tone, the awareness, attitudes within and without."

"Oh I see. Not a bad class at all. There's always the irreducible sediment of duds and troublemakers at this level. Lydia plays quite a good social role."

"You've no problems with sex confrontations?" Ice on bows and rigging, here.

"They've had a good understanding of their own physiology given them last year. Naturally at this age there's some consciousness and curiosity, and a quantity of experiment – we keep a close eye, you know. We can accept no responsibility outside the school gates."

"Oh quite." Excellent women.

Lydia was less terse than of wont; even voluble.

"Old Mother Carrère, the queenbossyboots, yes she did blither a bit. Gushing away about Mum being Czech, the impertinent old bitch. I told her yes, we got nursery rhymes in English and pompous old Pa reading aloud the Snow Queen – oh the splinters in my heart! The old bag was impressed, good mark for me. Infernally curious about what you do, I wasn't about to tell you're really PJ and about to peg her for criminal approaches to the young, the old les."

"Lydia, who's *old*?"

"Well, she has false teeth and you hobbling about with lumbago like you were a thousand."

"Lydia, what does the word 'lesbian' mean?"

"Ho-mo-sexual behaviour between girls – thanks very much, I don't fancy one tiny bit."

"And have you evidence, meaning that these suppositions

are supported by factual indications? Frivolous and malicious tattle; am I mistaken?"

"You're absolutely right as it happens, but poor old Pa, paranoiac as well as schizo, doesn't have a clue."

"Neither wishes nor needs to."

"Hoppity-skippety sublimated-unconscious-homosexual Pa."

"You mind your mouth, young lady." Glaring.

Nothing to raise the temperature there but what seemed to be hotting up were Russians.

He has been learning about museums – scandalised, if not much surprised, by the peculiar status and privileges of museum attendants in this our Fatherland (oddly, feminine in French). The Corots, stolen from the Musée Marmottan, are not his concern, as Salès has politely told him: this is a protracted affair, and she has to go to Japan again. There seems to be plenty of money for this. Not the sort of world he is used to. But Morandière is helpful, as usual, when asked.

"Oh, terribly penny-pinching in the administration. They'd never dream of creating a few more posts for attendants in the Louvre – or trying to change all that featherbedding; I'm off duty with my poor flat feet. But where Pres-tige is concerned, the Honour of the Foreign Office, millions will get splashed about. Hold tight, and you'll see."

At the humble level of such as Castang, Government is visible in the form of little memos about junior employees' canteen allowance. It is over in the fine broad streets between the fine tall houses of the seventh quarter that you see the haughty black limousines and their white-gauntleted motorbicycle outriders. So when he gets an abrupt, a rude summons to betake himself with zeal to the Ministry in the Rue Saint Dominique, he takes the metro like the rest of us. At the pompous portals there's a lot of frowning over his pass and status, and a messenger to see that he doesn't get up to mischief. In a small

and undistinguished office without any Louis XV map-tables
he is left to cool his heels for a good twenty minutes before
a slim fair-haired young man comes in, glares around, says
"Smoke!" angrily at the little cigar, fanning the air with the file
he is carrying. A thirty-year-old deputy assistant to somebody,
giving himself air and airs: it doesn't bother Castang much.

"Sit down and pay attention. You are being entrusted with
a simple, straightforward negotiation with a Soviet official.
There's no real negotiating involved: it's cut and dried." Abom-
inable young man. National School of Administration; they
come in hordes.

"It's not policy to do this through the Embassy: they'll
have an observer present and no more. All that's asked of you
is to carry out the instructions here in the schedule. Normally
Madame Salès would be thought adequate for a job of this
nature, but she's in Japan. And after dragging their feet for
a year these good people are showing signs of impatience, so
you'll substitute; it's no great matter.

"The secretariat has booked you accommodation in Leningrad. Now in turning over this dossier I'll impress upon you
that as a commissaire of police you are an accredited agent
of the Government, which is why you've been chosen in the
first place. You're regarded as responsible. I'll recall to your
attention that this is a confidential transaction and you'll obey
the rule of absolute secrecy: there'll be no gossiping with your
cronies over the apéritif. A press leak would mean your head,
am I clear? Very well then, off with you." This is Government,
these dreadful little boys drest in their brief authority? He had
kept silence while insulted five times in as many minutes by a
jerk of a clerk, as is only just.

"Heavens, man, haven't you a proper briefcase? That's
sensitive material you're waving about there."

Humbly Czech, Vera was impressed.

"So the job means something after all – Leningrad!"

"Don't you believe it. They could have sent a postcard but an errand boy is more consonant with their dignity."

"Yes, but the Rastrelli baroque, the lovely town, the Hermitage and the – "

"Yes, and economy class on Aeroflot."

"Tomorrow – oh dear, it doesn't leave you much time."

"Have no fear, Russians are two hours behind." He was packing a tatty bag when she reappeared flustered, with a 'present', an attaché case so that he would start to look like a negotiator – he was touched.

"Not Cartier," deprecating. "South Korean imitation."

"I'm not real Cartier either," said Castang.

Looking for polite euphemisms, travel-stained might do for the plane. It was the first Russian lesson: they aren't interested in the look of the thing but only in making it go, and he felt in tune with this sentiment. The first Russian smell, which is their brand of disinfectant, synthetic perfume added to carbolic. But their ideas are in the right place, this people. The stewardesses are polite, and they're pretty, and they're fresh-looking; and that's something new on airlines. Further there's weak coffee, and marvellous tea. The airport has a checkpoint marked 'Diplomatic Personnel Only'. Everyone else went through this too. The first of that ubiquitous troop of Intourist buses, and it's much more like the stewardesses one knows, rather frowzy and decorated with artificial flowers, and a doormat to boot. And the Hotel Pulkovskaya, just like any other holiday inn but for the guards on the door to stop hooligans sneaking in for drinks. The bed is all right, the plumbing works, the air-conditioning doesn't but the window does.

Lesson number two: impressive quantity, size, and majesty of memorials to the Great Patriotic War. To understand what it means to them, decidedly one has to be there. It explains so much of what has happened since. He had learned that this city stood a siege of nine hundred days, and knowing that one realised one knew nothing. In a way one felt admiration for the German troops who had so stubbornly fought an entire people which stood here and died, a million of them, and didn't let go. How long had the siege of Paris lasted in eighteen-seventy – six months? Bit paranoiac, are they, about foreigners? Nothing to what I'd be.

The next discovery was that he was ten kilometres from the city centre, along the far-from-inspiring Moscow Boulevard. Probably they had done it on purpose. So all right, the metro station is across the road. Hm, with an embassy observer getting in behind me. No no, prudence, dinner, bottle of wine, early bed and a bit of homework: morning brings counsel. He was quite right because the phone rang in his room.

"Commissaire? Ardisson from the Embassy. Comfortable, are you? Good, I thought we'd get together in the morning after breakfast. Eight-thirty and don't be late. Across the lobby, in front of the Intourist desks. Very well then, g'night." He hadn't learned much about Leningrad before falling asleep.

A horde of tourists was clamouring for tickets to the cultural-events. Castang identified a French head, square and sour; the willowy young men must all have been implicated in homosexual scandals by the KGB, packed home in disgrace. This one looked like a cop. Castang remembered being stopped at the Ministry gate and photographed. He had put it down to security until the cop at the airport said 'Just a moment, Commissaire' and tucked the visa into his passport. Clipped to the grey card with the cyrillic typing had been a photo he had never seen before, and doubtless this chap had a copy in his pocket.

"Sit here a moment, shall we?" Leather bench, such as hotel lobbies provide for the weary. The milling tourist uproar made it impossible to be overheard. "We've a quarter of an hour," glancing at a hairy brown wrist. "Car will pick us up. Their car incidentally, so if you talk, stick to social chat." Not very

Foreign-Office. Proust described those mannered intonations, up and down an octave, with so precise an ear that eighty years after they are entirely recognisable. This was more the public-relations man whom they have in television studios, to put you at your ease before the chat show. Castang was embarrassed by the attaché case, which he hadn't liked to leave in his room. The floor gouvernante must be KGB. Surely they always were?

"Nervous?" smiling. "Not very used to this, are you." It wasn't a question, but of course he was nervous, feeling sweat under his arms. Ardisson had a tie he envied rather, grey with little silver seahorses. "Bit like being on the box. Done that, have you?"

"Two minute interviews, to explain to the public that police-men are Nice, really." Polite grin, on both sides.

"You'll do. Ah, that'll be for us." A driver standing just inside the door, patient and bored. Ardisson knew the town well, and identified the dreary buildings along the boulevard. Russian jokes, about the shoe-factory and the power station. But across the canal, into the old Saint Petersburg, Castang was at once captivated.

"Yes, it is pretty, isn't it?" No; pretty isn't the word.

They crossed the Admiralty Square, stopped at a side door. There was the usual Russian old lady, wanting their coats and hats, and a young secretary to bring them upstairs. A big and beautiful eighteenth-century room flooded with the daylight from fine windows, a round rosewood table, and two elderly gentlemen doing the wreathed-in-smiles. The embassy man went formal, before withdrawing into polite immobility.

"Monsieur le Directeur; département de l'Art moderne. Mr Abrassimov from the Ministry." An old face, of extreme distinction, and a thin old body in a comfortable tweed suit. The ministry-man had black eyes and beetly brows to match, but looked like a chap who could see a joke. "Coffee?" asked the young woman.

"Might I have water?" Standing in the strong daylight of the Gulf of Finland was a picture on an easel. "Ah, this is the

Modigliani. I've only seen photos till now." Hearty laughter from the Ministry.

"So alleged."

"As far as I'm concerned" – good water, temperature just right – "any other allegations are groundless."

The old director put on hornrimmed glasses, looked at the canvas as though he'd never seen it before, took them off again and spoke in a gentle, rumbly voice and excellent English.

"Nice picture. Pretty picture. And, indeed, a good picture. But Modigliani didn't paint it." An enchanting smile and eyes full of vision looked at Castang. "I must beg your pardon. I read French well but I cannot speak it. D'you mind English? Or perhaps German?"

Castang had to assimilate two things, and quick. One is that there weren't many reasons for sending him, but he's supposed to be good at languages. And the other – is this the famous Russian technique? You destabilise the adversary, at the outset. The embassy man sat still as his chair, face saying nothing. Of course you can say Well, in that case, what we need is an interpreter or two. But Snap.

"My English is far from splendid. My German even worse. I take it that the essential is that we should understand each other. So if Monsieur the Director pleases . . ." And he saw that it did please the old man.

"That is courteous. Better – it is friendly. I hate interpreters," in a childish tone that made them all laugh.

"So we're talking about a good picture," said Castang.

"To be sure it is," said the old man, in a kindly manner. "A painter's sight is like his voice. A tone and a rhythm, a timbre and an inflection. He speaks to me, and I answer. We have . . . a magic telephone." The English was academic, accented; clear.

"We recognise, and comprehend each other. There is no language difficulty," smiling.

"This is not a technical problem, Monsieur Castang. That

has been discussed, and at great length. We are past all that. I am in no doubt. I never have been."

He had got up, to walk around the canvas, to taste its texture.

"A good painter. And made, quite possibly, with the knowledge, the connivance, of Modigliani. Such jokes are not infrequent. But you see – this joke picture is not what I want."

"We all have pictures like this," said Castang, gently. "You, me, or Paul Getty. That are accepted for years and then are downgraded. The Rembrandts; there used to be, what – four hundred? Barely half that, now. You've four million objects of art here: not all of them what they seem."

The old man's hand made a short chopping movement, of impatience.

"What are these stories? Vanities! A professor runs about, to spy on a Parmigiano, to write School Of, in his little list, and what importance has it? Be serious, please. A workshop picture – that is like a movie. Many have worked, to put it together, and we do not enquire the names of all the assistants. I hear the voice. When the secretary is speaking, I know that, also." He had gone for another of his little walks; to look out of the window.

Chess players are like this, thought Castang. Some stay still and others roam around.

"You're telling me that you don't want to lose face. Neither do we. You have a good book which describes this situation. A conjuror gives women wonderful Paris frocks, which disappear out in the street leaving all the biddies standing there in their knickers."

Mr Abrassimov was the first to break into a hearty guffaw.

"Bulgakov yes, you like this book? It's a very Russian joke. True, we are ridiculous for buying and you for selling. But the onus, my friend, is on you."

"No such thing as caveat emptor in art." The director was smiling gently, long brown fingers making patterns.

Good, everyone knows that once the knight made a fatal mistake on move seventeen the chess player will come in the end to concede. They know too that he will fight it out stubbornly to number fortyone, the time limit and the move sealed-in-the-envelope.

"Very well," said Castang. "I am instructed that the government of the Republic has nothing to refuse to its friends."

"Nothing!" said the ministry-man nigh falling off his chair with the laugh.

"Let us hear this nothing," said the director.

"We're not there yet. In recognition of good faith, we would like some conditions fulfilled."

"One is that our faith is acknowledged. Nothing is made public. The picture is good enough to be shown. You don't want to return it and you didn't buy it to put it in the auction the week following. The phrase is crude but you're stuck with it."

"And if I make the transaction public – you're stuck with it."

"So two is that your good faith is not to be brought in question. In recognition of which I am instructed to mention a figure. In compensation for the error of judgment."

"So let's hear your offer." Abrassimov, jovial.

"We aren't," getting cross, "bargaining over a cucumber in the market. It's useless – " He wanted the word 'chaffering', couldn't find it, used a coarser German word, instead.

The old director leaned forward, touched his colleague's sleeve gently, and said, "You are empowered."

"A realistic figure. We have a benchmark. The 'Girl in the Cravat' reached a sum at auction unlikely to be bettered. Still less when a doubt is cast on the attribution."

"Name it."

"One million Swiss francs."

"Accepted," said the old man.

Castang had not imagined a day in his life when he would come to be drinking champagne in the Winter Palace. Belle-Epoque too, the one with the bottle made after the Gallé design.

"Appropriate," said the old man charmingly.

Nor had he thought his career would include signing a paper. For and on behalf of the Republic. But without vanity. He was only a glove with another hand inside it. Still, it was something to put in the new attaché case.

He got too the young secretary. Well no, not 'got'. He had better not try! (What would have happened if he had?) She gave him the tour of the Hermitage, and lesson number three; that art in Russia belongs to them, and they feel very strongly about it. This is not like being in the Louvre!

That evening she took him to the Kirov: yes, this is the Maryinsky and that – pointing – is Karsavina's Theatre Street. It was an opera night, and *Aïda*. He found himself strangely moved – for a cop – and the young woman cried, saying simply, "I always do. Be grateful it wasn't *Otello*." Perhaps this was the real reason why he made no effort to climb into bed with her. Vera says of herself 'I am the sort of idiot who sheds tears in the slow movement.'

He had bought her, of course, a fur hat. (And the usual dolls for the girls.) She exclaimed over this, so that it was then extremely pleasant to give the parcel.

The old gentleman in Leningrad had produced this, with antique courtesy; 'For your wife.' Little souvenir, yes?

Inside there was a piece of paper, framed and glassed. Quarto size, a bit foxed. On this was a pencil drawing of a woman's head. Very simple, and very pretty, and signed in the corner 'Alexandre Benois'. But what nice presents they give! She burst into tears.

Far worse happened, three days later. A large boring brown envelope postmarked in Belgium. Documentation inside. Subscribe to *Fortune* magazine? No; another, grander envelope. And within this a flowery letter from Zürich asking for Instructions, together with a credit note for ten thousand francs. Minus porto charges, subject to negative interest – but still Swiss. The smallest envelope was sealed. This is your Code Number to be quoted in all correspondence. Oh Christ, a bribe.

"Nonsense," said Vera. "That's an ex gratia."

He worried about this for a whole day; still quite childish at times. Not supposed to let the KGB gain a hold upon one. He had it transferred then to the little pot. Vera's word for jamjars full of threepenny bits: his for complicated savings accounts, the house investment scheme and the pension fund, which greedy tax collectors mustn't get their claws upon. Who would have thought the Fine Arts this fruitful? Hm, Madame Salès says that art has nothing to do with Action, but she was in Japan and doubtless getting plenty of action under the counter.

Vera's imagination, which was lurid, ran to photographs of him with Russian girls in fur hats and nothing else.

"Too easy to fake."

"But I could tell."

"And who'd be impressed?"

"I should."

"Who knows? Keep watching for the postman."

Vera said little. She wasn't very happy. She found him much calmed after the uneasy beginnings. Too much so; altogether too sage. There he went, trotting off to his train with the attaché case (newness wearing off) full of bloody art and exactly like the other dim civil servants. She preferred the time of raped girls (might be staged) and robberies too which might not be all they seemed. The people who landed on the crim-brig's desk, often dirty, generally imbecile, always troublesome; but she preferred them to this artificial world, this leisurely existence. She looked at her Russian drawing, and she loved it. Still didn't feel happy.

She had been into the office, and met Madame Morandière; had much liked this kindly and sensible woman, who got her back-door entry to exhibitions, and into the Louvre when (as generally) they were on strike. Cards too to previews.

"The old gentleman whose place you've taken – he loved dressing up and going to parties. Varnishing Day – well named. Lots of champagne and caviare for the people whose eye they want to catch. He thought that was him. Now your man stays at home and does his work, and believe me, we're grateful." And so is she.

She should thus have been happy, and sometimes was; and more often wasn't. Is Paris a city for the very young, and the very old? She enjoyed it, and she felt in-between. It was the same at home. She was not vexed by the discreet flittings of her landlady, and the house had its points. The solidity, the seclusion – yes, appreciable; and with spring coming on she would enjoy the big overgrown garden. But she never felt it hers. At times she hated it, as she had never hated the hireling flat in the North which had been half the size, and much noisier. She felt lonely as never before. Was it fifty years too late to enjoy the Ile de France? She should have come here before the war maybe, when it was a countryside and beautiful, recognisably that of the Barbizon painters? Now, as well as ugly, it is Fidgety.

Living was expensive. The swarm of suburbanised Parisiens carried huge mortgages and the women worked of necessity more than freedom. Their children were alone all day, to her eye badly neglected and in compensation badly spoiled.

The girls complained at their shabby clothes. They had to have the same shoes and jackets as the others, and Carefulczech Ma found it all much too lavish. She wasn't worried by the over-sophistication of these brats. Henri had got into a sudden fuss about Sex, but she felt confidence in Lydia; hardheaded child, of strong character.

Vera was not what the French call at home in her skin, and she wondered why. Well, what woman would want to be home all day in this gloomy great flat which old mother Saulnier refuses to have papered and painted? Henri does not of course come home for lunch, and the journey makes the day much longer. The children catch a school bus and eat in the canteen; crisps and popcorn instead of proper food. So that she has to cook an elaborate Dinner to make up: too late as well as too heavy. This was all much too French, and made her feel much too Czech, and increased her deprivation, and her solitude. Fidgeted, she took to spending too much time in Paris, drinking too much coffee, looking at too many sub-Poussin sub-Raphael paintings, her eyes hankering for gritty northern pictures: more Breughel . . .

So that she didn't know whether to be pleased or sulky when invited to dinner by Dr Denis Manuel, and decided to be horrid.

"The French never ask one into their houses. It will all be hideously formal. Acres of polished table and the good silver candlesticks. Fourteen different things to eat, which one has to praise and it's always fucking foie-gras. And all that paraphernalia about The Vintage."

"Nonsense," said Castang who was pleased. "Denis Manuel's not a bit like that; alert and funny. I haven't met his wife but – "

"Quite sure she'll loathe me, and I'll loathe her. Anyhow I've nothing to wear."

Castang knows that all women do this, but one always supposes that one's own wife is worse than others. Vera is talented with bits of striking clothes (found cheap), and when called upon can make herself strikingly pretty. He won't listen to this flow of grumbles.

"So sit there," cross, "with the cat and the vacuum-cleaner."

Denis Manuel lived on the edge of the town, in a house looking as though a high wind had blown it cross-Channel out of Guildford or Reigate. But it would need, says Denis, to be a dandelion seed. Decidedly, too heavy . . . It has a gravel approach, and laurel bushes, and steps up to a porch. A notice with a painted fist pointing a finger like a pistol directs Patients, those low people, to the far side, a boxy annexe which is the Waitingroom. Dr Manuel's dirty and much-bashed car – he is always in a hurry – stands in front of this, but there are no patients, God-be-thanked, since it is the weekend and he is not on guard-duty.

"They will come ringing here," letting them in at the front door after 'a peep'.

Vera has had plenty of time to be ill in, but has not seen him before; thinks well of this untidy man, looking younger than he is, with a brush of foxy hair, large ears which prick, expectant way of padding about: a desert fox, a fennec. There are only two other guests; the Judge of Instruction promised to Castang, Monsieur Maurice Revel, and his wife: a slab-face but a kind face.

"Are we late?"

"No, we were early. I am always early. Unless everyone else is always late. I have to buy a new watch, maybe?"

"Hallo. I'm Michèle. Sorry to be rather sweaty; I'm cook."

"Always among the bacteria, no change," said her husband.

"Are you a bacteriologist?"

"She looks at shit on slides."

"Why thank you, Denis; just the thing to give us an appetite. Stop chatterboxing, busy yourself with the pop."

"It's these hateful twisty wires. Pop all round, or is anyone allergic?"

"These are supposed to be cheese straws but they got a bit burned."

"Hateful being the Judge's wife. What can you do to keep your end up, when you're stupid? I sneak off to Paris and help out in a dress shop. Corinne by the way, the wretch never said."

"Vera. They wouldn't even have me in a teashop so I'm hausfrau and paint on Sundays."

"Lovely frock."

"Fleamarket, I hung it in the rain for a week to get the smell out."

"But then lo, Schiaparelli, yes, I promise, I can tell."

"She couldn't wear the tchador despite being a wounded freedom-fighter just in from Syria. More pop? Those things have almonds in, I can't think why."

"Easy there with the dangerous drugs, Denis, you're spilling."

"Sneaking up behind me again with that footstool."

"No, in Fontainebleau, but the tribunal's in Melun."

"Threw me out of the criminal brigade. Overfriendly it was said with terrorists."

"Full of third-rate Rodin, smashed up in a rage by Camille Claudel."

"Well darling, if you need more time there's plenty more pop."

"Just usher, and I'll drag the pot in. Nonsense – just sit and be elegant. If you insist on working then you can light candles." They shrink and look pallid, for the moment before burning up into a steady flame and changing all the faces with new lights and shadows.

"Has this got shrimps in it?"

"What it has is a shot of pastis."

"Takes the Judge to discover that but what did you expect, Maurice – arsenic?"

"Michèle puts booze in everything, it's because of the bacteria."

"Then we've got some jolly good antidotes."

"Premier Cru they call it. Not sure I'd want to try the second."

"Denis tries to put you off so that he can lick your plate on his way out with the empties."

"Not quite; in the hope there'll be leftovers. Else there'll be nothing for an entire week."

So that Vera, who had dreaded a protocolaire stiffness, so that one can neither stay sober nor dare to get drunk, is now hoping that her hook-and-eye will stand the strain; made for a narrower waist than hers.

Dr Manuel boned a saddle of lamb; speed and clinical precision. His wife brought in a big 'bouquetière' of spring vegetables; he looked at this.

"Well soaked, I hope, in a strong solution of potassium permanganate." Revel, as a familiar of the house, comes swooping at her with a decanter. She will certainly get drunk, and like it. Henri, normally prim in his manners, has an elbow on the table and is house-on-fire with the judge – he hates Judges! But Maurice Revel might spit fire in his office: here he is a gentle man with an enchanting smile. And nothing could be less pretentious than these women.

Perfectly simple, thought Denis Manuel, pleased with his manoeuvre (and admiring of Vera, across the table) – one needs only plenty to drink – and what after all is a doctor for? Hm, my dear Michèle is already stocious. But she has worked hard, and made a good dinner. That Czech girl is a beauty. Medically speaking I'd like her face a little less drawn, and a bit more colour in it. Give her another glass. "Cheese," he said comfortably. There was only one but it was a good roquefort and who wanted more? This is a good sauterne, he thought, smelling the cork.

"What colour is it? Come on, the painters. Gold is cheap."

"Varnish." Henri being horrid.

"A Watteau girl on a swing."

"Sicilian lemons in an evening light." For Corinne is both romantic, and kind.

"Josephine Baker in yellow satin." Michèle is decidedly a bit drunk.

"First prize. Up on the table and strip."

"Denis!" deeply shocked.

"Just a change, from all my old ladies who've eaten too much mayonnaise."

"No apple charlotte for you, and go stand in the corner."

Vera drinks unsoberly her sauterne, painterly admires the play of muscle on Michèle's strong forearms, thinks it probable that with one more glass she wouldn't have hesitated an instant; wonders whether come to that she'd have hesitated herself. Funny, vulnerable creatures, women. Silly at the wrong moment.

It was a Saturday, but Maurice Revel was going to his office just the same; stopped – he often did – to look at it; to think about it.

French Justice is administered in buildings of much weight and majesty, varying little in style as our government veered from monarchical to imperial and then republican régimes: throughout the nineteenth century nothing happened to alter the courses of the Law. And precious little since. We are a legalistic people, with a relish for complicated formulae on paper. We adore the Letter of our law, hate to do anything that alters it. The most that is allowed is a scrap of tinkering; cosmetic, a little silver above a magistrate's ears: touch of distinction.

Other monuments – banks, or the stock-exchange – modernise the interiors of their temples. A show of progress; public relations veneer and a perfunctory pretence of respect for the public. We do not. The Palace (it is always a palace) of Justice is loyal alike to the fabrics, the mentality, and the aesthetic taste of the first Napoleon.

And of all the poor relations, at budget time, our department is the most indigent. Governments lavish with autoroutes or aircraft carriers can never find a penny for Justice. The Keeper of the Seals is felt to be sufficiently rewarded by the possession of these valuable artefacts: surely he doesn't want money as well. This is the Senior Minister. The job was always given to an elderly nonentity thereafter expected to be neither seen nor heard. And when, very recently, we got a Minister who was both seen and heard, precious little thanks he got for it, and a lot of abuse.

Castang, ten minutes later, wasn't thinking about it; didn't notice it much. He had lived all his working life with it. Had often laughed at it, sure; sourly enough. Since it was a Saturday, and nobody here, it struck him more than usual: the acres of hallway and stairway and stone passage, the shortage of lavatories. The handsome, massive oaken doors labelled XXXVII, more napoleonic, and thus more legal, than saying 37; lettered in gold paint with legends like President's Robing Room, but he scarcely bothered to imagine the goings-on within, splendour of furred robes and a wonderful cylindrical hat, like a cook's. And in England they have wigs, instead, but it's just the same and all of it Bleak House.

He pattered on, towards the corridor of the judges of instruction; pushed a door covered in padded, buttoned black leather as though it were part of a chesterfield sofa. Much favoured by the legal and medical professions. Nobody will hear the screams.

Maurice Revel was sitting in his office (the Cabinet of M. le Juge). He had worked at making it informal, and even pleasant. At least once a week he bought flowers. He had thrown out shelvesful of blackish leathery lawbooks which nobody ever looked at. He remained burdened with the trappings, and trapdoors, of office.

There's no point in being facetious. It is of course possible to imagine a President Disrobing (assisted by the chorus of *The Beggar's Opera*, the ladies-of-the-town). But a judge of instruction isn't funny. Maurice did not lack humour, but was too well-trained a magistrate to worry about it. Like Castang a professional. Worrying led to neurosis, and incompetence. But he thought about his job.

Denis Manuel was right; a good idea for these two men to meet and strike up a friendship. For a commissaire of police is as ludicrous as a judge. To this day he is empowered (flanked by a bailiff and a locksmith) to enter private property in the nocturnal hours, something utterly forbidden to cops; for the purpose of catching wives in adultery. Great fun, though Castang has never done it. Depriving himself of income: it is remunerated and there are plenty of vindictive husbands around. You can get out of paying alimony this way.

"Good morning, Henri." They shook hands, being French. Maurice looked lawyerly; middle-aged, middle-sized, unremarkable. A face shaped like a fourleafed clover; wings of darkish hair beneath some baldness, balanced lower down by a tendency to jowl, a shaved glossy pudginess on either side of a clever little tucked-away mouth. His eyes were a clear grey, friendly when not burdened by judgedom. "Coffee?" He had a stainless-steel Italian machine on the side table.

And while they are drinking their coffee, in silence, a lawyerly exchange took place. Caution, on both sides. The two men do not know each other well. A social meeting, with a lot to drink, had allowed them to be unbuttoned, to use first names. They are much of an age; Revel a year or two the older. But here they have their masks on. Like two fencers. There will be some footwork, to impress the other.

"I'm sorry to have dragged you all the way out here," offered Revel. "Seemed a good place, for a word. In confidence." Castang nodded. The Judge had something to say and needed his office for it; a place where he could be official, and also be Maurice. "Not a thing I'd want to hear talked about in company. Even at home." Castang is nodding away wisely while wondering if this is about what he thinks it is . . . They're a well- and an ill-assorted pair. Rather a comic couple they make.

For even if both devoted to upholding the law, they're on opposite sides of the fence. The police in European countries are subject to the authority of the examining magistrate. Even a commissaire can get told off like a schoolboy and as a rule there isn't much love lost. The executive and the judicial branches . . . and here they are; you'd almost say conspiring.

"I like it here on a Saturday," Maurice was saying. "I can think, then. No clerk, no gendarmerie shuffling about with sad people in handcuffs. The paper of course never goes away. But at least there are no interruptions."

This too holds a message for Castang. Officially everything which takes place in the judge's 'cabinet' is confidential, and the 'secret of instruction' a well-worn shibboleth. In practice things mysteriously become-known. Plenty of advocates and plenty of judges are chronic leakers to the press. Apart from the professional shop talk in wash- and cloakrooms.

The instructing judge is the hinge between the two branches. The principle is that he is independent of either, and can be subjected to no pressure of expediency or politics. It is laid down as a tenet that instruction may hold no bias towards either guilt or innocence. This judge sits on no tribunal and is never present in court. His enquiry establishes the facts, which he assembles and sends with his conclusions to the Procureur. Where there is doubt the subject will be sent for trial; that is what trials are for. Where the instruction establishes innocence the papers will be marked 'No case to answer' and the matter is at an end.

A good system, and very French. Brilliant in theory; complicated and leaky in practice.

"Denis Manuel told me – allowed it to be known is a better phrase – that you had come by a disquieting piece of knowledge, which you had then brought to his notice." This is all very careful, but Maurice Revel is by definition a careful and a scrupulous man. "The indiscretion is justifiable. You see, this kind of thing has happened once or twice lately."

"There are always a few like that hanging about," said Castang, "but they don't often reach the surface." His own criminal-brigade experience must be as long as Revel's, pretty near. "There's very little one can do about them." The grey area, of child abuse, is something both cops and courts have to live with. Physical battery, mental sadism, sexual assault, incestuous or not; eighty per cent of it escapes them. There wasn't anything remarkable about that child Sabine, except that she'd been momentarily the bosom pal of his own daughter.

"Exactly," said Maurice. "Complaints are rarely made, and even when they are, they tend to get hushed up before they reach my desk."

"Better off without them," suggested Castang.

"Yes – yes," in a high voice. "But one cannot close the eye to what one knows. Not very long ago an instance of this sort was suppressed, I'm sorry to say. Another – to my knowledge – could have been prosecuted. There was some technical doubt whether the evidence was sufficiently substantial. But I'm afraid, Henri, that in both cases it was not thought expedient, and that protection played a role. Of someone highly placed." There was a bit of a twitch, at the corner of the magistrate's eye; face of someone finding a fly in the soup, at a Presidential dinnerparty.

"Not only have I got no dossier," in a voice just short of the irritable, even the querulous, "but I've no firm ground for legitimate suspicion. Which doesn't prevent me," in the deep voice, "from possessing a fairly shrewd idea . . ."

Mildly, Castang repeated the crashing truism that some sleeping dogs are better left unpoked at. Ashamed of this even as he said it.

"Henri," wheeling his chair round to stare at the window, "not long ago a judge of instruction – a woman, too – left a homicide suspect sitting in prison for two years. Without once bringing the file to the forefront of her desk. She was expecting a promotion, you see: she wanted nothing to rock her boat. This suspect happened to be a black man.

"In default of any proper instruction he was brought to trial, where he was promptly found innocent – patently so – and discharged. He sued the State for unlawful detention, and the Court awarded him heavy damages. He had lost three years of his life. Nobody, to my knowledge, blocked that judge's promotion.

"Puts," in a different voice, "an indecently acute pressure upon us; not to be like that."

He has wide powers, the instructing judge. He can subpoena whoever he may wish as witness; call upon any expert opinion, technical, medical or psychological. Important resources of public time and money are saved in the avoidance of unnecessary trials, and, it may well be, bad miscarriages of justice.

The English nose, accustomed to the accusatorial system, tends to wrinkle. We do not fail to object that these private and secret procedures smell of an Inquisition. For in England a bad judge can be heard and seen, criticised, and perhaps opposed. All this is true. A bad instructing judge is worse than none at all. Some, as Maurice Revel is the first to admit, are too young, inexperienced and impressionable, for the laureate of the Magistrates' School may still be under thirty and know nothing of the world.

But safeguards exist. Any suspect has the right to counsel, should there be adumbrations of bullying or inducement. Still, judge and counsel are generally friendly, and a smell of plea-bargaining can hang about these proceedings.

"Your shrewd idea . . ." said Castang into the silence.

"Yes . . . yes." Dragged to it, and now that he's got there, hating this sluglike phosphorescent trail of hearsay. "There's a man called Dampierre. A member of the Academy."

"Haven't I seen him on television?"

"Quite likely. Makes a hobbyhorse of education. An interest in adolescent schoolchildren . . . Is there anything more difficult than to know how much weight one is to give to the tales of children?"

"Children hear and see all sorts of horrors, but are tougher than we think."

"Others are not so fortunate." The tone was level. Just a bit dry, just a scrap of sarcasm. "Your daughter was a witness to a nasty adventure. Even if not duly mandated, Henri, there's a thing or two I'd like you to look into. While loafing about with art frauds." Rather nasty, that.

Defensively, Castang had put his hands in his pockets.

Revel was looking out of his window, standing there silent a long moment. In front of the Palace of Justice the pavements leading to the tiered and pillared entrance converged upon a municipal flowerbed bordered by parsimonious hedges; horizontal juniper and cotoneaster: spiky things indifferent to the nasty habits of the public. Two gardeners were surveying the scene. Their rakings had disturbed a jetsam of cigarette packets, cola cans, plastic wrappings and hideous remnants of fast food. A strolling rat would give the dump a glance and leave it to the poor. The two were now leaning upon broom and shovel, in an attitude of municipal contemplation, like statues by Rodin. A third arrived towing a trolley loaded with dim bedding-plants, and spat in the centre of the border as though to provide a marker.

"I'll change places with them," said the Judge of Instruction, "any time of day." He sat down, pushed away his empty coffeecup and made a pass with his hands to exorcise the papers on his table.

"There isn't any evidence, and nobody makes any complaint. I want you to find the one and provoke the other. Then, perhaps, I can act."

Commissaire Salès was back from Japan. Contented? – apparently so. Not much to say for herself and nothing about her doings; she seemed more interested in the progress of the pink woolly pullover that Frau Morandière was knitting for herself. In fact the three of them were being municipal, exactly like the gardeners. She was counting her stitches with a tense face and muttering lips. Salès was shuffling papers about as though puzzled to find so little stimulus in any of them, and Castang perused the afternoon paper, stopping to read the juicy bits aloud. The professional interest here was that the Louvre had jam on its face, from an illegally acquired Murillo. They were enjoying the jam, because several distinguished advocates, an impeccable Swiss notary, and several art experts, had all somehow got involved in whitewashing a good deal of money, a lot of which had stuck to them, though all of course in the most innocent manner imaginable. It gave them a good laugh.

" 'A new illustration of false appearances, the lights and darks in the commerce of works of art, where social respectability rubs elbows with exquisite crookdom.' " Castang, quoting *Le Monde*.

"When good pieces turn up cheap," Morandière changing needles, "they can't ask why, because they might not like the answer. D'you recall the Raphael which the holy nuns had thrown in the attic, as being pious rubbish?"

"I did warn them at the time," said Salès, "that the young woman was up to no good. They were so dazzled by all the splendid guarantees by Maître This and That they wouldn't listen. And who'd blame them? How often does a piece of such exceptional quality turn up? Isn't a museum director anywhere in the world wouldn't commit parricide, let alone close eyes to jobbery over a few paltry million. Damn it, now I've got to go to Italy about the Flemish tapestries from Arles. The dealer in Milano says he Can't Remember."

"The chemical factory in Tours," Castang was ruminating onward, "wow, fiftysix reported cases of pollution and nobody paid a blind bit of heed because they were such good friends with the Prefect. I'd like to go to Italy."

"You can go to Arles," dry, "and examine how a burglary took place because the builders who were mending the roof never bothered taking the scaffolding down. Some detective work needed there, all right!"

"I got that faker for you, incidentally. A Miró, two Balthus and a rather ambitious Chagall. It wasn't very hard; he's only nineteen years old."

"They were very poor fakes. Even the old gentleman in the Academy didn't take much over five minutes to see through them."

"Speaking of the Academy does anyone know anything about Monsieur Dampierre?"

"Save that he's in the Academy," said Morandière, "and who needs or wants to learn more? Sudden shortage is there, of unreadable books?"

"He has a collection of medals," added Salès. "Without getting excited about it, a lot of them were certainly stolen, but who's going to ask an Academician embarrassing questions?"

"Has he now? Well, I think that I might."

"Don't get yourself burned." Madame Salès blushed suddenly. "I shouldn't be telling you that. But be careful. He has better friends than a pack of Prefects."

"If the Slyboots in Milano," wistfully, "has a very bad memory, give me a ring, and I'll come and light matches under his toenails."

"Italian laws are totally incomprehensible and I can only hang about buttering up the Sheriff's Office."

"I can't even remember French laws," idly turning the pages of the newspaper. " 'Genetic Sequels of the Battle of Poitiers' – what a splendid title."

The Lyceum is as perennial, as napoleonic as a Judge of Instruction. Domino effects beset these rigid, granitic structures: chip at a stone and the edifice might well tumble on your head. France holds on tight to this beloved feature of the landscape, and the Monolith, Bastillewise assaulted in 'sixtyeight, has shown itself astonishingly elastic.

Outwardly it hasn't changed. Its resonant historic name rolls out as heavy and splendid on the tongue, and it still prepares the élite of the nation's children for higher things. Uniforms and drumrolls have gone out, like public executions, but the aspect is still frowningly military; the Alcazar at Toledo. Even inside you won't see much change until the bell goes, and you see that half the children are girls. The professors, as well qualified as those in university faculties (and a lot more privileged), will still greet one another with a ceremonious sweep in passages. The grand manitous who rule this world are still called le Proviseur and le Censeur. The Gymnasium or the Prytaneum are not far off. Nor – thought Castang – were the genetic sequels of the battle of Poitiers.

All right, an élite is no longer officially allowed to exist. They had to quadruple their intake. To find classroom space

they now only take children for the last three classes before
the sacred Baccalaureat.

A Proviseur is now perforce a humble soul. He is per-
petually short of money, staff, and space. He spends much
time apologising for shortcomings, while full of reassurance
about a bigger and brighter future. Most of the parents pin
a pathetic faith to education, while convinced that schools are
full of delinquent hooligans stuffed with drugs. He was anxious
to be polite to Castang, even if a Commissaire is nothing much
as bourgeois notables go – about on a level with a Proviseur.

Quite a lot of Castang's interest was genuine curiosity.
What a long time ago it seemed – and in a Paris as removed,
as archaic as Nineveh. The grim old Port-Royal quarter, surrounded entirely by hospitals, prisons and lunatic asylums.
A small shivering child, working its way upward from the
eleventh class of the Petit Lycée. A severe entrance examination governed entrance to the sixth and the Grand Lycée.
We were unbelievably disciplined. Past participles beautifully
harmonised, mental arithmetic like lightning; two spelling mis-
takes in a dictation meant a zero. A quite magnificent level of
instruction, and as I remember no education at all. I survived;
I was 'a bright child'. Lydia cannot spell, needs an electronic
machine to multiply six by seven, and half the children in her
class read following the line with their finger. My irregular verbs
are faultless and I am word-perfect in the rivers of Europe. My
administrative prose style, a model of simplicity and lucidity, is
derived from Caesar's *Gallic War*. Lydia at thirteen is far more
educated than I was at twenty.

But the Proviseur is lecturing – I must pay attention.

"Going into the fourth is she, your girl? Then we've time
to look around us. No worries – with the College we have
a perfect sense of continuity. Special programmes we have
embarked upon. The child has a literary gift? Then next year
she may have the fortune to meet Monsieur Dampierre." And
this was what Castang had come to hear. A bit more than curiosity, hereabout. It is the school's big gun. The Academician.

Goldlaced uniform, cocked hat and sword. The equestrian order, even if he doesn't ride his horse into the town.

A practised patter. Monsieur had come to the Proviseur with a scheme. He deplores the lipservice paid to Maths – as silly as the old bias towards classics? – and is much concerned at the decay in the purity of the language: he proposed to encourage small reading groups. Between the fourth and second classes; catch them early enough for the flame to be spontaneous. Short-ish evening sessions, the official programme is not interrupted. The children simply love it, Monsieur Castang. A remarkable man, and most generous thus to give us the fruit.

Edified, Castang would like to learn more. No, Monsieur does not conduct classes as such, nor in the Lycée itself. Perhaps the atmosphere is a little depressing in the evenings. The chil-dren do not like to come back there (and the cleaning-women must be allowed to get on with their work). But the old coaching auberge in the town, that's right, the Golden Hart. They have these rambling suites of rooms for banquets, and one by special arrangement – a cosier atmosphere, not so blackboardy, you follow me. It cuts at worst into their television-watching time, and that we'll agree is no great loss.

Castang quite agreed. Not at all, not at all – my pleasure.

He has not gone to Paris this morning, having other schemes. Monsieur D. lives somewhere in the offing, but where, pre-cisely? Damn, the map is not where it belongs, in the glove compartment of the car.

This was countryside, and the nameless, crooked sort of road that went with it. Directions asked, of various people met, tended to be vague. A big villa. But it's hard to see from the road. No, it's quite small really but it stands out. Norman sort of style, you know? Sort of stripy? He caught a glimpse then of the peppermint bullseye look behind a high green hedge; braked and reversed. There was a gateway, and gravel overgrown with grass. That is no villa; cottage, he'd call it. Still, he was off the road. Does no harm to ask afresh. Can't be far out. Nice little house. Only one storey, but attractive among the trees. Like the witch's house, that you can eat.

The noise he made had drawn attention. Windows were open to a damp spring day and the sort of drizzle which wets you, after you decided that it wasn't worth putting on a raincoat. A woman's head showed and a moment later the woman appeared on a wooden verandah.

"Sorry to bother you. I'm looking for Monsieur Dampierre's house."

"You're not the first." Nice contralto voice, sounding amused. "Vain old man. Why can't he put up a notice? But you're out of luck. He ain't there." She broke suddenly into song.

"I see him going by just an hour ago

    With a girl called Nelly Bly . . ." Her accent was funny too: something further east than Vera's.

"I can come back, that's no problem, but where's the Sorcerer's Residence?"

"And I'm the witch," giggling. "You don't see it, through the trees. This used to be the lodge. Fifty metres along there's a gateway between two holly trees. If you aren't afraid of being turned into a bat. And you ring up for permission. Or you would if the phone were listed, which it ain't." She had sharp, bright eyes.

"But I have a magic password." Entering into the spirit, since she showed no sign of impatience. Whoever she was, she wasn't usual. The bright eyes were going over him carefully.

"I'll buy your password. For – a cup of coffee?"

"That's hospitable." No French woman would have let him in to the house.

"Perhaps. Come on in, then." He followed through a french-window into a large corner room with a second window looking out to the roadway, explaining 'Nelly Bly'. "I was working badly," busy with a coffee machine, "and you appeared. Useful – maybe. Sugar there and that's cream if you don't mind canned."

"How, useful?"

"No no – the password, first."

"That's easy. People peer out from behind bars, and say they're busy. So I hold up my card – like this – and say 'Police!' They let one in, then. Curious or frightened – or both." She put her head back to laugh; a fine throat.

"I knew it. Not that you were a cop, but that my instinct was right. There's character in your features." She put her cup on the arm of a sofa and made an odd gesture, with her thumbs and middle fingers formed into a frame, through which she looked at him. "Now prove you're a cop; what's my job?" Castang is married to a painter; there was no smell of oil or turps, but there was a large working-table set to a slant.

"Designer."

"Not bad. One more try."

Castang's street skills were dimmed by lack of practice. But more recently he had learned to look at pictures in a way cops know, at details of ear and hand; at the way paint goes on, and is built up. And he was 'on trial'.

He was looking at a woman of forty, a strong forthright face with no makeup and dark hair combed back into a single long braid. Plain, but striking. A large body in firm planes like the face, muscular under the softness; dressed in trousers and shirt, and over that a bush shirt of coarse cotton, with many pockets and a row of coloured pens clipped in one of them. Plaited leather sandals on her feet.

The room was sparsely furnished, with little to tell but that here lived someone with a clear visual taste and a good colour sense. There were books, and pictures, but it was a workroom. There were sheets of paper on the table with pencil drawings and written annotations. She had lit a cigarette and was staring out of the window. There was a slav look to the planes of the face, bigger and heavier than Vera's. The hands were heavy; no rings. He remembered the fingers making a frame.

"Theatre, or movie, or both."

"Good, Mr Police Officer. So do tell me what you want of my landlord. Registering a complaint? Not making one, surely?"

"Not going to tell you; it's none of your business." A gurgle of laughter as she slapped her cup on the saucer.

"Idle female? Nosy Parker? Writers see things as a paragraph in fiction. We're the same. The postman comes; it's a scene; how does it compose? I look at you through a camera. Or my landlord. He's an interesting man. If you get to meet him, observe the way he walks – or talks. But he leaves me alone, I leave him alone, we aren't palsywalsy.

"And there he is, by the way." She had not looked, but the sound came of a car motor slowing, changing down for a turn. "Big Mercedes. Cream-coloured. I try to keep my senses sharp. Peeled, do you call it? I call it dusted," illustrated by expressive hand movement, 'dusting'. "It's my trade. Perhaps you've given me something: I don't know yet. But come up and see me some time," in the deep, Mae-West voice. "Nothing is ever what it seems."

She gave again her little hitching bubble of laughter. Water comes up from a hole in the ground, thought Castang. One can build a little stone surround, and it's a spring. Ferns will grow in the cracks. And perhaps it is the source of the Danube.

She had sat down behind her working bench, put on reading glasses. Another of her sudden scraps of ridiculous song lipped over, like water. "'Getting to know all Ab-out you . . . Day – by – Day.'"

"My name is Castang," he said. "I am a commissaire of police. I work in Paris. I live over the other side of the town, and I'm in the phonebook, and it could happen that we could help one another," with his hand on the door. The eyes glinted at him.

"My name is Maria Varvara. By coincidence, I also am in the phonebook. Have a nice day now." He turned the car on the weedy gravel and got a perky wave of her hand, on the way out.

Two holly trees, yes. And a narrow track, asphalted. Inside the wood it opened out, into a parking space, and beyond there was a gate, very locked and with a notice saying *Ring*. He peeked through. Immediately beyond, a narrow plank footbridge crossed a brook, a metre wide between deep clayey banks. Here was a fellow who really cared about his privacy, because one could guess that the brook made a complete tour of the house. Here on this side of the water a sturdy mesh fence protected a high yew hedge. Effective, and an assailant getting through that would still have a scramble to cross the brook, and there might well be an electric wire in the bank. One could conclude that Monsieur Dampierre was rich, and had things worth protecting. Like objects of art.

Castang had seen castles on artificial islands. Moats were decorative. There could be some sort of lake or lilypond on the far side here, but what he could see was no castle; a smallish house, and not even old, in the Norman style of alternated beams and plaster in narrow vertical stripes, with the top storey mansarded in the steep-pitched roof. Imitating a castle, with a hanging turret on the angle facing him; hexagonal and too small to be anything but a bathroom. At the far side a bigger, octagonal tower had been built on, in a chessboard pattern of beige and white stone. Nicely done, with the pepperpot top brought into skilful proportion with the main block. Tasteful ensemble, if mannered and precious. Suitable to middle-aged gent of cultivated nature and plenty of wealth. One could guess at three big rooms downstairs and four bedrooms on top with as many bathrooms. One didn't recall hearing mention of a Madame Dampierre.

The house stood on a knoll of grass. Well kept; there could be a nice terraced garden behind. All highly desirable.

He went back to his car. The cream-coloured Mercedes, some years old but well looked after, did make him a bit jealous. He got his briefcase, and a businesslike look. Rang the bell and waited till a rusty female voice said, "Yes?"

"Castang, Commissaire de Police, calling on Monsieur

Dampierre." A silence, before the latch clicked. A smooth flagged path to the door held open by an elderly biddy with a mistrustful eye.

"Credentials? . . . Wait here please, and I'll let him know." Time to study a panelled hall, real marble chequered red and white, and a grandfather clock. "He says he'll join you in the library, in just a moment." She held a door open – closefitting, heavy hardwood – left it open. Vanished on felt slippers. The house was quiet; he could hear the clock tick in the stillness.

The library was what it said. An English style, of glass-fronted mahogany, brass reading-lamps, leather armchairs. Impersonal; the books looked as though nobody read them, the chairs as though nobody sat on them. Like the waitingroom of an expensive doctor. He hadn't time for more before a small noise made him turn.

Monsieur Dampierre had a peculiar way of coming into a room: a sidelong fashion of keeping close to the door and holding on by the handle as though it might come off. He held Castang's card in his other hand. He spoke in a muffled voice between closed lips, as people do who have bad teeth, and with a jerky delivery, pausing as though he had conquered a stammer but was afraid of it breaking out. Sniffs accompanied this, and snuffly laughs when there was nothing funny. From a well-known speaker in public it appeared excessive. Everyone has masks.

"Monsieur Castang, good morning. Won't you siddown? What can I do to be of service to you?"

"Kind of you to give me time. I'd have rung but the number's unlisted. No great matter – as you see on the card – Fraud Squad, Beaux Arts."

"So I see and am quite curious. All the way from Paris?"

"We've had a number of items signalled in *Stolen Art*, which is a publication you may have come across. A few fine, early American coins, and we're wondering whether anyone's been attempting surreptitious sale." Just enough of this was not nonsense.

"Well now, that's courteous of you and perhaps you'd like a – a drink?" Apology, even shame, at allowing the Demon in the house. He looked about, as if wondering where the drinks were kept, headed sideways for a corner cupboard, pottered incompetently with a decanter.

"Smoke if you feel like it. I don't myself collect Americana, but we'll – look for you."

He was a small thin man, looking smaller in an English tweed suit. He would be in the lateish fifties, bald in front with a dark tanned forehead and hairy ears. There were mild, bright blue eyes behind oval glasses in gold wire frames: he looked much like Mr Kipling without the big moustache. Behind the fumbling diffidence was a humorous alertness. A bony hairy hand gave Castang a glass of port; it had bunches of tendon and big oval nails filed and polished. Expensive clothes. One expects an Academician to have plenty of money.

His books sold well: Castang has not read them but has heard them praised. He now remembers seeing the man on television: decisive and professional, with the punning, joking talent which is the French literary manner.

"Can't say I've laid eyes on these you have here. One does get offered sly things from time to time. Any dealer would know it wasn't – my line. Small circle – specialists – do sometimes go outside if one hears of something to – pounce upon, but own collection mostly Renaissance medals. Want to see?" nodding towards a tallboy cabinet with the shallow drawers for what Castang calls butterflies.

"Pleased to, but I'm no connoisseur. How'll I put it? – I'm the criminal technician. My work is mostly the means used for fraud or robbery, rather than judging intrinsic values."

"No bad idea. Great increase in volume of fraudulent handling. Forces one to take expensive precautions. Not surprised to hear, chap like you, drafted in to stiffen um, prevention. My pictures, nothing much, one or two minor eighteenth-century masters. Got some pretty – books. But obliged to turn house into a fortress. Insurance premiums – outrageous."

"I had a case not long ago," struck by how long ago it was. "Rare stamp dealer, a professional; and professionally cleaned out."

"Not a bit surprised. Isolated here. I'm a careful man." And well protected, thought Castang.

"Home already!" said Vera.

"Nothing wrong with that, is there?"

"Surprised, that's all."

"Startled is the effect desired. Surprised would be the lover bareass in the clothes cupboard."

"Idiot – only just in myself, as it happens. I've found a job – no, just social work a bit."

"You haven't started cooking? Right, find a tin of cassoulet or whatever for the girls, and we'll go out to the pub. Why, why, I feel like it, that's why. All these explanations. I can do social work too, can't I?"

"Yes, well, I still want to change my frock; not going out like this, even to the pub. What are you fussing for? – oceans of time."

"Because I have a particular reason for wanting to be early."

. . . "If we have to eat out, why here? This menu doesn't look at all inspiring; why shouldn't we go to that nice riverside place, Whats-her-name's house – Sabine?"

"I've a reason for that, too. After a few drinks you won't notice the lousy food."

"All right, I've understood, you're on a job and it has nothing to do with art, but what's all the mystery? Get me another drink, I've got to go to the lavatory."

"Vera – just tell me when you come back whether you noticed anything unusual?"

. . . "I don't know whether you'd call it odd. The place is full of schoolchildren."

"Monsieur Dampierre of the Académie Française is giving one of his special literature classes."

"And this is the point?"

"If this job can be done at all it'll be devastatingly tricky."

"It's to do with that child Sabine?"

"I went to see the parents, yes, the riverside restaurant. Very snotty the wife was too; held me at bay, and told me pointblank to mind my business. The handicap, in a thing of this sort, is that covering it up is in everyone's interest. Above all, no scandals. It's natural for people who depend upon local trade and goodwill. And the same applies to Denis Manuel. A doctor knows all sorts of things but had better keep his trap tight shut or he'd lose his entire practice. He put me on to Maurice Revel. Three of us with a vested interest in saying and doing nothing.

"Maurice has talked me – much against my inclination – into some police work; informal and very inefficient."

"I'm getting confused here. You've got a suspect?"

"I was a bit upset about that girl Sabine – just a year older than Lydia. Maurice tells me that indirectly he heard of another instance. His hands are tied – no evidence, and no authority. Now you take a guess at what has been going on."

"You're telling me that the man, teaching the girls about *Madame Bovary* here in the back room . . . ?"

"Keep your voice down. Circumstantial pointers but no evidence. Voice suspicions and we'd both be carried out of this district, feet first, Maurice and me both."

"But you mean you're going to dig, to keep a watch? He takes home young girls, for what the papers call 'ballets roses'?"

"Dig," said Castang. "What with, a garden trowel? I'd breathe deeply before using even a plastic toothpick. I should dig a hole and sit in it with a periscope? I can watch, sure. Maybe he comes out of here and has a girl beside him in the front seat of that big nice Mercedes. And what does that prove?

I met him this afternoon. He's a very sly bugger indeed."

"Oh God," said Vera, "and I'm drinking here on an empty stomach. Feed me with a tough steak. And canned petits-pois. And those very hard, shrunken pommes-frites. And a bottle of red plonk. Let the blind be led by the blind, say I."

Castang looked at her with sympathy. She's just nicely-pissed.

"What I have, maybe, is a kind of listening post. He lives in a country house, about twenty kilometres off, barricaded like the forts of Verdun. There's a lodge to it, hired for purposes of thought and quiet by a Russian film director. If one kept an eye out – but it's hard to see how to get further. Nobody'll talk."

"What's he called?" interested.

"It's a her. One of these Stepinskaya names so she calls herself Maria Varvara."

"I've heard of her; said to be good."

Like Academicians, thought Castang. Everyone's heard of them, and they're said to be good.

Drunk or not, Vera was useful, since nobody thinks anything of a woman pottering in the passages of a country hotel. While a man, conspicuous inside a building, can tack about unnoticed in the parking lot outside. The reading group, a dozen children in chatter with the great man, dispersed and she could peek. Nothing to see; a semicircle of chairs and a litter of coffeecups. Two girls in need of a pee. And outside, the knot scattered, to the McDonald's across the street, or to bicycles. No one got offered a lift in the cream-coloured Mercedes.

They compared notes.

"Ten, eleven children. It's a privilege; they aren't going to cut these sessions."

"Only three boys but that's normal; the boys are more math-minded and think literature a bit sissy. What age d'you give them?"

"Fourteen to fifteen; the fourth class."

"There's an older group, in third. Mm, the idea is to catch them young; mm, both ways."

"You've been detecting?"

"Nothing much; the Proviseur of the Lycée. Oh, and a woman in our street, who had a flat battery one morning. History teacher, quiet sensible woman, and to Lydia a sadistic fiend. This is the major problem; children see things differently."

"Pompous remark. No thanks, I don't want a huge ice-cream."

"I might pick at cheese a bit."

"Give me one of your cigarettes." Vera doesn't smoke 'except in restaurants'. Not a totally useless evening – she had exaggerated the horribleness of both the steak and the frites. But you wouldn't write it in your diary.

Quite early when they got home; a bit after nine. Of course the children are still looking at the television. Castang sat down in front of the set, leaving the programme out of sheer idleness. When Vera got back ten minutes later, from exercising discipline on the toothbrush front, he said idly, "Look at this."

"Turn the tripe off."

The 'sociology' might be that they belong to that high-minded group, said to be between two and five per cent, who disapprove of the box. Reality is that they're more likely to find the thing boring. When she finds it on she stares blankly with an eye and a mind elsewhere: he will switch it on, to be found, ten minutes after, sunk into a light doze. He will set the recording machine, for some cultural delight programmed at three in the morning, and then forget all about it. Since the children are sent to bed at eight-thirty – but this also is a rarity, in France.

So that now they are repairing a neglected area of their education.

"The children were looking at this . . . you sure as hell won't get that on Czech television."

"I suppose that must be accounted standard fare." Castang, who 'hadn't realised' and told himself he should have known, was rather more taken aback than she was.

"You hadn't realised?" Madame Morandière was amused. Carlotta Salès, conscientious woman, was already out and at work, but the other two senior-members like a cup of coffee and a chat, before settling to their stride . . .

"There's pathos in this innocence, I agree. There, I scarcely look at the thing."

"I can never get away from it." Her children are older than his: eighteen and sixteen. "True, I don't take in much."

"But a thirteen-year-old . . ."

"Water off a duck's back," robust. "Look, there are two sorts of programme – the dramatic violent ones, which all take place in the dark, so you can't tell the goodies from the baddies, and can't hear a word said anyhow; and these softedged things you complain of, but they're just as unreal. The sun is always shining and the girls are always naked, and real life never intrudes."

"Lydia has certainly a sense of reality." Looking at a repro-duction of a Greek legend, classically delineated, she had asked (exactly like Pamela Widmerpool) 'Who's the naked guy with the stand?' Thoroughly sceptical about the swan screwing Leda – 'Oh I see; myth . . .'

In his twenty years in the criminal brigade, Castang has seen enough of pubic hair to be able to say it's no great treat to him. Still, he's a man, isn't he?

As in crim-brig days he has bought a school exercise-book to note it all down in; facts and suppositions, evidence of things seen and of things imagined: the true coincidences and the false ones. Like every policeman of his generation he has had the Boston Strangler held up as a text: their row of four nigh-perfect suspects while poor Albert the 'Measuring Man' was under their nose for the whole year, but the computer had him classed under the wrong heading . . . His daybook, his diary; he is humourless about it. Over and over, he tells himself that whatever the circumstances may look like, he hasn't any evidence, and the circumstantial is just not good enough.

They had been mightily entangled in their own scruples, there in Boston; ridiculously but rightly so. How right to be distrustful of the psychiatric experts: a dozen tempting strangler-types, damned lucky to have no hard, factual evidence like a hair, a thread, or a button against them. While nobody wanted to believe in Albert: he 'didn't fit the pattern'. Lewd-and-lascivious behaviour; the measuring man had lifted several hundred skirts in the Boston area. But that's not murder, is it.

Wasn't this affair here perhaps a much ado about nothing? True, both Maurice Revel and himself have struggled with their scruples. There would be a criminal charge. 'Attouchements', 'Attentat à la pudeur'. Slipping your hand up a skirt while teaching her Latin is a serious offence. And these girls, who looked at the eternal-sunlight movies in which the unbuttoning of frocks and the lifting of nighties was common form . . . it might be water off a duck's back to most but there would always be a few who would think it amusing to tempt, to provoke.

It worries him because his thoughts have been turning to entrapment. Fancy stuff with concealed cameras and microphones is mostly inadmissible, legally: evidence obtained by improper means. But the police use it often enough, when they lack anything better. Pin it on him, the police are apt to think. It's damning, illegal or not; we've got him, and now watch the bugger wriggle. So that Castang too has used such means. Set a bit of bait and wait for the crocodile to swallow it. After that, you let the judge of instruction worry whether it's admissible. That's his work: you've done yours.

But psychiatric patterns . . . Standard thinking used to be that the sex criminal progressed, from flashing, say, to fiddling with little boys and girls, and might well end up with raping. This is all a bit too glib for some authorities. Maurice Revel thought there might be some evidence of rape, but how are we to tell for sure? By laying some bait, said the cop. We don't know enough, said the magistrate.

Anyhow; what bait? Nobody is going to make a policewoman into a convincing imitation of a schoolgirl. Porn video-tapes do, but not in real life. It would be possible, and even fairly easy, to find girls of around fifteen with all too much knowing cynicism. It wouldn't work. This sort of predator is sly, and quick to smell deception. This man is highly intelligent.

It takes a genuine innocence to stimulate this perversion. Alice perhaps wondered what made Lewis Carroll's trousers stick out that funny way in front.

These meditations were interrupted by Carlotta Salès pottering about. The third time, surely, this morning? – what was making her so restless? The tortuous procedures of Italian justice; but that was a commonplace, and one she was well used to. Sitting there brooding in a nest of paperwork; snappy when spoken to: curse, no doubt (hereby showing himself as unimaginatively selfsatisfied as the male can be). Making no headway with his problem – on government time too – he let his mind idle in neutral, like a driver at a red light, gazing at any pretty woman in the field of vision.

It looked as though Salès had been gingering herself up whilst in Italy. For lack of anything better to do? She had a snazzy new Milanese haircut. A tall, thinnish woman, she had her hair cut urchin-short. This had been smartened and the fringe, cunningly uneven, gave a new emphasis to her eyes. He hadn't-really-noticed, before. The eyes are not slav, like Vera's (or Maria Varvara, dressed in wolfskins, swigging at the sour mare's milk), but they have a slant at the corners. Taking a guess there must be Vietnamese blood there somewhere. One pictured her in a flowered silk jacket, the padded kind which buttons up to a tight stiffened collar. Frogs. And when she smiles, which is not often, the eyes narrow fetchingly.

Biting his ballpoint, the lordly male allowed his dissipated imagination to tilt towards lechery, unbuttoning the chinese jacket. Nice long neck, finely-boned shoulders. There were too many women around with shoulders like American football-players, and the same sort of clothes.

Salès has been doing something to her clothes. She is as a rule determinedly dowdy, so that even Frau Morandière giggles at the 'good navyblue skirt', inescapably schoolmarm.

Something supple there this morning; call it lithe. Been popping into the little boutique, in Milano.

Imagined male experiments with buttons disclose a fetching undergarment. He had bought this for Vera (in winter given to woolly vests, alarmingly Czech). 'That thing,' pointing at the window: it has straps, comes to hip length, not a petticoat. 'A caraco,' said the salesgirl grinning. A plain heavy silk, and 'beautifully comfortable' knickers went with it; expensive, and Vera much pleased. But it all had to be kept-for-best, and best doesn't come around often. So that one might as well take it off Salès, since the mind's a blank anyhow; deplorable behaviour from the senior civil-servant on taxpayer's monies, but the narrow straps slide off these slim rounded shoulders.

Salès hasn't much tit. In fact two fried eggs sunny side up, if ever I saw them. But you Haven't seen them – it did occur to Castang to pull himself up: he pushed the 'diary' aside, pettish, and dragged the official typewriter into place, for the parsimony of the administration has economised on a secretary. He has dropped cigar ash into its bowels – the administration last bought typewriters in 1950. Cursing, and manoeuvres with an old toothbrush, took his mind off the steamy manipulations.

The decline in live births has caused European governments to encourage the immigration of Moslem populations. High birth-rate, and a docile labour-force. This is why France is indulgent towards Arabs, and Germany towards Germans whose grandparents were born in Tadjikistan. Meanwhile, European women – blissfully sterile – become sex objects in an exaggerated way they hadn't exactly counted on. Commissaire Salès was surprised to find herself in this category. A fortnight in Italy has been known before to work havoc with the northern European female.

Does that sound crude? – she has been thinking about it. How old is she? – still skimming thirty. She had spent several years proving herself the technical, intellectual, commercial equal of the male animal. She had been disconcerted. Italian policemen appeared to hold her in a higher esteem than she was used to from French colleagues. They had also higher expectations. Maybe it is the mere fact of being French; the far-off hills are always greener. Hiding behind her own typewriter, Salès seeks objectivity and isn't doing well with it. All right; hell, be subjective.

One has to be careful with jokes about Italy: the English have been making them since long before Robert Browning. Recall Noël Coward. He saw the bar on the Piccola Marina, where love appeared to Mrs Wentworth-Brewster, with a gentle eye. The collection there of frauds, whores, and thieves is not malicious, or not by modern police standards.

Commissaire Castang is not a good witness; he is distracted, and worried. Madame Morandière is an excellent witness, in her cubbyhole appearing to see nothing. She sees and says what she chooses; which isn't much.

So that we're left with Carlotta herself, as witness. She is a trained policewoman, and a considerable authority on her subject: she has a very good eye for a picture. In Castang's eye she is still on the periphery of vision; how good is her own eye for things nearer home?

One must forget also the clichés about France; the stony-hearted egoists. What is France? Part of the European peninsula, and the way through to the others. The French are peasants, their feet screwed in to the land with bloody-minded obstinacy, but they are few now, getting old. Madame Saulnier, Castang's landlady, is a good example. For all her lifetime in the most bourgeois quarter of Paris she is simply a peasant woman. But look at all the others, ask who of them are French – look in the phonebook. They have come from somewhere else, and have paused in their journeying. They don't know where they are going; they are frightened people with long memories of injustice and oppression; they are insecure, and they lack the smugness of the island-race: they are much more like Americans. The words you will find most often repeated are 'fear' and 'dare'.

Paris is like a gigantic railwaystation, and one feels there the nervous excitement, the anxiety, as well as discomfort, impermanence. There is a little corner of a carriage, temporarily your own, with the smell of your overcoat; a claim pegged out by a magazine; some waste paper, a half-empty bottle of mineral water.

All French people make for themselves this little nest, characterised by fear of the outside; a bunker, much fortified. The American mania for being neighbourly, for making a private life public, is the exact converse and thus the very same. 'Je suis bien dans ma peau,' they say; I'm comfortable in my skin. But no further: beyond that, a profound and pronounced unease. Nothing lasts, as they say, as long as the impermanent.

So what and who is Carlotta Salès? Behind her typewriter, she is asking the same question. The name is French enough, but scratch and besides the Vietnamese grandmother Castang guesses at, you might come up with anything. She has been wondering whether the instinctive sympathy with italianate ways might not bespeak some Piedmontese origin. And it's a Toscan eye which looks at pictures.

She is a lonely person – as lonely as Castang had been before the meeting with Vera. She has a sister somewhere; last heard of in Montpellier: and a vague notion of cousins in America – South. Her childhood had passed in a small boring town in Normandy. Nothing to get sentimental about, but she had lost her father early. Dead? – no means of knowing; one rainy morning he was gone. From what she knew of Castang's background, which wasn't much, they had something in common: one got out of the ruck through grey matter and perseverance, why not say ambition? She supposes that if one were to analyse, she'd find that this police career had given her security: an illusion it may be but there'd been a clear and coherent (and these two words are as common in the French mouth as 'fear') picture of things. The delight in and longing for law which characterises Franks – 'Dieu et Mon Droit' is a slogan written upon English passports, but it's a very French sentiment.

Carlotta lives by herself, and keeps much to herself, in a rabbit-warren old building of a sort still frequent in central Paris, in the Tenth, just off the Faubourg du Temple. One goes through the archway in Bâtiment A across a scruffy courtyard to Bâtiment B. There are a lot of stone stairs. Above are unsafe-looking balconies, washing lines, moribund-seeming potplants. There are ingenious ropelift arrangements for hoisting heavy shopping, and lowering the garbage. There are smells of frites, drains, cabbage, and the household disinfectant called eau-de-javel which is the true scent of France, with that of centuries-old dust.

She is well enough paid to afford somewhere smarter, but is content here. It is not far from the Filles-du-Calvaire metro station, and she can walk to work if she misses a bus: think of Castang with an hour's weary ride to hell-and-gone in the Val de Marne. Her rent is low for the amount of space; three good-sized rooms and the balcony gets sun. Here she has her collection of little bonsai trees, the apple of her eye. There is no street noise and the racket of radios and quarrelling neighbours is supportable since the walls and floors are antiquated, and that means thick.

This style of living lends itself to the French talent called 'bricolage': the English do-it-yourself fails to convey slap-happy improvisations. Heating, plumbing, or electricity are alike eccentric, illegal, and probably dangerous. And this is one reason why the Paris Fire Brigade is both so good and so much loved by its people, as no police force ever could be or will be.

Nearly everyone will have ripped out the old kitchen sink; cemented in some smart modern sanitation. Carlotta is attached to her early victorian bathroom, likes her cast-iron lavatory cistern (oval moulded plaque with the maker's name). The neighbours could be Kurds from the wastes of Turkey, could just as well be Woody Allen and Diane Keaton. One does not enquire. And nobody knows her to be a police officer. She is, though; enough to have much solid steel and trustworthy locks, for the protection of the nest. Once in the nest, the bird is secure and comfortable. She has nothing valuable; one or two pleasant antiques. The pull-and-letgo in the lav is ivory, said to have belonged to Sarah Bernhardt: that sort of thing. She has a couple of nomad rugs and one good piece of furniture, a roll-top desk, near Louis-Seize, in reality near-empire. Her bed is a Japanese futon on the floor. She is kind to the children of the warren, talks to them, and in gratitude any Turk will give her a hand with a housekeeping problem. But few of her friends have ever been past the door.

She has respect for property, and that includes herself: it's not especially valuable but is the best one has. A meretricious man (there had been one, a lot earlier; he didn't last) called her mean with her body. Castang, more generous, sees her as fastidious. She keeps it fiercely scrubbed, scarcely a puritanical obsession, and does not wear perfume in the daytime. Her bathroom holds no secrets; she has bother sometimes with skin allergies. She shares no beds, male or female; there might be a kind-offer now and again but the idea does not really occur to her. Not so much 'unprofessional' as a source of needless complications. But an abusive word like arid she would rightly find cheap.

Personal friendships are few. She is not the extreme case of the schoolteacher – say – who goes from a crowded classroom to no company but the cat. She is lonely, but she does not suffer from solitude, and has no cat. A tolerably selfsufficient existence and a useful one. Giving a lot of thought to what she wished from her life, now that it is thoroughly organised, has not occurred to her much yet; she has been too busy.

As a professional she has a few goodish unimportant pictures. In the office a poster or two of 'good' pictures. Castang will find one, think of it as 'her portrait', by the Parisien Italian Modigliani, whom he has had to look at carefully, both before and after going to Russia on the gentleman's behalf. It's well known; the reference is *Liegendes Frauenakt auf weissem Kissen* (Staatsgalerie, Stuttgart). Recumbent Female Nude. She's soberly painted, in a classical attitude like a Titian Venus, a simple strong composition. A calm face with a flicker of amusement. She is both tent and intent, as well as competent. He didn't need the poster, having found the model.

Perhaps the episode can be traced to some remark, heard or overheard, made in the Questura in Milano – or the Soprintendezza of Fine Arts. The sort of remark that an Italian man may let fall without giving it weight. It is not really derogatory nor even disparaging. 'Ach! – French women . . .'

She loitered in, standing in the space between her office and his, as he was packing up.

"Walk with you? – as far as the metro."

"Good."

"In a hurry?" she asked, on the street.

"Not a bit." Their hours are laxly kept, but there is often overtime, and it isn't paid them.

"Perhaps you'd like to come and have a drink?" Which seemed to her to take a long time to say.

"Sound notion." Castang is briefer.

"I don't live all that far. We could catch a bus?"

"Treat you to a taxi," since there was one cruising. It took away whatever she had planned to say next.

"Bit of a climb, I'm afraid." It was a mild surprise to him, no stranger to ramshackle Paris houses but nobody knew where Salès lived; she didn't talk about her life, outside.

"Well – perch, then. Whisky all right? Ice or what?"

"Just as it comes." She pottered in the kitchen while he looked about with approval; she'd made it nice, here. He wasn't keyed to any thinking. He felt touched, a scrap; a friendly gesture, that she'd come round to accepting him as a good colleague and looked for a way to show it. It pleased him. He pulled his weight now, at this work, but only just. Compared to her he would always be an ignoramus. She'd put water in her own whisky, brought some green olives, which he didn't want, took a 'blond' cigarette (she doesn't smoke in the office): thanks, he'd rather his own, the darker french tobacco.

Castang isn't exactly daft. Wary of invitations from women who live alone. But this is just his colleague. He hasn't seen her any other way: the 'tit-fantasy' this morning was as unimportant as it was insubstantial; like blowing a smoke ring without meaning to, admiring it in the brief instant before it shreds into the air. He also observes a sound rule, good in the police or in the Beaux Arts, concerning not dipping pen in company inkwell.

Adultery, like homicide, has the trick of seeming like a good idea at the time.

But whatever, don't sentimentalise. Avoid cant. Do not fall, like too many people, into the marshmallow theology of Travis McGee and begin saying that if you feel good afterwards it's moral. Ernest Hemingway is generally credited with that one but he too had the mentality of a threeyearold, crying when he didn't get it. There are only two attitudes that a man can have while standing up straight.

One is Vera's. Damned Czech morals. Stalinists all the way. Either they're being Catholic with nostalgia towards bonfires, boiling lead, red-hot pincers; or atheist in the same intolerant fashion, pushing anyone who disagrees out of a thirdfloor window. Vera gave her word, kept it, expected others to do the same. If not, bear the consequences. Above all, do not attempt to justify with any pious hypocrisies.

The other is to say straight out that morals don't exist. In Ron Ziegler's memorable words, confession is bullshit. Hedonism has its problems but is, at least, consistent.

One can't apologise for Castang. Adopting the think-about-that-tomorrow tactic, he knows that the man condemned to execution wakes up and says 'Not today.' But Tuesday fortnight always comes.

There is a trial, first. It doesn't all happen in a second.
First, Castang who hasn't been thinking is disconcerted. Salès
sitting on the sofa, talking body-language. Of course, he has
found himself before, and often, in these false positions, and
knows how to handle them. Even if the temperature has gone
up, and the barometric pressure, one can still say no. Indulged
women believe the offer of their body to be irresistible, and
the result can be the opposite to that intended. Carlotta was
not an indulged woman, nor a vain one. A woman making a
timid, awkward offer, and as though expecting a bucket of
cold water over her – one isn't excusing, to say that he was
touched. Police officer or not, one can't not have emotions.
Even a doctor has feelings, if he's any good. The man who
has suppressed all emotion is well on the way to becoming a
firstclass shit.

A purely hedonistic world is where people grab whatever
they can get; nasty because they believe that something offered
free conceals a trap: indeed that nothing ever is free, since
there's nothing around except greed and selfindulgence. Ray
Chandler, in Hollywood, remarked that they hadn't found out
yet how to option the night air. But they'd get around to it.

It makes, between men and women, a ridiculous, odious
and a boring world. Worse, a world with no humour. The
words we possess for a clinical description of a man and woman
making love are miserably unfunny. Castang and Carlotta had
a moment of trust, which was honest, and also funny. If she
had not been so tangled, so terrified, he would have finished his
drink and looked at his watch. If he had been coarse, knowing,
greasy, she would have doubled up as though punched in the
stomach, rushed to the lavatory, locked herself in and been
sick. The words would diminish them, and us too.

Paris went by, outside. Uncaring, and dull. It is true that
the colours seemed brighter, on his way to the metro station.
But the effect wore off on the steps down. He would have
liked to stay for dinner. It is annoying to have to say No time
for cheese, and sorry, I'll skip coffee.

There is not much time ever. Tuesday fortnight always comes: it is now. It took this country many years to emerge from barbarism, and once, many years ago but also today, Castang had to be present at an execution. That's the rule: even when no longer 'public' the law lays down that those instrumental in this legal decision should see and know what they do. Not the jury: it was thought that the scene might be a bit strong for their stomach. But the professionals: the President of the Assize Court, the prosecutor, the defending advocate, and the chief of police investigation. A sorry group. Do they all at least have one brief moment of laying selfsatisfaction aside? Castang did not ask the others. He had died, and had been surprised, afterwards, to find himself alive. An indelible mark which comes back to him now and again. Like in the train going home. When not just another screw, to make love is also to die.

Carlotta was terribly hungry; sat still naked at her kitchen table and ate a whole tin of sardines, with the olive oil. He hadn't let her dress.

"I don't want to dress, so I do so looking at you. Childish? Yes, it is."

"Do you have to go?"

"Yes."

"Will you come back?"

"Yes."

She stood a long time under the shower, as hot as she could bear. Screwing up courage, which took a long time, she set it cold with the teeth set too. Dry, she put on a dressing gown, and took it off again. She didn't want to put on clothes. She still felt so appallingly hungry. Looking at bread made her feel sick and she thought about the Italian place down the road because of a longing for a big dish of spaghetti, and got the giggles at the idea of walking in there naked.

Castang, feeling sick on the train, stabbed out a just-lit cigar, a waste because they are expensive, and foolish because he should never have lit it. There had been several foolish things in a row, the only sensible one having been to take a shower while still with Carlotta, which saved taking one when he got in, which would have looked funny. Because his turn is at night. Hers is in the morning. Vera is an economical woman and hates damp bath towels. And this way you don't get under one another's feet, and that's important when you share the bathroom, and the bed, and life. Only dying you do on your own. He did avoid being sick, on the train, but it was a nearish thing.

"Aren't you rather late?" Vera was still in the kitchen, seeing to it that the children, for once, did the washing up properly, not just leaving everything Encrusted. It would be much easier to do it herself. But if children don't learn vile jobs early they never will: roughly her own upbringing.

"Something came up as I was on the verge of leaving." Perfectly true, and with the double meaning Shakespeare isn't above pushing into dialogue. "And later there are fewer trains," hastily. Undeniable. But Vera thinks neither of denying nor prying. That is the most horrible: trusting herself, she always trusts him.

"Your dinner might be a bit desiccated." Thank God, he is now hungry. "Homework please, you two." Discipline! In the livingroom, whether she's reading or painting her nails, it's on a hardish upright chair, because that's where she's comfortable. Lydia likes to work sitting on the floor, with a pop record going and a schweinerei all around; Vera won't allow it. Emma sprawls with her face on the table, cheek touching the exercise-book in which she is writing. Vera doesn't allow this either but the obstinacy of her daughters equals her own. Even Castang gets told to sit up straight. Hm, the voice of authority. He eats his dinner in silence. The juice has got a bit over reduced. It's a healthy, stolid, central-european stew; something for the man to go down the mine on, in Ostrava. Plenty of garlic – good for the lungs. Breathing all that poison every day. And smoking into the bargain. Plenty of beans too. But be grateful – yes he is – for that hardy, tenacious, straight-backed wife.

"Beans make one fart," complains Lydia, who has reached the age of being fastidious, and makes a fuss about cups 'with germs on' and sharing her sister's bathtowel. This argument would be more cogent, says Vera, if she washed rather more often. Emma, who is like the good soldier Schweik, is too clever to complain, and is still at the age when farting is funny.

Eight-thirty – Emma, bed. Nine o'clock, and the hell with the television – Lydia, bed. And will you please not spatter toothpaste all over the washbasin.

Around ten Carlotta decided she needed spaghetti after all, and got dressed.

At about ten-thirty Castang too quite often gets told that it's time for him as well because of needing the sleep. He doesn't always pay attention, but will sit with a bit of reading and a bit of smoking and maybe the radio playing. Eleven at night is the time when occasionally the television might bear watching, but that is just too bad: he will potter off, and quite likely find his wife asleep, in pyjamas that come up to the neck and down to the wrists, and all the windows hygienically open. Sometimes he finds her reading. Sometimes he might even find no pyjamas, and a smell of perfume, or Madame enjoying a delicious, forbidden cigarette. This is a rarity of late. Is that an excuse for going to bed with Carlotta? No it is not.

So that at three in the morning he is awake, and would prefer to see things 'in a sensible light', but of course this is the time when one does just the opposite. Between waking and sleeping one spirals slowly outward into space but the needle has stuck in the groove, so that on and on, repeating the same foolish notion, the same imbecile reaction . . . in his case he was tying a tie, in front of the bathroom mirror, feeling a dry, sandpapery face, noticing how drawn and pasty the face looks.

But why a tie? – he has put on a dark suit, too, for the nightmare is that he must get up early, and dress for a formal occasion. This is the day of the execution.

A courtyard; a rank of people standing, with strained,

unnaturally pale faces. Never mind about the tie, because they will give you a white shirt, with an open collar. They will rip off the collar; that is part of the ritual. In just another moment a ritual phrase will be uttered, in the silence.

'Au nom du Peuple Français, Justice est faite.' Is it true that Danton – whether or not one admired him as a character – made a gallant, and very parisien, joke? – 'This verb is not conjugated in the passive voice, since one does not say "I have been guillotined." '

I must get out of bed.

Castang went to the open window but the draught cut through his thin cotton pyjamas so that he put on a dressing gown, pattered out across the cold tiles of the terrace, opened the french-window. The big walled garden with its still trees is unpleasantly like a prison courtyard.

It is the time of false dawn, overlaying a sickly hue, lower on the horizon, which is reflections from street lamps, and over the silence comes the faraway mutter of the autoroute which continues all night; a growling tearing noise which Emma says is that of lions being fed (and she refuses to look at lions). Close up, he makes out the sleeping trees, a silverish sheen on overgrown grass.

> They shut the way through the woods
> Seventy years ago.
> Weather and rain have undone it again

– no, it is not one of Vera's English poems. It is something else.

> I wonder what she is doing at this hour,
> My Andean and sweet Rita
> Of reeds and wild cherry trees.

Surely it is César Vallejo? He is trying to remember further and cannot. Rita has been ironing. The poet recalls her skirt with lace; that her body smells of spring sugarcane. She looks up at the sky and shivers, and says 'Jesus, it's cold.'

Who is she, Rita? The pale oval face, the thin dark hair

and long body are those of Carlotta Salès. But the reeds and wild cherry trees belong to Vera. She has been training herself to draw them, sitting upon a river bank, with a chinese brush, a bottle of indian-ink, with her little frown of intense concentration before she takes the brush for a bold, controlled stroke.

And this face overlays the first. And he has recalled the last, abrupt line of the English poem.

But there is no way through the woods.

And that will go very nicely with the sharp Spanish throwaway. Jesus, it's cold. Castang went back to bed. He knows now what to do. Carlotta is a sensible, a balanced woman. Yes, it will hurt. So does the sting of the razor.

"You look a bit hollow-eyed," said Vera.

"I didn't sleep very well. Too hot, perhaps?" Not possible because there is a glint of melting frost on rooftops, and a hard clear sky. It is far into spring, but a whiplash of cold air from the north has blown away cloud: it will be bright and sunny. A clearcut, commonsense day. The faces in the train are calm and free of tension: it does them good to look out at spring sunlight. Just a whiff, on clean, shining Paris streets, of the sharp north-easterly wind. A day for sensible decisions.

South Wind is the one for foolishness. No Santa Ana blows upon Paris, but once or twice a year, all the way from northern Africa, the south wind lays down the fine sand. So that you can draw silly faces on the roof of the car, as Lydia had that morning, finding the spring frost on the shady side of the street. It was nothing much. Might nip the darling-buds a scrap, but not so as to chill hearts.

Still, the sight of Carlotta, her back to him, standing at her desk reading mail . . . He says nothing. He had prepared a pompous little speech, and it has melted away – like the frost – or stuck to the roof of his mouth – like the sand. She turns around and he says stupidly 'Bonjour', and her eyes screw up and the small, secretive smile takes hold around the corners of her mouth; and it is not going to be easy at all. In fact, like the man in Dickens, a book Vera is fond of, he is 'suffering grinding torments' – and serve him right!

It is Vera's free day: once a week she says the hell-with-housekeeping, and follows her fancy. To go to Paris perhaps, and dally in streets, and gawk like any tourist, with a lovely feeling of this-day-is-mine, to lick at slowly, like an ice-cream.

No! The Paris streets will be gritty and draughty and the feeling is wrong. Nor is it a painterly day: the light is wrong, for the Ile de France. But it is a Chinese day, and she will draw. There are bamboos in the garden, but she knows of a corner, by a little river, where there are reeds. Also wild cherry trees. She stands, though, irresolute. Something is wrong with the day. Her senses pick up other worlds, but what this is she has not identified. For work she must have concentration, and uninterruption. Messages, whatever they may be, must be isolated, cleaned of static, decoded. This radio wave must be put out of her mind, because it buzzes about, and distracts her.

There are security measures first, because we live in a tricky world. Go along the path and make sure of the gate. The children do not shut it properly: it hangs a bit and sticks. Lydia never loses anything, has keys safe in her bag: there are squalls of rage when this is verified. 'Ma snuffles in my private affairs.' Emma who will lose anything, gloves, scarves or purse, has keys tied round her neck . . . Henri is forever going to do something about this gate, and never does. Because if it is open, so are your windows, to air, and in the street, it might not be just 'les gitans', 'the tinkers'. The tinkers are a lawless, suspect folk dreaded by local housewives. They come asking for iron. They operate Mime-like transformations in their den, a slummy barrack where nobody else will risk their skin. And why don't the police Do Something? ask all the militants of the National Front: there are plenty of them too, around here.

There are worse people around than The Tinkers. Some

women keep large dogs; Vera doesn't want a dog even if
Emma does. Others have guns; illegal but the police are
tolerant about the shotgun, the pistol (only Dad's wartime
souvenir), the ubiquitous twentytwo rifle. Vera does not want
guns, either. She knows where Castang keeps his service pistol,
which he rarely carried even in the criminal-brigade days, and is
now on a par with the wartime souvenirs. 'There will be no more
Parades,' he said, with a theatrical emphasis, and Dad's gun,
in its holster, hangs on the broad leather-belt in the wardrobe,
next to his winter overcoat.

It is a lie, if a brave one, and Vera knows this. The gun, an
unadorned police-positive, standard Smith & Wesson revolver,
.38 calibre, four-inch barrel, is a symbol; of authority, and also
of demotion and humiliation. He brings it out once a week to
oil and clean the action, 'like winding the clock at Sunday
lunch-time'. A week ago he buckled on the belt, found that
his waistline had slipped a notch, and made a sour joke about
desk cops.

The pistol is loaded. Vera will not touch it nor even look
at it. But it's there.

She stopped to look at the garden: this is for her symbolic. She had been brought up a country-child; ever since
she can remember there had been a garden to work in and
animals to handle. Her grandparents were peasants. Even as
a student she had bicycled out there for the weekends – and
ferried back a big packet of earthy, goodsmelling vegetables
on the carrier; a bunch of dahlias in a string bag, on her handle-
bar. ('These aren't vegetables,' says Vera contemptuously, in
markets, braving all the townbred-Castang jokes about going
out to shit on the compost-heap.) And in the cottage she had
had a garden, but in the Northern town only house plants and
windowboxes on her balcony. She wonders whether she will
ever have a garden again. One could do things here . . . but
it is already May and heavy work is needed: Henri is forever
saying he'll . . . but it's like re-setting the hinges of the gate:
he never will.

She brought her shopping bag with drawing materials, and
flung it in the car. Castang makes vulgar jokes about 'Mary
Cassatt's painting-stool'. She does, too, have a painting-stool;
it's her pride-and-joy (found in the fleamarket), and she says
defiantly that maybe it was too Mary Cassatt's since it dates
from that period. A simple marvellous cylinder of smooth
hardwood, the four quadrants of whose circle open out top-
and-bottom and the heavy comfortable webbing seat has four
pockets which slip over, and you can't-get-anything-like-that-
now.

Beyond the little town there is countryside. Not that Vera
would call it countryside: you'll see nothing so vulgar as cows
there. Today's farming means that any marginal or awkward
piece of land is untended and has run back to wild; drains
blocked and fields gone sour. Nobody comes here, along this
piddling streamway – an obscure feeder of the Marne. It is
not picturesque. The access is all banks of coarse bramble,
and beyond there are boggy bits. Nobody had ever gone Hoy
at Vera for exploring, here.

The stream had worn a bed below field level, but there
was a shallow bay where cows used to come down to drink.
Poles growing from long-ago-cut trees gave a dappled shade.
There were coots, moorhens. Later in the summer it would be
hot and there would be gnats, horseflies . . . The growth on
the banks was rubbish stuff: willow, aspen, alder; but gazing
at leaves (and as Don Juan recommends, at spaces between
leaves) she found a wild cherry tree. A poor place, long shot
and fished bare, interesting nobody. She had parked her car
upstream, a hundred metres away, and three times that by the
path. A by-road – a pretty, old stone bridge, but there was little
traffic. Listen hard enough and you might even hear birds.

The river may come to life again some day – when the men
have left. Without pollution there would again be fish. Herons,
perhaps a kingfisher, an otter. Is everything quite extinct, in
this sad country?

The water was still alive, barely, and made some volume of

sound. One would hear the plane, overhead, or a truck along the road, but little else. One might hear a footstep but Vera, concentrating upon trees, heard nothing.

Thus she was knocked flat, with no warning at all. She found herself on the ground. She did not cry out; had time for only a gasp of astonishment before an arm, crooked under her jaw, made yelling impossible. A hand, gripping pinchingly under her armpit, dragged her from the water's edge to the slope of the bank.

She has had lessons from her man; the standard police lessons. 'If something' – like this – 'should ever happen, remember first, not to struggle. Because then you're likely to get a bash. Which might mutilate you. Or you might be strangled. Stay still, don't yell, try to keep your wits.'

Yes, she remembers this, and stays limp. She can see sky, and something black which looms. The choking pressure on her throat eases, the dazzlement lessens. The man is kneeling above her, shuffling to change position. She tries to recall the second lesson.

'Try to think; if you do get humped it isn't the end of the world, and better than broken bones. So stay loose and watch for your chance because you've two good ones. Eyes, or balls. It's violence which excites them, so force yourself to give the illusion of a welcome. Even a caress – then you're sure of winning. Because then he's as vulnerable as you are.'

'But I don't think I could. Can one force that much, against all one's instincts?'

She was wearing countrified corduroy trousers, so old they hardly stay up at all, and they didn't. A button popped, but what's a button? The man had little to wrestle with: her legs had gone completely numb and required no pinning; she felt dead from the waist down. Quite possibly, this was her old traumatic paralysis, reinduced by shock.

This heavy immobility, and the man's impatience, did her a good turn because he released her arms; he was using both hands to drag off her tight underpants. He spread her legs and lurched forward to climb on to her. It brought the face close to hers so that she could see eyes wide open and glaring. She was right to think of instinct as stronger than reason, for instinct doubled her hand into a fist with the forefinger and little finger outstretched: it is the antique gesture with which the peasant wards off the evil eye. The hand struck like a frightened rattlesnake.

The man screamed most horribly. The body collapsed limp, on top of her, disgusting her with a bristly jaw. He ejaculated across her bare inner thighs, her exposed vulva: she was overcome with the disgust.

She could move her shoulders and she scrabbled with an arm, seeking purchase. It was not easy because she was on a slope with her head lower than her feet. But the man did nothing to hinder her. He made a raucous sobbing noise and lay collapsed upon her with the hands covering the eyes and the knuckles pressing into her jaw and throat.

Groping around, her hand touched a leg of the overturned painting stool, and thinking only of her own squirming, retching disgust Vera reached out with her other arm, brought the X of the stool into its compact and heavy whole, wrenched her head off the ground and brought the cylinder whirling round in a crash upon his head. Instinctive, convulsive, and shortly, to a lieutenant of gendarmerie, perfectly explainable. The man fell sideways, taking pressure off her.

But what followed was not at all easily explainable, and nobody could understand it until she was helped – as she often is – by a book she was fond of. Enid Bagnold's *National Velvet*.

Velvet, a child of thirteen, has a little brother aged six, who is impelled, quite wantonly, to stamp upon an ant.

'Why did you do that?' cross at this barbarism.

'It wanted to be dead!' And suddenly overwhelmed, the little boy goes on stamping. 'They all want to be dead . . .'

It is much to the credit of the lieutenant of gendarmerie – a civilised man – that he understands at once.

After a while she was able to move. After a further while, spent upon her hands and knees, she was able to do something about her clothes. The elastic of her knickers was broken so she ditched them. The trousers – Vera is the sort of woman who, if she scrabbles for long enough in the accumulated rubbish in her handbag, finds a safetypin. Public decency was insecurely maintained, but so is sanity. It took a long while before she was able to walk. Her sketchblock was in the water, ruined. But she would not come here again. Or no more than once; she realised that.

For the paralysis, the emptiness, has given her a precious gift: time. Time gave her thought. She was after all a police officer's wife and has a good memory of Henri putting out an arm, to stop a running girl, one night after the cinema, in a town of the North.

This was not a northern town but it is still the French countryside and five kilometres off is a village, and fifteen beyond that is the town, and in the town a gendarmerie barracks, and three-quarters of an hour later she limped in here. She was the running girl, and the Castang practised in police routines, and the Vera too who had steadied and supported that girl past police, and doctors, and administrative form-filling.

"I want your officer, please. Here is my identity card."

She has also one of Henri's business cards. Castang is no subscriber to the traditional distrust and rivalry – even hatred – between the Police Judiciaire and the Gendarmerie. Vera knows something of this but it doesn't come to mind. It was a puzzled, even a suspicious officer who received her. Formal politeness; a stiffish military salute. It is a soldierly outfit, a world of close shaves and polished boots. The PJ, all neglected beards and downtrodden tennis shoes, is irritating just to look at, and Vera is dishevelled.

"Lieutenant Lawless. At your service." A good Irish name. These are not uncommon, in France, where wild geese came often to enroll, under French arms. His christian name is Etienne.

"I haven't quite been raped but it was pretty close. I think there'll be some evidence. Scratches on my thighs and stains. I mean it has to be photographed." They are both embarrassed. Young Lawless frowns a little. It is a pity she does not know the story of Lytton Strachey pointing an accusatory finger at a stain on Virginia Stephen's frock, saying 'Semen?' in stern tones. Shrieks of laughter from both the sisters. Vera is not like this at all, and anyone more unlike Lytton than Lieutenant Lawless . . . "I mean," uncomfortable, "I'd be happier . . ."

"We'll need a doctor."

"Yes please. Denis Manuel if he's at home. He ought to be."

Military discipline. The Polaroid shakes a bit, but like the barn door, it'll serve.

"I think – I'm afraid – the man might be dead. I'm sorry, you see, I hit him."

Etienne Lawless had begun by thinking that this was a bourgeois affair, a crime among notables, that would have to be swept under the bed. But he is beginning to grasp.

"I know you'll want to take me back there. I don't mind, if you are there too."

"In a little while. Taking your time, Madame, and in your simplest words, tell me what happened."

"I hit him and hit him and hit him. He wanted to be dead!" Yes, dangerously near hysteria. But it was her one real relapse.

Denis Manuel arrived, so blessedly matter-of-fact that she would not again lose control.

"Just two minutes if you would, Lieutenant, alone with my patient. Let's take a look then, my dear. Tra-la. A-ha. How long ago was all this? Excellent, nice and fresh, I'll just take a swab and then you can have a nice wash. You pop into the lav, Vera, while I have a chat with our friend . . . Oh good, you've got polaroids – splendid, no judicial errors here."

"She insisted. Unusual woman . . . Uh, the husband."

"Desk job. In Paris. I know him, 's all right, a good and reasonable man."

"She asked, you know, voluntarily. One thing I don't want, a PJ stink . . ."

"No no, I'll be your guarantee. And she's very hardheaded. If she says there's a man, then there really is, and we better get our ass out there. Whatever we find, that's an ironclad rape, Lieutenant, you've your photos and I'm your witness."

A little gendarmerie car. A station wagon, with a stretcher for the if-need-be. Two stolid soldiers, with measuring tapes, and a can of plaster for imprints, and evidence-bags, and the trusty Polaroid. One forgets that the word 'lieutenant' means placeholder, substitute. Etienne Lawless is a good officer. Denis Manuel has plenty of forensic experience. It is Vera's first scene-of-crime, and she cannot help hideous shudders, and putting her palms before her eyes. Denis has thought of giving her a shot of tranquilliser, and decided she would prefer to manage without. She is a proud woman, and she tells herself that she must behave as Henri would wish, and expect of her. The man is there, where she left him.

"Go sit in the car, Vera."

"No!"

"Then stand there and be silent, and let me work. Got your photos, Lawless? Not dead. Or not clinically. Coma, depressed skull fracture, get him into Reanimation with no more delay but on the face of it . . . All right, Lieutenant, you'll agree, that tells its own tale." Vera's painting-stool goes into the evidence bag, and a gendarme who has waded a bit downstream returns in triumph bearing the hideous rag which had been Vera's knickers, that morning.

The tinkers? All that would be needed is the suggestion of a 'swarthy tint' to the man's bluish-pallid skin. But Lieutenant Lawless though humourless is a conscientious, thorough young man. It's in the day's work; be it taking polaroids of a woman's genital area, seeing to it that his evidence will pass the sniffi-est of judges-of-instruction, retracing the steps of the loitering vagabond 'up-to-no-good-that's-certain'; being rather stiff: the Gendarmerie likes to say that the big difference between us and the PJ is that we do not blur evidence, just in case it should involve local notables. And Vera is thinking of how to keep-it-from-Henri, and wondering whether she dare ask the others to do so.

Denis Manuel straightened up, gave an expressionless sweep of the hand to say take-it-away-boys. Reanimation, and I don't hold out much hope for the eyes, either. Lieutenant Lawless has taken the scrapings of the man's fingernails for one glass tube, and come awfully polite to ask the same of her. Labelling scrupulously, turning to her, to Denis, to his sergeant.

"You agree? You agree? You agree? Sign please . . ."

"Are you all right?" asked Dr Manuel. "I'd like you more warmly dressed."

"Yes. Thank you."

So now Lawless. Not the tiniest bit humorous-and-Irish. Quite the contrary; exceedingly-humourless-French.

"I must thank you, Madame, and I must apologise for exposing you to this, and I must congratulate you also because I have to say that the prima-facie case accords in all respects with the account you gave as it was taken down in verbal-process. Now if you can manage one or two final miseries – can you walk all right?"

"A bit shaky on the pins but managing, thanks."

"What I'm thinking of, to satisfy the Proc, and avoid, maybe, some damn judge dragging you out here afresh, is could we have a re-enactment, for perfect consistency in the distances and angles?" But Henri would ask the same, of her, or of . . .

"Pay no heed to discrepancies, what with shock or confusion, but if you're up to it – Sergeant Jonas will act the part of your aggressor." Sergeant Jonas, a professional of twenty years' standing, was prepared to be quite as solemn as his superior, and only said 'Ow' when he caught his hand on a thistle. But Vera, with a gendarme on top of her smelling of aftershave and mysteriously mothballs, got the idiotic galloping giggles and Denis Manuel had to put her in the car and say 'Swallow, child, swallow.'

"Very good," said Lieutenant Lawless, and for the first time he gave her a beaming smile, and this was very Irish: blue hair, blue eyes, and delightful crooked teeth, and the moment she could stop crying she felt miles better thank you, and if it be known devouringly hungry.

"Purely," Denis told her, "in order that Lawless should feel quite happy with all his rhyme-endings in order. You were perfect. You need only repeat it for the instructing judge, and they're not likely to bother you any further. Even the court appearance will be brief and formal."

Kind Denis! She felt too dulled to say she knew it all by heart. That maybe one woman in five could get through a comparable situation without feeling more badly torn, worse used than by the rape itself. You could toss up a coin, perhaps, before deciding which would be preferable; the stiff military maleness of the gendarmerie or the greasy familiarities of the police.

Privilege! An instructing judge, if not Maurice Revel himself, would have had a word said in his ear. The President of the tribunal would be gentle, softspoken – and would have the court cleared of prurient-public and indecent-press.

'You wouldn't mind telling the court what you were doing in this lonely spot?'

'Painting.' For she had faced plenty of vulgar humour in the past and not least from the police. Castang's jokes about Victorian maiden ladies – 'Ho, the church spire, as immortalised by the vicar's sister.' There would not even be a patronising note in the 'Painting – I see.' Not even 'Painting what?' Forcing her to the 'Er – reeds. And a wild cherry tree.' Nice opening for the sarcasms of a defending advocate. But the President would protect her. It wouldn't be needed: lawyers know who butters their bread.

Castang is not as a rule vengeful, not really inclined to abuse his official position. She knows though of occasions. Once, after a lawyer had been over-zealous in crossexamining, Inspector Orthez (chosen for his brutal appearance) had strolled up in the interval to say 'Nice work, Maître. Incidentally, if you wouldn't mind coming down to the office tomorrow – we've a slight problem with your alimony payments which seem a bit overdue.'

'Well,' had said Henri, defensively, 'fellow's got to learn there are forms to respect.'

Dr Manuel, with patients to see to, was offering to drive her home.

"I'm all right, Denis. And I've two children coming home wanting their dinner. Not to speak of a hungry Henri. Not a word there – please!"

"Good, then we'll drive back in convoy. If, Lieutenant, you can now dispense with us both."

"No problem," saluting automatically. "An open-and-shut affair. Not a thing the Proc will want to worry about."

Denis Manuel, thinking about his other patient, got home from the round and picked up his telephone.

"Fellow the police brought in this afternoon – skull fracture, and eye injuries."

"The road accident, was it? Oh, that one . . . dead on arrival, my docket says."

"Really? I'd thought he had a fair chance."

"Check it for you . . . hold on, I'm on the other line . . . okay, that's both right and wrong, he's on the machine but the graph is flat. Alive-but-dead, quoi?"

"Sounds a bit early to say that."

"Well, they won't unhook the machine, until the professor takes a look, this evening. Ring you back, shall I?"

Hm. Better have a word with the precise and conscientious Lieutenant Lawless.

"Yes, I know." That depersonalised police voice. "Hospital told us. We've looked him up. Can't find any relatives. A vagabond – a record for shoplifting. They've said irreversible coma:

well, I can't give an order like that myself, as you understand, so I've had a word with the Proc, and he didn't even hesitate. Even if it wasn't so, the fellow would be at best half blind, a charge on the state, facing a rape indictment. I mean, just work it out."

"Very well; thanks."

Dr Manuel was working it out; there are plenty of methods of legal execution without bothering with guillotines; but is this one a medical dilemma? Not, apparently, a legal one.

The phone rang.

"Hospital. Just thought you'd want to know. I went back to see. The professor took a look, and thought the chances thin. But there's been apparently some legal authority to cover it, so the Chef gave the word to disconnect the life-support."

It is quite frequent, and of course in medicine it is clear enough – once the braincentres are dead there is no point in maintaining physiological life. Some people think that there's an ethical problem here.

No, we will not tell Vera. She wanted to make me promise not to tell Henri. My eye I won't tell Henri! Monsieur Castang will be in his Paris office. Now who, apart from Vera, will have that number? . . . Maurice Revel might have it.

A lot of work, and not just for the secretary. But he is a good doctor.

A soft, warm woman's voice. Madame Morandière, had he known it.

"I'm afraid he isn't here. Can I get him to ring you back?"

Damn, and now I've a waitingroom full of patients.

"Tell him nothing to worry about, but he should ring Dr Manuel before leaving for home. I'll be here till seven. You'll see that he gets that?"

Madame Morandière would. Naturally, he was in bed with Carlotta, but she wouldn't know anything about that. Or not officially.

"Denis? What is all this?" Professionally a listener, a non-interruptor, a non-fusser, recipient of other people's tales on the phone, often tangled but not now. Castang managed a professional non-reaction.

"That's quite clear. And Denis – thank you." But he could not prevent the arrival of an unoriginal thought. How all occasions do inform against me! Though he puts it differently.

Well now, isn't that just lovely! . . .

"What's all that?" asked Carlotta, who had been hovering.

"Nothing. That's to say domestic disturbances. You know – somebody loses the car keys again? Still, I'd better make tracks."

"Somebody, now that I think of it, has to go to the Rue Drouot," looking at her watch and sighing, "and it looks as though it's going to be me. Putting a good face upon dereliction of duty," showing him the good face, and a conspiratorial grin. "But I don't feel like going home, not just yet."

"Quite so."

"Auctioneers – very dull company."

"Make sure they stay as dull as they are now."

"Give me a kiss then."

"Carlotta, have some sense; anyone could walk in."

"I'm in no mood for sense – I'm keeping that for the auctioneer."

"Look, I must run."

"How boringly domestic."

"I always am." This was rapidly becoming insufferable: he snatched his hat and bolted.

Clichés, about coals of fire, hounds-of-heaven, grinding torments, pursue him down metro passages and into suburban trains, their tongues hanging out, panting with eagerness to get at him and tear him. These hounds – they'd got on to his track rather fast, hadn't they?

Selfpity, that pleasurable emotion, does not dislodge the sharp splinter lodged in a tender place. Maybe he should start calling himself lucky? This would finish badly anyhow. He has just honesty enough remaining to acknowledge that left to itself it could finish much worse.

Castang had taken Carlotta to an extravagant lunch. Then he had taken her back to her flat and to bed. Looking out of the window at suburbs he could see, with a clarity abruptly hideous, her body naked upon sheets of a pale rusty red colour; a very beautiful body. The splinter, which is where he sits, causes him to shift position a great many times. They have done their best to make the seating of the Regional Express Railway vandal-proof (nothing can quite manage *that*); but said nothing about making it red-hot. The best he can manage is to recollect other passages in his life of which he is not proud.

He was home an hour before his usual time; ahead of the school bus. Vera was in the kitchen, grimly going about the work of dinner. That is like her. Hell or high water, the work gets done. And there is another coal-of-fire cliché, but placed adroitly, burning close to where he keeps his prostate gland.

Her face was a battlefield. She has the complexion called thin-skinned, which goes with thin blonde hair: that straight, stringy hair she complains of, too fine to take a perm, too soft to stay up in a knot. In the early years it was long. Then she tried it short; a disaster. Now she has it collarbone length, and says it never looks properly washed. Right now it has grown out to be a bit taily, and must be cut. But a good cutter is expensive, and this is another grievance. Women have a lot to put up with. Carlotta's hair – Ay!

There are red patches in Vera's face; the eye-sockets look bruised with blue shadows; the nose is wax-white and red at the end, but in the event, this isn't funny.

She glared.

"What are you doing home so early?" She hammers the words with sharp taps, like an Arab, upon copper with his little mallet. Her soft voice becomes soprano in anger, but not scratchy. Which Carlotta's, in emotion, does . . . "I see . . . Someone has told you things, and that can only be Denis. Fuck him."

"He had to tell me. He's quite right."

"Dramatising. Nothing is wrong with me. What-so-ever.

There was a minor incident. It doesn't even affect the car insurance. I had a small shock, and I'm now completely over it. I don't see why we have to talk about it." Making for the lavatory, limping a little, shutting the door with a snap. Vera always shuts – and locks – this door. Now Carlotta is the sort of woman who walks across the room naked, and sits upon the lavatory in full view . . .

Vera shut the door again behind her and said, "What has Denis told you?"

"Simply what he saw. Observed. Like a good cop. He didn't go reading any meanings. Rang me at the office. Like a good friend. Short catalogue of facts. States of mind aren't his business. Or they are, but he recognised they'd be mine too. So no rage, please."

"Oh Henri . . ." crying. "I thought I'd killed him."

"As I see it, you weren't given much choice in the matter."

He cuddled her, while feeling shame that the cop stayed uppermost. Before leaving the Faubourg du Temple, he had had a shower.

"But because there's something horrible . . ." – she doesn't cling; she never does – ". . . oh, why does one have to go and make it twice as – "

"It's the way of the world. Consequences. They're unsought, and unforeseen." Coals? In some parts of the world there are fire ants. Now where has he learned this valuable information? From a *Reader's Digest* no doubt – in the office – while supposed to be working. "Look, Vera. You are crossing the road. A car, going too fast, swerves to avoid you, mounts the pavement, kills an old woman with a shopping basket. She was in the wrong place."

"Oh, Henri, you're forever telling me that violent crime – "

"Yes, is the fault of the victim. Don't read too much into it. If I stick the carving-knife into you, consequence of never-ending nagging, yes it's your fault; you've ground me to a shred. So now don't go grinding yourself to shreds, it'll do you no good."

"I don't intend to," quiet, and standing upright. "I had a shock, and I've feelings of guilt, and I'll cope with both, and please make no fuss."

That is very female. Now it's him making the fuss.

"I'm very sorry. But what if it had been Lydia? I thought too about that girl – you remember the one in the North, we'd been to a movie? And just because I've a red nose – "

"You ought to be in bed."

"I won't."

"The reaction is classic, and recall that I'm an experienced officer and know all about it." She changed the water on the potatoes, put in salt, and set the pot on the fire.

"I haven't been much of a wife to you, have I – these last months?"

Saying either yes or no to that is a quicksand. The fire ants are getting up his trouser leg too.

"And then I go and get raped – almost as though I'd done it on purpose."

"As I understand from Denis, you weren't. Or was the idiot breaking it to me gently?"

"No. Don't make me talk about it . . . Oh, I will talk about it."

The experienced criminal investigator knows something about crimes which happen accidentally-on-purpose; something too about provoking a confessional mood: fidgets.

"Talk or don't talk, but don't hint." Irritably, because of ants.

"The truth," said Vera, "is that he got my pants off but I – he didn't get into me because I hit him." Bleak. "With my painting-stool."

"A solid piece of heavy wood," thinking about it.

"That's the trouble. My legs went bad again. I couldn't walk, for some time. So that I could think, and get clear about it, instead of rushing about in a panic. I mean, I went to the gendarmerie, and they were polite and efficient."

"I am glad to hear it," said the Police Judiciaire, in a prim voice.

"I made them, uh, him take photographs, and then Denis came, and looked at me, and said I was all right."

"Vera!" seriously. "Say it out, loud and clear. You have nothing to reproach yourself for."

"They said the man was still alive. I thought I ought to ring the hospital. I kept saying I had to cook the dinner first."

It is a relief to be able to laugh out loud at Vera's scale of moral values. But she is calm enough to hear the truth, and the sooner will be the better.

"The man's dead. Cry if you like, but tell yourself that defence from rape isn't only a legal argument, but a moral one too."

The door banged and Lydia came bursting in shouting, "Where's the grub?" – pulling up sharp and saying, "What's wrong with you, then?" Like any child of her age she is both shy and secretive, but she's not a bottler-up: like her mother she's a blurter-out.

"Nothing at all," said Vera at once. "You know me, I cry sometimes out of sheer stupidity."

"Have you two been fighting?"

"No."

"How come you're home so early, Pa?"

"Looking for a career in the law, Lydia?" mildly. "Go and wash and mind your own business."

"If Ma cries, it is my business." One does not always tell the truth to adults, but telling it to children is a good rule. Or as much as one can.

"If you want the truth then your mother was out drawing, in the fields, and had an unpleasant encounter, and this has upset her. Rather naturally, I came home early."

Lydia wide-eyed. Equally typical, Emma has slipped out and off to her room. Not that that one isn't curious, but if there's something nasty afoot, she would prefer not to be told.

"Were you raped?" with much interest.

"No. If I were it wouldn't be funny, would it?"

"No, but since you're always telling me not to be, it would be interesting."

"Right now, please let me get on with this sausage."

"You look awful – did he hit you?"

"Will you kindly fuck off," said Castang, exasperated.

"No need to be rude," flouncing out. "And vulgar," slamming the door.

"Now those goddamn sausages are burning," opening the window, which was to shut the stable door.

"I can't cope," said Vera. "I think after all I am going to bed; I feel awful. Denis gave me a pill. Just leave me alone." He nodded, struggling with the sausage. But when he straightened up she was still there.

"I promise faithfully, I'll be perfectly all right in the morning. But will you look in, later? . . . If I can't sleep, will you please come into bed with me? I need healing."

He nodded again. The fire ants had got under his clothes all over, by now.

Silence at the dinner table.

"I don't much like this sort of sausage," said Emma. There were three different sorts. Food is important. She had no comment on Vera being missing, seeming content with Lydia saying 'Ma's got a headache so you, little fool, will kindly be quiet.' "But when they're black they're quite nice." A useful discovery.

"To be filed for reference," said Castang. "Had a good day, poppet?"

"Fair," ambling off towards homework; virtuous but vague: a ruse to dodge the washing-up, which he allowed.

"Lydia, you wash and I'll dry, okay?"

"Can I have some wine, please?"

"Yes."

"I got a three for math again." Unwelcome information for which she judged the moment well-timed: he'd find out sooner or later.

"You and I will have a serious word, young lady."

"Nothing to fuss about. They've changed all that. It's no longer that racket of you're shit-hot at math or you're a dimwit. My marks are good, everyone says so. I'll get ol'granny Dampierre for the private parties, next year, if I'm a Good Girl."

"We'll see about that. I find you rather too frivolous, on the subject of rape. I'd like to be sure you realise what that involves."

"I don't want to talk about it." Lydia is modest on occasion.

"Neither do I. You always think you know everything. It's not just physical hurt or invasion of privacy. What tears a woman up is the humiliation." She looked prim and said nothing. "Ma had a narrow squeak and you see what it did to her. Just bear it in mind."

"So what else is new?" Mutinous, at a lecture. So be patient; that's not cheapness but shyness.

"Lawyers argue distinctions, of intent or behaviour, but the result is the same, and very nasty."

"Oh do belt up! I'm not a child. I could have a baby right now. Well, perhaps not right now. Incest being frowned upon." Irrepressible, so that he had to keep his face straight. "I mean – all these pious sermons. Yes, horrid, and I quite see. I know all the rules: don't provoke, don't get into ambiguous situations, don't get caught out alone; after dark the satyrs swarm. Even without you and Ma marching behind me, two enormous flatfeet, I'm well aware, and you better believe."

"There are coffee stains inside this cup. Wash it some more."

"Mad niggers in the Metro."

"That'll do!"

"Am I supposed not to know?"

"Just wrap up, Lydia, and don't push me too far."

———— ∞∞∞ ————

Vera was asleep. Drugged, since she is not used to even one sleeping pill.

Castang had got rid of the ants, but this was a relief.

He switched on the television, switched it off again, and reached for the phone. Even on the formal, stilted terms which will pertain between an officer of Police Judiciaire and a Placeholder in the Gendarmerie Nationale, it does no harm to be polite. Cordial, even: stretch a point, and call it warm. He has nothing to be selfimportant about.

"Slight headache," said Vera in the morning, "and the arse is a bit stiff."

"Denis with his ever-ready little valium pill – would you like me to take the day off?"

"Heavens, no; a long hot shower and I'll be as good as new."

So that he went off to catch his train, not looking forward to the day in front of him.

Because if there's a good way of putting an end to a love affair, Castang hasn't heard about it. Done in the heat of the day, or done in the last light after a cold, clouded sunset. Do it now and the blood will spurt. In his boyhood there had been an English song, of that gloomily sentimental nature dear to the soldiery.

'Five minutes more – give me five minutes more!' As with an execution, Tuesday fortnight will always come, even if it be three months hence. He has made his mind up; he is not going to face Vera's eyes, not even until Tuesday fortnight. He doesn't know either how to face this woman he longs and longs to be in bed with. So be professional, and hope that she will be, too.

On his way through the streets, he was again a small boy on his way to school, upon the gloomy pavements of the Thirteenth District, lined as they are with lunatic asylums and frightful medieval hospitals – not to mention the prison of La Santé. ('The time has come to show yourself extremely brave' – the machine is waiting in the courtyard.)

He practised his irregular verbs: *coudre*, je couds, j'ai cousu; sharpened his mental arithmetic, in preparation for the terrifying professor who likes to spring what he calls 'the cold shower' upon squirming children; and always early in the morning, like the executions.

And the poem, to be got by heart.

'Err – er.'

'Where did Victor Hugo write Errr?'

'Booz s'était couché, de fatigue accablé.
  Il avait tout le jour travaillé dans son aire.'

'The meaning of *accablé*? . . . It's what you are, you nasty child: Overwhelmed!'

But no magical incantation is going to help him now, not even a list of Latin verbs governing the dative case.

'You are despicable. You seduce me, you desert me. Throw me away, like a handkerchief on which you've blown your nose.'

Of course Carlotta said nothing like this: in fact she said nothing at all. The only reaction remotely resembling all these clichés he had rehearsed was that the blood left her face, which stayed white with huge eyes looking out at him. She turned around and walked out.

That anyhow is reacting like a pro and he values it.

He did not see her until the late afternoon, when she came in and spoke to him in a quiet, levelly professional voice.

"Henri, you're needed, to go to America." He thinks this is a very good come-back, and only hopes his face does not betray his sentiments.

"I was putting it off, actually," went on Carlotta. "There's no point in that now . . ." Quite.

"Don't imagine it an important matter," chill. "It's trivial. Quite foolish, actually." I have got the message, Carlotta, thank you.

"We have agreed to this at the insistence of the American banker who owns – yes, it's an extremely valuable picture. It's for the big loan exhibition, and he'll only let it go under stringent conditions.

"God, the fuss there's been, I don't know how many planes and how many insurance companies are involved, but it's staggering. This one is also highly fragile like a lot of them, we aren't getting the big one from Boston at all, because it simply cannot travel.

"Now the preclusive rules laid down by this old boy are as follows – it is allowed to come only as personal hand baggage, it's not very large, of a senior police official, that is you, who will at no time let it out of his sight or hand while in his possession. You'll be watched all the way by an American guard unknown to you."

Faintly, "Dear Jesus."

"You'll fly Swissair out of Geneva."

"Why?"

"No idea, unless it's the only carrier he trusts. Plainly, he's quite dotty: oh yes, and you'll wear a gun at all times, that's cleared with Security. This was all booked for Friday. I've had it changed so that you can fly tomorrow, two extra days in New York with nothing to do but look at pictures in the morning and whores in the afternoon."

It seemed on the whole an adequate vengeance.

He made a long telephone call home and –

"Where's Lorenza?" he asked Frau Morandière.

"Gone back to Italy," in a placid voice. Nothing to read upon her face, either.

"How very professional of her."

"Showing you a good example." That was the only remark made which could be called snide.

So *lontano degli occhi, lontano del cuore*, which is about all the Italian he knows. He has some passable English, defensive German, quite adequate Spanish – which he supposed might help him in New York. And he recalls a piece of early-american-folklore called the Ballad of El Paso: 'I-felt-the-bullet-go-deep-in-my-chest'. One feels no such thing. One would go sprawling on the hard ground as though from a gigantic kick in the whatsit. What you feel in the chest is simply Lorenza-goodbye.

In no sense could Castang be called a travelled man. He has pottered about in Europe. He hasn't been to China, or Japan, or even Bangkok (said to be well named). A real provincial stay-at-home. Lorenza Lotta glides about, with condescension, snapping her fingers for the footman in Hongkong or wherever, but he is just a great Peasant and has never been even to the United States. He is ready to be impressed by New York. It is all rather more like Istanbul than he'd bargained for.

His bag was unpleasantly heavy. Vera had fussed about the climate. Suppose it's hot – it is the month of May – suppose it's high-humid. Or suppose it's cold . . . she'd packed a lot of clothes, remedies against frightful diseases like air-conditioning.

He liked the glimpse of Greenland. The fly-in, Long Island would that be?, caused a flow of adrenalin. Immigration brings one down to earth all right. Do not cross the white line. Sweating in these appalling passages, inching forward in the long queue to be searched, stripped, shaved, and doubtless gassed, clutching this fucking suitcase; Castang feels a right Emmy Grant.

All this humbling of the mighty is highly salutary, thought Castang, since one has plenty of time for history, say, once in the toils of Immi. Time your arrival to coincide with an Air India Boeing, and meditate. If it comes to arrogance, the French and the English are hot contenders for first prize, or were before American complacency put them both in the shade.

This good lady in the sari, sitting beside me on the airport bus and gazing mirthlessly out at the Van Wyck Parkway, is she thinking 'Very like Calcutta'? And this is Forty-Second Street? The Arab quarter of Marseille on a rainy afternoon. Castang standing there, still with that goddamn suitcase; as the English say, like a spare prick at a wedding, because there's not a taxi in sight. There are plenty of Arabs saying 'You gimme five dollars I get you taxi', but cop-sense has him scorching

out into the street to snatch a cab. It's exactly like the Gare
du Nord; only fewer police. What there are, so loaded down
with heavy machinery of law-enforcement, it's a wonder they
can walk.

"That's right," said the cabdriver approvingly, "never give
those assholes a penny."

"But if I were a little old lady? In a sari?"

"You're a little old lady in a sari, my advice would be,
hadn't ought have left Calcutta. Everybody got their problems.
Uptown or down?"

Excited, bewildered, depressed or gingered? First time in
New York is the same for everyone; for Castang too. Relish
it? – he does. Acquire the rhythm; learn the language. What's a
submarine sandwich, and what's an imperial gallon (and why)?
Anybody French starts with the food, so, bee-el-tees and the
battle against bagels (lost before begun, that one). It would
take more than cream cheese to make lox comestible; and so
forth. But pastrami's fabulous.

Courtesy of the French government, he has been booked
into one of the monstrous holiday-inns jammed between Park
and Lexington, and before you get to the park: this is good
because he radiates out in all directions, and like a good
cop, on foot. For two days he trudged. Zigzagging to and
fro, crosstown. Up or down, he thought, would quickly give
substance to the idea 'Very long, Manhattan', just like 'Very
flat, Norfolk'. Isn't it the villages, rather than the town – ?
'Very dull, this Avenue.' Two days isn't much, alas. But he
got his moneysworth, from feet, and shoeleather. Next time
he'd find a bike to hire: rollerskates are exhibitionist. All
right, Broadway may be as dull as the interminable Rue de
Vaugirard, but he discovers the Cherokee Apartments and the
John Finley Walk, as well as Chelsea; Canal Street as well as
Riverside Drive. Not a tourist since he has no camera. Why
no pictures, Vera will ask jealously, and be told that carrying
a gun *and* a camera . . .

Villages – they aren't, any more than they are in Paris.

Spaces between? – like the lights and shadows between Vera's leaves. Frontiers; yes, Castang is always at his sharpest on the borders of things, of places, of people.

On the third day he has a lunch date with his contact, his go-between; Mr Bryan Dubesky. He has eaten swordfish and bluefish and Maine lobster, and drunk a lot of California wine – but this is different, this is now a flossy hotel on the park, and even if it's only the snackbar – under a fancier name – he has to wear a suit, and a tie, and hope the gun isn't showing. Mr Dubesky comes waddling in wearing extravagant check trousers (a mistake since his legs are too short and too fat for his stocky body and thick throat and sly, intelligent, toothsucking face), and he says he'll have a hamburger, and he wants it rare, and he wants a drink quick (something with pickled onions in) and you all fixed up, fella? – you – really – want – roast beef? Shaking his head, as though Castang would bitterly regret not having the tuna salad sandwich in the deli along the street.

"Now you just leave it all to me, okay? We meet the Man tomorrow for lunch, at his club, up near the park. So don't let the gun show neither around there, 'cause he wants to look you over, and you better believe he's sharp; even if he's had this bypass operation, there's nothing missing up here, right?"

"When it comes to the inspection, no problem. I slip you the goods, Swissair desk at Kennedy tomorrow evening, and you're on your way. Into the hands and no other of Missis Cash-in at the palace of Or-say and no other, right? She'll give you the signature, that's your discharge – this fucking hamburger isn't rare, here waitress, did I ask for a steamed chinese pancake, I said rare, so would you sweet and kindly make that so?"

Castang has been lucky with his weather, and works his way down Sixth to the Village; a bit too selfconscious, the Village, but at least there's less risk of meeting Mr Dubesky.

Little bits of the puzzle were falling into place. This is New York and over there is Paris, and not a lot to choose between them, on the whole. You could be French, or American: what did it matter? Neither was a town to be poor in; but if you did not have the dense carapace of money, you might do better here. Though you had to belong to a tribe; as he never would. Be born in Vilna, or Palermo. But don't be born in Paris, because you'll never belong anywhere else.

Castang, the solitary individualist, sitting drinking in the Village, moves the glass around, the cigarette packet, the ashtray, and considers them. One is him, one is his job, one is his wife: you move them around but they belong together; they are his identity.

If you were a Breton, or an Auvergnat, you came to Paris – or here – and the tribe knew you, accepted you, found you a job and somewhere to live. There was a quarter, a language, a church, a newspaper.

But who ever heard of a quarter of Parisiens? The only thing that binds them together is Paris itself, and that's why they can never leave. Vera would be Czech, here: what would I be? I'd be sitting here in this goddamn Village with all the other phonies.

Castang has often asked himself the Questions. Who am I? Where do I come from? Where am I going? Had never found the answers, until here. Here in New York he was able to accept his own solitude. So that when you marry, you must marry a Vera, and then there must be no cheating, no compromising, no giving in. You must understand Carlotta, and all the millions in Paris with nothing but their own tiny fortress. But realise that the brief moments of belonging together create nothing, generate nothing but more hunger. Go to bed with a Carlotta and it's the ski-jump. You cannot brake or turn back. There is nothing in front of you but that desolate ninety metres of void.

Afoot early next morning, because it was his last day, and because the sun was shining, he met – no, wrong word – the thundering herd of girls. Swept off the pavement isn't right though they do mow down, clear along the avenue, but Castang has been a street cop.

He knows how to stand blockishly, making himself bigger

than he is, immobile with a sardonic eye, so that even the most blank-eyed girls, the ones with walkman-plugs in their ears, flinch a fraction and step aside without willing to. Between eight-thirty and nine, Fifth or Madison, the heels go taptaptap, all the way up the avenue, in a greedy rhythm which echoes in the canyon. Who are you? asked Castang: no need to ask where you're going, but do you know why?

Waiting, very deliberately, for the green light, Castang crawled crabwise across the avenue, parks in the coffeeshop, gives himself up to the contemplation of a Vera; who walks rather slowly, limping just a little, with eyes on roofscapes. Chimney pots, gutters, attic windows, television antennae. But as long as there is sky . . . An express lift to the thirty-eighth floor will show you no sky, but since you can always hear about it on the radio . . . He likes the coffeeshop, the coffee's not so weak here, and you get it straight off, before you need start worrying about eggs and stuff, and the Spanish-speaking girl may not smell of spring sugarcane, but perhaps at home she has a skirt with lace. Wild cherry trees are for those who know how to find them.

This waitress has quiet, unanxious movements, and on this third day she recognises him, and she stands still, and the smoke from her cigarette goes straight up like the campfire at dawn, and she catches his eye and brings him a third cup of coffee, and he will never see her again and leaves a dollar under the saucer, and is glad to be going home to his wife. He has bought her a book of the Jacob Riis photographs, and T-shirts for the girls, with obscene exhortations on the chest.

On foot the Club was a pleasant stroll, halfway up the park. Stay on the bus up Madison and you can go a long way within the shadow and shelter of money. On Park, it's block after block of suspicious and watchful wealth; smooth steel and concrete shafts, slippery and impermeable; nothing on the sidewalk but yawning doormen under marquees and chauffeurs walking dogs. But the Club is quite low, the dingy victorian Gothic of its origins a symbol of perfect, placid arrogance. No need here of electronically-fortified portals and lounging security men with large guns. The sheer weight of all that money is quite sufficient.

There was still a hawkeye gaze, and Castang felt it. There seemed a great many servants just to take his hat, to stare at his tie and enquire the password. An adumbration of disapproval hung upon his heels, crossing the vast hall into the silent cathedral of the gentlemen's lavatory, where he peed, washed, and titivated in a heavy stillness and as though watched from behind mirrors. Wearing a gun is not gentlemanly behaviour. As soon exhibit your penis. He recrossed the lobby with mayoral dignity, as though about to lay a wreath upon the tomb of the Unknown Soldier; without being at all pally about it the concierge said, "Mr Barton will join you in the library." He went up the stairs like a walk-on part in a Wilde play – probably *A Woman of No Importance*.

Nobody was in the library: probably no one ever was. Castang sat, hitching his pants. A frock coat would have provided better concealment than the summerweight suit (Lanvin Hommes). Crossed his legs, for his shoes as always were highly polished and no cause for shame. Hid behind the massive fence of the *New York Times*. Presently he became aware of an elderly gentleman standing in the doorway.

Castang knew him only as old, rich, and eccentric. He was plainly also ill, with the face of a recent severe heart operation and the careful movements of the convalescent. This was all Castang ever learned, except that he had also courtly, Edwardian manners. He rang to order drinks, and talked pleasantly in his slow extinguished voice, like a man entertaining a guest and not a hired bravo. He mentioned the history and architecture of the club, he touched on the view from the tall first-floor windows, he dwelt lovingly upon his nigh-vanished New York. He talked about Elsie de Wolfe! – whom he had

known-as-a-boy. About fine arts – recommending Castang 'not
to miss seeing the Frick Collection'. He got carefully to his feet,
and Castang passed him his stick.

"Thank you . . . go down, shall we? Dubesky . . . will join
us, there." Castang, much impressed, offered an arm on the
wide, shallow stairs.

"Civil of you. I appreciate it. I'll manage. Because, you
see, I have to." Halfway down he said, "I like – France." He
meant, no doubt, Talleyrand's France, and Elsie de Wolfe's; not
Castang's, but it was touching, thought that polite functionary,
who had perceived that if he were to fail the test of these old
eyes, as sharp as those of the servants but much shrewder, the
old gentleman would be quite capable of refusing to let the
picture go.

The diningroom was sombre; dark polished mahogany and
white starched linen. All the waiters were head-waiters. Talleyrand at the Reform Club – eighteen-thirty.

"I eat very little. You must take whatever you like. The
beef is good. I will have a Dover sole, a glass of chablis. You
will choose, a really nice claret. It will – give me – pleasure."

That animal of a Dubesky arrived late and gobbled his
food. Only the very best clubs manage to combine the plain
and excellent raw materials, impeccably served, with quite
such awful cooking. Still, their claret . . . Dubesky drank
the Comtesse de Lalande as though despising it for having
no pickled onions in; saying I gotta hurry, I gotta pointment.

"Just a moment." Mr Barton did not use this voice towards
club stewards. "You will confirm with me. Here. At four o'clock
precisely. That is understood?" Dubesky nodded, sucked his
teeth, said "Kennedy" to Castang; bolted. In the silence
a waiter paced gravely forward, picked up the fallen napkin
as though it were a dead rat, laid it on the abandoned
chair.

"May I smoke?"

"You are going to have a real cigar, with your coffee.
You are going to tell me – a little – about yourself."

*

The magnificent Larrañaga lasted all the way down to the corner of Fifth – it was a bright sunny afternoon, in Central Park.

No, the old man was not mad. Insanity was close to the surface in this city, as a few steps into the park show. But the degree of control varies.

"Let us go into – the ballroom. Nobody ever comes there, and we don't want to shock anyone."

It was indeed ghostly. Three hundred women in the complicated evening toilettes of nineteen-eleven waltzed timeless upon this parquet, beneath these chandeliers. Tertiary syphilis has got Oswald. 'The sun, Mother, the sun!' The old man, still talking about Edith Wharton, pointed to a tall pierglass and said mildly, "Don't break it." Castang invoked blessings upon the shade of the Comtesse de Lalande, wheeled and drew his gun.

"A bit slow." It was John Wayne addressing Victor McLaglen – you've been at the whisky again, Sergeant. "A little rusty." Kindly; all these campaigns we've seen through, together.

"It's the cigar," apologised Castang, speaking between his teeth. For the first time he got a smile.

"But competent. With a competent weapon." The old man was amused, making his monkey show off its trick. "I feel now more comfortable, lending my picture."

"I'll answer to you for it." All his life he would remember the ballroom, the shadowy figures reflected in the tall old pierglasses – and pulling his gun, on Edith Wharton.

At the airport Dubesky was spot on time. He handed over the saddlebag suitcase, saying, "That's it, pal. Sign here.

"And now we've got to get you through the machine." A cop with a bulgy Irish face and belly, big Colt magnum in an open holster. A security man, with the face of blank blottingpaper common to all security men. The technician with his eye on the screen, while the bag goes through the tunnel, and Castang through the gate with his non-plastic revolver. For them Dubesky has a special muttering confidential manner, and something palmed; a visiting card of the Man's and presumably a C-note for-your-trouble, since these just-doing-my-job-buddy faces look at the ceiling, and Castang walks through like a letter in the post.

"Okay," said Dubesky. "Cointrin and Roissy airports are both told to expect you. Got no use for Europe myself, but have a good trip."

Go back to the old man and bow three times. If they let you in the ballroom, curtsey . . . But the pallid young Swissair man was making Swiss faces and looking at his fucking-Rolex, because Castang was last again, as usual.

No letter in the post (addressed to Madame Cachin at the Musée d'Orsay) could have gone smoother. Castang ate, slept, read. He was mercifully wide of the movie screen. He never knew whether 'the guard' was a figment of Carlotta's imagination. When some six weeks later he saw the pictures he wondered which was his. Since the notice says no more than *Private Collection*. Still, he has learned things which in their way are as valuable as pictures.

Nor must one forget the material reward. When Dubesky took him all confidential by the lapels of his jacket (odiously so and with breath smelling of gin, also – a New York smell – of dust) he got a confidential envelope tucked down into his inside breast pocket, and when he came to count there were ten hundred-dollar bills, so that Wall Street had not done much worse than Russian museums, if more predictably.

"Rather mean?" said Vera. "The thing must be worth a pile of millions."

"Not really. Just a tip to the chauffeur. Also there were enriching experiences," thinking of Señor Larrañaga, and the Comtesse de Lalande.

"New York?" expectantly.

"Oh, that's a back number, like Paris or London. You want to get with the action, you must swing with Seoul. My guess is, we should have got in from Bialystok around nineteen thirtyseven, we'd have been just in time."

"Coming and going."

"Might still have been the cold water walkup on Delancey, but we'd have caught Lester Young at his best."

"And the Count," entering into this.

"The Duke."

"Cootie Williams and Tricky Sam Nanton."

"Louis before the emphysema."

"Sad when you think of it." But it's the same with all empires. Just as they are celebrated with fanfares they cease to exist.

"And did you eat lox and bagels?"

"And what a shocking disillusion."

"I'd like to be rid of my nightdress, but one moment, this bed's full of crumbs."

Benny Goodman, on the tape, is making an enormous splendid noise (it is nineteen thirtyseven) and in just a moment Harry James and Ziggy Elman will be doing the Jewish-wedding music.

"So?" said Maria looking out at her door. "This is a surprise.

'The old music master simply sat there amazed
As wide-eyed in wonder he gazed and he gazed.'

But if you go on wiping your shoes like that you'll wear the mat out."

"One of the first lessons a cop learns," returned Castang, "is that be he in uniform or in civil, he has always trodden in the dogshit. There are people who make you take your shoes off at the door. And the ones who make you walk upon felt soles."

"I've always wanted to make a film about this. Entries. The outsides commonplace, shabby – and inside. There's a poem about a little man in a dark suit, but when he gets home –

> 'A splendid Titian blazing on the wall
> And twenty naked girls to change his plate.' "

"You've come to a good shop." Castang is remembering an old cop called Monsieur Bianchi, who used to do Enquiries on behalf of Families, and who'd seen things nobody would believe.

"We can do extraordinary things – put a camera almost anywhere in any light. But we can't yet see through walls."

"This is one of the things I've come to see you about."

"Just one?" feigning alarm. She was moving about, getting a drink. She had a smart frock on. Sturdy serviceable calf muscles, a deep solid bust. She can be an attractive woman, he thought primly.

"Sorry about this," thought-reading. "I was at a party with some magnates, who've been wondering whether to give me some money."

She kicked off the high-heeled shoes, flexing her toes. "Better." Like this she has a light-balanced, feline ease of movement.

"And did they give you the money?"

"They'll think about it some more. I need hardly tell you about the pains of the movie industry."

"That audiences are dim? But not as dim as the magnates? No. So are you very busy?" She shrugged.

"It's built in, to be kept waiting about. While I have one idea in suspension, I've others on the drawing board."

"What I mean, you might be here on base, for maybe a few weeks? Or you're off to look at locations and things?"

"Explain the purport of these cop-questions, pally."

"Does it happen to you, to work on what they call an-original-idea by Bloggs?"

"You've got one for me? I'll always listen."

"Maria – have you ever thought of making a film about child – call it abuse?"

"Not for public consumption. I know a few who'd be interested."

"I'm serious, funnily. Make a presentation, can I?" An enquiry in the interest of the family – one of the most difficult aspects of police work. Monsieur Bianchi knew how to get past any door. He was so reassuring . . . "I start with a hypothesis.

"We suppose a man; we adumbrate his uh, circumstances. He's a clever man, he's in the public eye, he has a public reputation, he's much admired. He has a habit of inviting young girls to his home. Swim in the pool, that sort of thing. A few people, outside, feel some disquiet at this.

"There might have been a few murmurs. Some scraps of circumstance but it's nothing to build on. These are private lives in private houses, and one treads warily."

"You mean," suggested Maria, "you might get sued for defamation, or malicious prosecution."

"Or whatever," agreed Castang. "And a fellow like that has several layers of protection. Political friends; not just people who write books. If one has witnesses they're reluctant, at best, to say what they know; their central concern is to protect themselves from insinuation, or the finger of gossip, or even having their comfort disturbed. And as for minors, even if one could question them, children will clam up when faced with anything they can't cope with. Or say whatever comes into their head.

"In a situation of the sort a cop thinks of setting a snare, and where do you find the bait? Dress up some fat policewoman to look fourteen? This is an intelligent, alert man."

"The scenario's all right," said Maria, "but where's the original idea?"

"Postulate a young girl, really in this age group. She has to know what she's doing, and be ready to act the part. She has to be perfectly convincing – what experience have you of directing child actors?"

"I get it," blowing smoke across the room, "you think to protect the child by placing her in an enacted role, and you think I could give her the freedom and confidence. A reversal," thinking about it, "of the usual technique. Instead of persuading her to forget the camera you wish in fact to remind her of it, give her the illusion that it's there. I don't know whether it works, whether it's possible for her to behave unselfconsciously. At that age, half child and half adult, you might get the worst of both worlds. Quite a neat little problem."

"Because it's not like in a theatre. The man is not acting."

"We won't fence – you are talking about my landlord. You haven't mentioned the physical difficulties; that house is as well protected as its owner. I don't see how one would sneak a camera in there. What kind of evidence do you have to have?"

"I was thinking in terms of a microphone, some little relay with a range of from there to here."

"Possible – you'd have muffle, distortion – but if you get a tape, how do you prove it isn't faked?"

"Have witnesses here to it."

"I get mixed up in this, and it comes out in public, as seems to be your plan . . . like you say, witnesses curl up at the edge and I'm not sure I wouldn't too, thinking of the impact on the industry."

"Nobody forces you to do anything but think about it."

"Charley, you think about it. Have you got a possible girl?"

"No more than maybe."

"A child actress," thinking about it, "will take risks no adult would attempt. The child hasn't that fatal vanity, that selfimportance . . . And if something goes wrong what do you do?"

"All I can think of," admitted Castang, "is kicking the door down."

"The more people involved, the bigger the risk of leak.

You know, you've had a bad idea and it might turn into a good one. You in a hurry?"

"No."

"I have a lot of work coming up this summer."

"I may have a thread, and perhaps you're Ariadne."

"I don't like it. And I don't like what you tell me, either. I'll help you if I can."

He likes the sturdy way she says it.

"Henri, this horrifies me." Word pronounced in a buttoned, legal voice and in no way cavernous, because M. Maurice Revel rarely allows emotion to seep through, but still carrying due weight. He is a man stubbornly honest but burdened by respectability; an open man but within the rigidities of legal training. If it is not indispensible to change a tenet then it becomes indispensible not to change it.

"Maurice, I accept responsibility for the idea and its execution. I do rely upon you to find me legal justifications, because I can just see myself arguing this with a Procureur; and one who takes an iron-ribbed view of the law's never looking at things it doesn't know how to cope with." And the Judge, seated at his desk and drawing careful lines across a piece of paper, is looking alarmingly legal.

Oh dear, this interminable debate in France about the reforms of the Penal Code. One third is in favour, one third says it is quite enough to modernise the Code of Penal Procedure, and one third, in general the oldest, doesn't want to change anything at all.

"We'll both lose our jobs," throwing the pen down and pinning it to the table with a flat palm: it must not be allowed to roll.

"That, I agree, approaching fifty, is a scary thought."

"They can't sack me." As a magistrate Revel is constitutionally immovable. "But they can disgrace me, put me in a null-and-void job." Castang knows that he must be thinking of Monsieur Pascal, 'the little judge'. This tiny, resolute man, in a difficult murder enquiry, maintained his belief in the guilt of a wealthy industrialist and local notable. He stuck to his certainty in the face of adverse opinions from all his superiors in the legal hierarchy, and was made to look a simple-minded figure of fun. The trouble was that he might have been right.

Castang himself is thinking of another affair: a young, and by all accounts brilliant criminal-brigade Commissaire was thought by an instructing magistrate to be a great deal too friendly with his underworld informers. He booked this PJ officer for passive corruption. The trial turned into a nasty confrontation between the magistrates and the police, who formed a block behind their colleague. But Castang has no criminal brigade. He will find nobody to back him up. He will still suffer from the rooted distrust with which the judicial profession views the police. He needs some support.

He knows that Maurice Revel is his friend; also that this prudent and experienced judge is thinking of the many ways in which suspicion becomes envenomed. The struggle for power is political; the crude opposition of left and right. Reactionary police officials denounce liberal magistrates as a pack of damned socialists. Crusty old Presidents of Assize view a social approach to methodology as profoundly unsound. The prospect will bend stout hearts into limp compliance. Maurice has not gone limp, but his feet are a bit cold.

"Your proposal is probably immoral, almost certainly illegal."

"I don't see why," said Castang. "Establishment of infraction. Like an adultery. The Commissaire of Police when duly mandated by the aggrieved and deceived husband may enter the domicile even in the hours of darkness. Employment of a locksmith shall not be deemed breaking and entering." This preposterous provision is still on the statute book.

"When duly – where's your mandate? I can't give it you."

"I may not be attached to a criminal brigade but I remain

an officer of justice. As a father I am the legal guardian of a minor child."

"Damn it, you cannot be both judge and accuser – good God, Henri," as the implication struck him, "you aren't thinking of using your own child!"

"Truly, I don't see any other way," said Castang soberly. "I – mustn't say we, smells of conspiracy – have to put before the Procureur a fait accompli, that he can't wriggle out of. A flagrant delict; witnessed, written up and on the slate. Then the fellow can be arrested and held under the fortyeight hour rule before being presented for a preliminary hearing. Naturally he denies everything. But my word as an officer of justice is good in court.

"And if I apply to the Proc for a search warrant I shouldn't be surprised to find some further evidence. That kind of man is given to taking photographs and gloating over them later." Monsieur Revel is shaking his head and waving tick-tock a warning forefinger.

"Won't do, won't do; it stinks of entrapment. Put-up job from start to finish. Elderly party exposed to temptation by teen-age siren" – the Judge exposed to contagion is falling into police telegraphese – "a momentary lapse into weakness; culpable no doubt, but an advocate will point instantly to a set-up. I, as an impartial instructing magistrate, would be bound to see his point. You can't enter the scene. Another commissaire of police, motivated solely by legitimate suspicion . . ."

"Well yes." Castang agrees, because he has to. He is not anxious to confide in the regional service of Police Judiciaire.

"Gendarmerie," he said suddenly.

Revel smiled. He would not have suggested it – he is not going to suggest anything. He would not have done so anyhow, out of tact, because of the no-love-lost. There are plenty of reasons for this. The Gendarmerie is a military body and does not obey the same authority as the police. It is better disciplined and often more competent. It is also better equipped. Besides jealousies, there are envies. The lowliest gendarme is deemed to be the equivalent of an officer of Judicial Police, whereas a cop is merely an Agent.

"There's a young man called Lawless."

"An upright and competent officer," said Maurice primly, "in whose dealings I have felt confidence."

"I liked the way he handled – I hadn't told you, but my wife had a narrow shave from a rape."

Into "Really!" Revel injected shock, sympathy, and a scandalised disapproval at hearing it mentioned, in just the right proportions. It's a specific bourgeois talent.

"You see?" said Castang. "We keep these disreputable episodes in the family. We don't go blabbing them about. We may never know what suspicions and even certainties other fathers of families may hold regarding our academical friend. We make the first step and who knows what mightn't come scuttling out of the woodwork."

"This is the point, Henri. *Do* we have adequate certainties? You know that I cannot justify this proposal with mere clouds of suspicion. I may be well aware of your beastly habits, which all policemen share, but I mustn't be told about them."

"I think we do have enough certainties; even if most are children's gossip." For Lydia has – but he mustn't tell Maurice, who is still throat-clearing and looking grave. "I couldn't conspire – yes, that's the word – to put another child in a position, uh, while refusing to imagine my own daughter . . . Maurice, erm, I don't want to go into this, but I have given thought, you know, to protecting the child."

"I don't want to be told," said Revel unyieldingly.

"Only mentioned it because of the uh, legal approach."

In the case of a flagrant delict a law-enforcement officer takes, naturally, matters in hand, makes his arrest, and has fortyeight hours to do his paperwork before presenting his case. But if he can show grounds for legitimate suspicion, he can apply to the Procureur for a warrant. This is more tactful, all round.

Prosecutors belong to the most rigid, the most protocolaire

hierarchy the profession can show. Their ambitions for advancement depend upon the favour of the great, and they are thus abnormally timid about offending the powerful. If Castang, a nobody, has one of the grandest personages in the Republic brought in for sordid reasons, a horrified Proc will smell the scandal as far off as newspapers in Rome and London. He may well find legal pretexts for squashing the charge because he's frightened for his own skin, and will pin up Castang's, instead.

The horns of this dilemma, upon which Brother Henri is impaled, are that to frighten a Proc he must have evidence, which he cannot get without frightening said-Proc worse still. Revel's support would be invaluable. Maurice knows this very well and keeps silence. Critical remarks, even in the hearing of your friends, about craven policies, run contrary to the unspoken, and severe, rules governing the magistracy.

"I asked you to try and get some evidence," says Maurice unhappily, "not push an entrapment scheme down my throat and hope thereby I'll get the Proc to swallow it."

Shrieks of mirth and merry giggles; teen-age fantasies and inventions for which the word spiteful is too strong, but to which malice adds a decorative baroque perfume: this is quicksand. You trust Lydia or you don't. If you do, you must accept that her tales are not mere invention, even when heavily embroidered.

"Caroline Cunnilingue . . ." Castang's ear had only caught this in flight but he had been startled enough to be pompous.

"Lydia, I've told you before about bringing home these playground obscenities. Whatever next!" Only too plain – Felicity Fellation – but he throttles that, just in time.

Squashed, she had kept a prudent silence until a week later, when she happened to be helping him load the trolley, on the weekly shopping expedition in the supermarket. A ripe giggle in his ear, a jog from a childish elbow, a hot tickly whisper and a meaning look.

"Caroline Cunnilingue!" An exchange of schoolgirl greetings.

" 'Jour."

" 'Jour. Ça va?"

"Ça va. Salut."

"Saa-lut." They don't kiss, meeting casually in public, as they would upon a 'social' occasion, but give the limp hand-touch. Castang's sharpened curiosity makes for more detailed observation. A year older than Lydia, which would put her in the third class; a tall pretty girl (casually disdainful towards a child so much her junior) with splendid golden hair, and something oddly expressionless in the face. She strolled away pushing her trolley. Fine long legs, nicely tanned though it was still only June. Expensive clothes.

"Looks a nice girl to me." To sound artless is one of the police crafts.

"She would!" with a sniff. "A well-known horizontal. Men detect it," with a comical precocity. "Marie-couche-toi-là."

"Really?" with his concentration entirely upon packets of macaroni. "I don't believe it."

"Pooh, half the Lycée has had a go."

"Yes, that's what they always say about the pretty ones; one half wishful thinking and the other half jealousy."

"Jealous! Me? Of that! I've more selfrespect." Head-tossing. "Makes no secret of it. Was aborted, even; last year."

"Yes, well, where's the evidence?" snubbingly. "Don't discuss such things in public."

. . . "Gossip!" he said. He had waited till they were in the car, and used now a prudish voice knowing how much it would annoy Lydia.

"Oh poor Pa," with the immense condescension they use when really cross. "Look, she doesn't go with just anyone, that much is true. But fact; there was a teacher sacked for touching her up. Fact, she was taken to England in the middle of winter. Fact, she even had a session with old Nanny Dampierre, who gets a bit sentimental over that type, and will stroke their knee absentmindedlike, given half a chance, and she makes it a whole one."

"I really doubt that. I doubt it very much."

"Common knowledge."

"Common knowledge isn't evidence, I have frequently occasion to remind you."

"You really are the most pompous old – " Lydia did not quite dare say 'prick', knowing that he would be quite capable of a ringing slap, back-handed, while driving. "Fact!" she screamed. "She boasted about it and he dropped her like a hot potato. He yatters on about ol' Madame Bovary but he gave her a lift in that ice-cream Mercedes with the cosy leather inside and felt her up."

"Good gracious. What do the parents say about that?"

"They don't even notice. They're rich," as though it were a disease. "See her clothes? She has a thousand a month just pocketmoney. They're divorced, of course."

"That may explain her behaviour but is no business of yours or mine."

"Carries a packet of condoms in her handbag now, as well as pills." Castang is aware that his daughter is also Vera's daughter, and that she shuns these commodities as not consonant with her selfrespect. "Look look!" excitedly; outside the butcher's. The traduced Caroline, in company with a woman in tight lilac trousers, was climbing into a posh white BMW coupé. "That's the mother. Big executive in the papermill. Another poufiasse." The French language is rich in synonyms for harlots.

"Takes all sorts," said Castang mildly. "Rather smart, those trousers. We could buy some like that for Ma." Lydia gave him a look.

"Are you off your nut?" He didn't know which pleased him most, her loyalty or her good taste.

He was beginning to take his idea seriously, but of all the obstacles, some formidable, the prickliest would be Vera. Broach this subject, which he hadn't, and he could argue his head off for a week on end; she'd go on saying no, no, no. There would be no reasoned objection; an immovable female obstinacy. He'd have to bide his time.

June dragged on, with the whole of France thinking of nothing but its holidays, save those unfortunate school-children who have to sit their university entrance examination. France is a country of obsessions and the Baccalaureat high on the list. It was the kind of summer which comes only once in ten years, pleases farmers not at all; the fighters of forest fires in the Midi less still: even the tourists found it far too hot. There were horrid tales of old ladies dying of heat-stroke in Athens; Paris sweltered, and the Beaux Arts, which do not flourish in summer, languished pallidly. Carlotta reappeared, was taciturn, re-disappeared, and was towards him extremely polite. She had quite forgotten – she said considerately – that she had booked holidays in July, a long time ago: did he greatly mind taking August? Not at all, he said with matching courtesy; where was she thinking of going?

"Hungary, I think. What about you?"

"My wife wants to go to Scotland and this seems a good moment."

"Sounds quite lovely," in a high, formal voice.

Lydia, to everyone's surprise, got a good school report; sadly weak in math, but yes yes, we've heard those arguments.

Castang rang up Maria, wondering whether she was away. There was no recorded message on the phone, which she answered just as he was hanging up.

"Sorry, I was in the garden."

"Castang here. Right place to be but I thought you were in Spain."

"Off there again next week. Bloody paperwork."

"Are you booked solid? An evening for dinner, maybe? At my house?"

"I'd like that. Tonight or is that too sudden?"

"On the contrary."

He had bought a big tent. Fine arts being at a discount, he had spent many hours of public service upon detection work: subject Scotland. A large tent: thus, even if it does pour with rain . . . It had been put up 'for practice' in the garden, and the children sent out to sleep there. He had feared adverse comment about this from Madame Saulnier, but when she appeared – in the same clothes she wore all winter – she had smiled quite benignly and merely remarked that he'd have to resow the grass, afterwards.

"Why not have dinner outside?"

"All right," said Vera. "But it'll be a very simple dinner. I hope your biddy isn't too grand."

"Perfectly simple woman."

Maria did not let him down, appearing (busty and slightly overweight) in a wide-skirted halter frock, cool and becoming. Vera who had feared she might be haughty (there is also the mistrust Czechs bear towards Russians) was conquered. Maria can talk Czech! Castang basks in the credit for this masterstroke, of which he had not had the least idea. The children, at first wary, were magnetised; Lydia refuses to speak Czech, being selfconscious; Emma can patter a bit.

"What do you do?" asked Emma bluntly.

"I make movies."

"You *do*?" Lydia, on a high note; this is glamorous.

"Not very glamorous, a stupid actor got bitten by a mosquito or something and came out in colossal bumps. A sharp camera fell on my head and my hair was full of blood. Now I'm thinking of making a test. Using you."

"But I'm not an actress."

"That's a bullshit word. Everyone's an actress; I'm one myself."

"Can I be one too?" Emma wide-eyed.

"Yes, when we find the right part. I need Lydia now, for a specific purpose."

Castang bustles about with drinks. Vera's two sorts of cold soup, gaspacho and vichyssoise, have been exhausted by the hot weather, but he reads cookery books at work, and the Beaux Arts came up with a suitably glamorous recipe. Vera has made a grand big fish, and Lydia was so taken with Maria that she even forgot to complain about the bones.

Maria smoked Castang's little cigars, and volunteered for the washing up after the children had been sent to bed. She spoke plainly to Vera. Castang had the sense to say nothing at all.

Maria is not in the least put off by the no-no-no: she gets that all the time from producers afflicted by creative ideas.

"But this is – I must tell you, I had myself a nasty experience."

"You were protected by your experience and your common sense. She'll be protected by her innocence and by training. I've looked at her and listened to her. Well balanced and a good tough mind; she'll respond well to direction. All she needs is confidence and that I can give her."

"But this is a – "

"Vera, believe me: you can trust me, can't you?"

"But if she were subject to violence."

"We would know; we'll hang a microphone on her. If there's even the remotest peril we send a commando in. But I know this man well, he's my landlord. He won't use violence. Flattery, and a lot of sly little tricks, and we can arm her against all those."

"But Maria, she's only fourteen."

"Think about what you and I were like at fourteen. Much tougher than we looked." Vera thinks of the harsh discipline of the gymnastics school, and has to agree.

"Still," she objected, "all that pretence of sophistication is just gossamer. Certainly more vulnerable than we were."

"Agreed – look, we'll rehearse her. Nobody's seizing her by the leg to fling to crocodiles. I'll work her with an actor

– somebody good, sensitive. And don't think my motives are anything but selfish. I've been wanting for some time to work with a child actress and here is my chance to learn. There's nothing sentimental in my attitude; it's brutally materialist."

"I prefer that," said Vera.

I am the sentimentalist, thought Castang.

"When can you think about these rehearsals?" he asked. "She'll have to go back to school in mid-September."

"And I'll have my Spanish passage wrapped up and tied in August; be back here for cutting and editing so early September will be fine, and if you know where you can borrow a garden with a private swimming-pool, better still. Don't get Lydia confused with Lolita. And I don't want either of you there. Trust me, and the moment to begin is now."

"But she's not," said Vera shrewdly, "the actress you'll be looking for."

"And you're not well cast as a movie mum. Ever watch the child tennis-players? Mum glued to the sideline clutching Johnny's sweater, worrying about that weak second serve, and anxiously counting all the millions in her bloodsucking little mind? No, Lydia's not real movie material – producers look for something with fuzzier edges."

"And more like Lolita," said Castang speaking for the first time.

It rains a good deal in Skye. Literature has been known to get lyrical about the sunlit seas and singing sands, but the realities have sent the teeming millions rampaging off to wherever you like as long as it's south of Barcelona; and that is as well for a countryside too fragile for them. But now and again the anticyclone wanders distracted off its path, the rain buckets down upon everything south of the Loire, and the ten people left behind in Oslo take their shirts off and wiggle their toes, while neither love nor money can buy you a pair of gumboots in Nice. This happened now: instead of turning blue Sutherland toasted.

"Speed bonny boat," said Vera happily.

"Genau," said Castang who quite often uses German words under the impression he's talking English.

Weird things happen at these eccentric moments. Hardheaded German businessmen buy tumbledown hovels in Sligo for twenty times their market value: Inverness is a riot of roses: all the mussels in Brittany are pronounced unfit for consumption: the sea is at twenty degrees round Mallaig and swarms of jellyfish attack Aberdeen. Lydia announced multiple sightings of seals and Russian submarines, Emma saw the Loch Ness monster, and a redhaired girl from Glasgow called Julia was arrested by the police for indecent exposure. Castang's skin, in winter yellowish like a cheap cigar, became brown and then dark brown: Vera's which is white turned quite a pretty ivory; and the children grew amazingly healthy from eating nothing but chocolate bars and packets of crisps. Altogether, a successful holiday. It was gleeful, on the way back, meeting all those furious faces crammed crossly into Volvo stationwagons heading north. Daily temperatures in Stavanger have been higher than in Marseille for nineteen days running, and for once the French and the English are conjoined in rage.

Just as they got home the sun came out and Castang grumbled at having to mow the grass.

France had now to get back to the serious business of La Rentrée. A nerveracking affair this re-entry, because everything in France always is. In the provinces one won't notice so much, save that the prices which have been put up for the tourists now refuse to come down; but among the bourgeois of Paris there are severe withdrawal symptoms, linked to being tanned without catching skin cancer. People do silly things like reading newspapers, which are suddenly twice the size since all the journalists got back too from the farflung, and seized with new zest upon politics, economics, and the peculiarly French version of Literature, meaning books which nobody reads but everyone feels they have to talk about: the unreadable writers are content with this state of affairs.

But officially the Re-entry is all about schools. The children of Europe went back to their classrooms in mid-August without hysteria. French children, their last-year's neurosis greatly fortified by the long holidays, begin in mid-September. Every year there is the devil to pay; expensive devil too, presenting the bill before we've paid for the holiday.

This is the big moment for manufacturers of shoes, stationery, and this year's carrier-bags. Unveiled are the autumn fashions in pencilsharpeners and indiarubbers, grammar- and geography-texts, and the very latest in pedagogic methods. There are not enough teachers; there are too many teachers: both can be true simultaneously, but it doesn't matter because there is no money to pay them. There are too many children, and in the wrong age groups. This culminates in long sentimental television sequences of howling tots being dragged to sacrifice. The State naturally is as irresponsible towards the brats as towards tenants, landlords, farmers, stockbrokers, and the police.

Castang, back at the office, is plunged into a long unlikely tale of faked high-value postage stamps, some of which might have been stolen from the little shop in the Place d'Armes in – good heavens, Monsieur Brun: Castang had forgotten all about him.

Farther-sighted and less wasteful than the government, Vera has bought her children dull but sensible shoes in Inverness, and clothes which being Foreign arouse envy in the hearts of other little girls. Buzzing about among schoolbags and the infernal geography book (don't think Emma can use Lydia's old one) she had forgotten about Maria's need for a swimming-pool, and rings Castang in a flap.

"Try Michèle. That's right; Denis Manuel's wife." Michèle

has no children, mourns about this, talks of buying an Indian baby on the black market, legitimising the adoption through bribery of the right civil-servants – adoption procedures are complicated and obstructive. In theory she would then be happy ever after but has never screwed herself up to it; assuages guilt through conspicuous extravagances. It would be cheaper to get fecundated in vitro? 'Thank you – and find myself with six!' The pool has been only a partial success. 'I swim and swim, and I even stop over-eating, and do I get any slimmer?'

But it is ideal for the present purpose. There are high hedges, and no nosy neighbours, so that she can lie about naked.

The problem is that Denis, being a doctor, knows how to keep his mouth shut, but Michèle never does.

"The entire hospital will be ringing with it," said Castang, "and if Lydia is a movie star she'll want to be one too." A lecture on discretion?

"This has to be quite quite clear. Any whisper at all which might later be remembered and repeated, and we'll every one of us be saying Well now, isn't that just Lovely! Denis will find himself an abortionist in Ajaccio, and I'll be tapping you on the shoulder, in the supermarket. Mind unbuttoning your coat then, Missis? Quite literally, you know. This country won't be big enough to hold us."

"I promise; I'll be deaf, I'll be blind."

"Yes, and I also want you dumb."

Maria has dropped into song: Castang has learned to see it as a good sign.

"'And my Imag-ination
    Will make my dream come true.' " He tells her – she's even getting to look like Louis Armstrong . . .

"'Sweetheart, I assk no more than This-ss.' " Faking the diamond ring and the big silk handkerchief.

He has been allowed to come along 'this first time', to give Lydia an initial confidence (like taking a child to the dentist) 'but if you as much as cough I'll throw you out.' Lydia enjoys that!

Maria is both more comic and more impressive than he has known her; a professional now, at work. Her voice bounced on the water. A small woman with short dark hair was sitting on the tiled surround with her bare feet dabbling in the pool: this is Cathy Vandamme, the sound engineer. She has a clutter of electronics strewn about, 'bits of black things'. Cathy is not taking it very seriously as yet. She knows what they are thinking of doing; she had to be in the secret, but for this first time, again, it is really to give Lydia the feel. The child has not been told, yet, what will be expected of her. Maria will give her all that in due time.

"Maria is experimenting, wants a child actress about your age and build, and offers you the lollipop of standing in for tests, to see if it'll work, before she writes any scenario. One thing, though: you mustn't go gabbing about it. Least of all at school; it's a professional secret of hers and mustn't be known. You know what's meant, by industrial espionage." Lydia, much impressed, nodded vigorously. She has Vera's stubborn, secretive streak. Even at fourteen, her promise once given, she's less likely to be indiscreet than Michèle . . .

Maria, Cathy, he himself, are equally sceptical. It's an iffy scenario: what guarantee have they that the child-seducer, himself still largely hypothetical, will look with any interest upon ugly-little Lydia?

Oddly, after seeing Lydia, both women had become much more optimistic. "I think it may well work," agreed Cathy, of whose common sense he has quickly formed an impression.

True, the child has bloomed, in Scotland. Bold – overbold – in water; she had nearly got herself drowned last year at Biarritz. But the twelvemonth since had added centimetres to her height and depth. Startled, Castang realised that his daughter was now a young woman. His eye, however trained, was not detached; the holiday had rounded her out, filling in the saltcellars above the collarbones, giving shape to sticklike arms and sharp shoulders, a columnar depth to the scrawny throat. In the September sunlight, wearing the lavender bathing-suit new in June and already a bit faded, the nasty child looked a handsome girl. Her skin had a glow, from northern sea and sky, one does not find from baking on southern beaches; her eyes are brighter and bluer. He suddenly sees the point of Louis' ridiculous song.

"A kiss to build a dream on," he muttered: Maria's eyes in her broad diamond-shaped face crinkled up with amusement.

"I'm wondering whether to have her hair cut. You'd have no objection?" She has brought a camera along, parked it casually, is taking sighting shots, framing, with a little handheld device.

"Need no operator," she had said. "I'll bring an actor, next time maybe, but the fewer people in this the better. For her, it starts by being fun. When the serious appears, it'll still be fun. Time she comes to realise a sordid, even a tragic element, she'll have learned the meaning of effort, the holding still, the repetitions, the not brushing a fly off when it settles on her."

As yet, Lydia has no clue about anything; sits there as stiff as a post, paralysed by selfconsciousness, attitudinising: a vague idea that she should pose, as though advertising some-body's shampoo.

"Lydia – sing! Anything that comes into your head. La la la."

"Please – I don't know how." Instantly Maria breaks into a filthy ditty, Cathy Vandamme joining in, bellowing and laugh-ing. Mercifully Denis' consulting rooms face the front, and are soundproofed . . .

" 'There's an arab in the alley with a hard on,

'Cause the woman in the window's got her pants down.' "
If Vera might have been unamused at this, Castang knows that the industry functions on uproarious obscenities and that most of it is a limbering process, a loosening-up. 'Goes back,' as Maria says, 'look at all the double meanings in Shakespeare

or Molière.' Their common language is a bastardised English; she utters fearful-sounding oaths in Russian. As soon as Lydia gets the tune she pitches in, in her clear childish soprano, and Cathy grunts 'Good!' fiddling with her meters.

The camera is there because it's there: Maria moves it about, adjusts it, looks through it, tries out filters on it; there is film in it and Maria may shoot a bit if she sees occasion, but it serves no real purpose save to get the child used to it.

The moment work begins Maria is transported by a powerful electric charge; bawls, cajoles, acts: suddenly still, she softens her voice to Russian whispers fit to carry across a mile of snowclad taiga. She is dressed in sailcloth shorts and one of her loose tops with a big pocket where she keeps her book with drawings and annotations. She is teaching Lydia the simple moves, how to walk on and off stage, how to stand, sit, and get up again. She is like every real professional; having accepted an idea, however dotty, she carries it out wholeheartedly, neglecting no tiny detail.

"Rest. Lie down and stretch out – yes, like that, with one knee up. I'd like her to take her clothes off," she mutters sidelong at the discreet Castang, who is learning how to get out of the way in a hurry.

"I doubt if she will, with me here."

"No matter, I won't hurry her. Like to take your top off, darling? Those straps are tight and it spoils the line."

"Please, I'm not allowed to." Lydia's English has a Glasgow accent learned from redheaded Julia; who took the lot off, paying no attention to Castang and getting reprimanded by the police. 'Now young lady, yu put it back on or I'll be handing yu a Summons.'

"I understand; no strain."

A good five minutes later, while squawks and mutters come from the recorder of talking-while-swimming, Cathy says disgustedly, "No pleasing you, is there? Yah, back to silent movies."

Maria, who was striding up and down the side of the pool

with hands on hips (Vera would have been reminded of an early gymnastics instructor), put a large high-arched bare foot – with coquettish painted toenails – in the small of Vandamme's back and kicked her headlong into the pool. Lydia gave a squawk of glee, hideously distorted by the amplifier. Maria, all impish grins, said, "That'll learn her."

Cathy swam about underwater, peering to recover some little black thing, surfaced, wiped the water out of her eyes and said "Russian Untermensch" in a placid tone, and climbed out shaking herself like a dog.

"Now look at me! Ay de mi, my daughter, my ducats, my ducats and my daughter," pretending to wring out the sopping T-shirt.

"I saw you," said Maria meaningly.

"You saw what?"

"Peeing in the pool." Lydia giggled at this schoolgirl wit and Castang pushed a grin back into the bridge of his nose.

With deliberation Vandamme dragged off the clinging top, undid the shorts and spread them carefully to dry on the tiles, went to stand on a dry bit, making a thing of polishing the splashed meter with a paper hanky, naked as an egg.

"If it had been a dry pool," said Maria, "we might have managed to let a bit of light into that tiny black skull." Cathy turned round and put her tongue out. Castang admired this polished act. The police have a few routines too, with forgetful or recalcitrant witnesses.

Within three minutes Lydia was stealing sidelong glances at her father. Emboldened by a blank face and look of hebetude she reached up her back and undid the clasp, displaying 'reasonable tits' but white, since Vera does not permit topless children; Czech modesty. And I won't have any arguing; Julia is not my daughter.

"Easy fixed with a bit of Leichner," said Maria.

"Very good indeed, for one day," breaking for lunch, and surprisingly content. "She's going to be all right."

They were washing their hands in a restaurant washroom,

sharing a pullout towel. Only pizza and a couple of beers –
'No need to go to a lot of expense.'

Seeing Lydia in friendly conversation with Cathy Vandamme
Maria can be confidential, a moment.

"Docile to direction while bloodyminded over anything she
feels to be false or wrong – I'm optimistic. Another like that,
I'm banishing you – and then I'll bring an actor. I've talked to
Erich Mertens. He's a kind and decent man and will be perfectly
sensitive towards the child. Gay or ungay he has children of his
own. A thoroughpaced professional, utterly reliable."

And Castang hopes the same will get said of him, upon
occasion.

For it has occurred to him that he is being narrowly subjective
about the entire matter. Maurice Revel takes a legal view, and
Maria's interest is largely technical: so that he himself – wasn't
he being unduly personal about it all? True, he thought of
himself as taking a balanced view of his two daughters. Not
like the sculptor Maria had mentioned, who slept with both
his sisters and two at least of his three daughters . . . 'Did he
get into the *Guinness Book of Records*?' asked Castang.

Lieutenant Lawless is wondering what all the fuss is about.

"You meet a lot of sophisticated people, in the PJ. The
city slickers, uh? Ingenious – imaginative." A romantic view!

"We're the country mice. Seven-tenths of our work is Saturday night drunks. Simple stories of plain people.

"Take fraud – you get stock-exchange smart guys, computer
bandits, smoothies. We'll get some little mail-order scheme, a
small ad; you send me a hundred francs and I'll post you a tin
medal, a sprig of dried rosemary, and you'll never get cancer,
see? Or your hair won't fall out, your breath won't stink. A
peasant is no stupider really than a doctor or a lawyer, but
one can subdivide credulity; a sales talk is tailored for a specific
target. The fraud seems so obvious, and people still fall for it.

What's exotic to me is everyday to you, and vice versa.

"You got a child-abuse thing here, old man having it off with young girls. I can't say I get excited."

"No," said Castang.

"I had a farmer not so long back, two little girls twelve and eleven, took turns in his bed, any infringement of the rules they'd be stripped naked and beaten with the leather belt. Schoolteacher, young girl fresh in from town, sees it her duty, etcetera. Which is worse, the welting or the incest? Young judge thinks both are pretty bad, which they are, so the old man is jugged, the daughters are put in care. The farm goes bust, the old man killed himself, local people just about crucified that teacher, and it didn't do the girls a bit of good. See? – end worse than the beginning."

"Yes," said Castang.

"Village not far from here, young girl about fifteen, smart and likes to dress up and paint, got gang-raped, badly. Eight or ten local boys. We had to jug them, naturally. The mothers come storming in here furious; those are good boys, and true, they weren't hooligans; that girl's a cock-teaser and got just what she was looking for; some truth in that, too. Her parents were honest folk but they had to leave the district. Job lost, house lost, girl lost, life in ruins. Ask the judge for civil damages? Get awarded some paltry sum; these are all poor people."

"So what do you do?" asked Castang.

"More I see, more ways I look how I can avoid legal action."

"I agree. Which is why, most of the time, we take none."

"I defer," said Lieutenant Lawless rather rapidly, "to your senior status. Uh, your greater experience."

"Or something or other," said Castang. "More other than something."

"Listen, you don't mind my saying, I can think of a few reasons why . . ."

"Why I'm not popular in criminal-brigade circles."

"I didn't say that. Was thinking though, no denial, this is pretty far out. Ho, you say, the military mind. I like to have a line of retreat, not to get stuck out on the bare ground getting mortared. Say my commandant calls me on the mat, I tell him there's this PJ commissaire, he says What PJ, what's that got to do with us? You don't have any clear official standing."

"Forget the PJ. You're acting on the complaint of a parent."

"I set all this up? On the uh, unsupported allegations of a member of the public? Fellow like this, Academy and all? I wouldn't, you know. I'd be knocking and taking my cap off, coughing and saying It's been brought to my notice that. Fellow gives me the big laugh, and I say Yes, naturally, but you do understand, my duty is to issue a word of warning, okay?"

"This is the point," dry. "Stop him laughing."

"Yes, but it's like I see a chap break in a car, make off with a camera, I shout Hey and he pulls a knife. I draw the gun. Halt or I fire. He bolts. The law says I've got to put a warning shot in the air.

"I know that house, Mr Castang. It's on our list for insurance purposes, contains a lot of valuables. You've seen it, and you tell me how we walk in. Time we get in, the fellow's had time to set up the breakfast table and be there drinking coffee. 'Here's a silly girl, Lieutenant. Take her home, you'll be doing me a favour.' "

"No, we've evidence. We'll have a microphone clipped to her."

"Isn't that enticement? Badger game, no? Girl invites the bloke up to her room, gives a scream and this big muscular type walks in and claims he's her brother?"

"It's a badger game when the brother suggests a little down-payment. Demand with menaces and inducements. He might offer us a bribe at that, if sufficiently flustered, but I'd guess he'd be too fly."

Lieutenant Lawless looks at him, amused. A full round face, glossy shaved jaws that will be jowls if he eats too much; the hair receding on both sides of a high forehead: sharp little eyes. It's an Irish as well as a French look. The Celt anywhere is a convincing talker.

"I'll be happier too," said Castang, "if I can get the Proc to see it my way."

"I'd be easier in my mind," agreed Lawless. "Another small thing is bothering me – what makes you confident, excuse my saying it, he'll take a fancy to your daughter?"

"Yes, that's the dodgy bit."

Castang can see much sense in these arguments. And more in the virtues of a nice quiet job in the Beaux Arts. Had any of those bourgeois breathed a word of complaint? Sabine's parents, who ran the expensive riverside restaurant? The famous Caroline? No, it would be bad for business! Maurice Revel says he knows of at least three cases in which children have suffered acute psychological injury. There's never much we can do about incest. But where are we to draw the line?

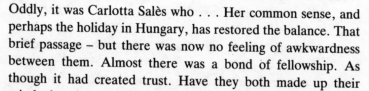

Oddly, it was Carlotta Salès who . . . Her common sense, and perhaps the holiday in Hungary, has restored the balance. That brief passage – but there was now no feeling of awkwardness between them. Almost there was a bond of fellowship. As though it had created trust. Have they both made up their minds that they are after all adults?

They were talking in her office. It was the usual shuffle of whatever was on their plate, and agreement how to share it out. He felt the sudden impetus to tell her what was on his mind.

It was in a way 'her doing'. It had been natural enough for Castang to have felt bothered by the 'Sabine' episode. His own daughter at a new school; a sharper eye on her companions, her behaviour. The meeting with Denis, the friendship struck up with Maurice Revel. But it was a safe bet that he wouldn't have done anything about it much, had he not felt guilty about his escapade with Carlotta.

He hasn't thought this out. Ludicrously, he had had the idiotic notion that Vera would not have been raped – don't dramatise, nigh-raped – if he had not been in bed with Carlotta at that moment. He thinks now only that she is after all a trained police officer. Vera takes a subjective view, a bit marked by that bad experience of sexual aggression. Maria, an artist seeing anything in terms of dramatising it, is not a good witness either. What will Carlotta make of his motives?

Carlotta slowed down; thinking about it.

"You think about crossing someone highly placed. About incurring displeasure, and perhaps malice. I've had this threat made to me too, three or four times; of losing my job. Or it can be jealousy. One can be too good, for the tastes of some. There's no greater rancour than that of a mediocrity, who feels overshadowed. But it can happen too that one is supported, higher up. Perhaps by someone who feels respect, silently, for whoever stayed vertical in the crowd of sycophants.

"And I should hope you would. Not having a wife or a family, I don't offer advice to those who do. But if you find yourself between a stone and a hard place, you should find people you can count on. I don't know much about your wife, do I? A bit about you, though."

She picked up a file of papers and made for the door, her heels tapping, rather sharply. And shut the door behind her, with a snap.

Feeling that sort of respect which she had mentioned, he bought Carlotta some long-stemmed roses, of a pretty pink shade. She was pleased. Observing them later, in a vase on her desk, he was struck by the unnatural perfection of these revolting objects: they were in all their features identical to those made of sugar by high-class pastrycooks. Still, Castang told himself, it's the thought that counts, they say.

Maria elaborated, over a drink a week later.

"Erich made her a number of inventive proposals. She cried a good deal, slapped his face, told him he was a dirty pimp. And I was another. She's coming on fine. Quite the little seductress on camera and that we mustn't have, so I've told her what this is about; in reality there'll be no second take."

The schools uproar has settled into routine. The little literature group had been given the pep talk. This famous and busy neighbour was indulgent enough to give time and trouble to tedious little boys and girls. So best behaviour and no cheeky backchat.

Lydia reported the chuckly, indistinct old gentleman Castang had met. But one had to admit, it really was interesting.

"We had all about Guy de Maupassant, did you know he was – I mean it comes alive, not like being in class, about society, and what the bourgeoisie was really like – and the painters – oh and the siege of Paris and the Commune, the German generals sitting in the Rothschild château at Ferrières, the amount of champagne they drank you wouldn't believe . . ." Magical old Dampierre had made her a true-believer in just fortyfive minutes.

But he has to be good, thought Castang. He is a man of genuine talent, and who knows what obscure distortions are magnified by this power into something which is the more dangerous for being to him beautiful. It is no crude pornography. He must feel, and the girls must feel, that a marvellous, unique experience is offered them. Creativeness. Something the world cannot understand.

Castang cannot tell a good fake, and doubtless never will. But Carlotta Salès can. Oh well, it's training, as well as instinct. 'Look, Henri, Paul Gauguin was doing well, bringing in good money, attached to a loyal patient wife, devoted to his daughter Aline. And still no good, he couldn't find it. He got a chilly reception from the bourgeois in Tahiti. Went out to those far villages, penniless, bananas, he wasn't you know just comforting himself with the little brown girls. Now look at this – now look again at that – can't you see the difference? A real one, even a minor one, is a priest as well as a king.'

Castang! – aren't you exactly like those pettifogging pricks in Tahiti? Sub-prefects, tax-gatherers, little colonial worthies. An embourgeoised moralist? And a feeble little hypocrite; you took Carlotta's clothes off and then thought better of it. I don't think you've anything to be proud of.

Maria is teaching Lydia objectivity.

"Erich is a good man," his daughter told him, scornfully. "He's kind and patient and I wish I could say the same about you!" One in the eye for Dad.

"Maria's nasty as hell. She hit me yesterday. I was asking for it too. She boils, because she's an artist. I understand why Ma gets frustrated." Ah-h.

After the third evening class, "It isn't me Granny Dampierre fancies," with adolescent cynicism. "Carmen Vannier."

"Who's she?" Justified in gloom.

"Pretty, which I ain't. Terrific hair. I must tell Maria to do a few shots of her by the poolside and we'd have a clip for a shampoo ad, sell that with no trouble at all."

He takes the trouble to have Carmen Vannier pointed out to him at the bus stop. Indeed, ravishing child. And her parents work in an advertising agency! He wonders drearily whether to say a word to them, and the heart fails him.

October dawning, and the maples beginning to turn, not a real sugar maple, just a good decorative tree for polluted suburban areas.

"I'm not sure," said the newly-Maria-trained-Lydia, "that Granny Dampierre isn't viewing me with a favourable eye. 'There's an arab in the alley with a hard on.' "

"Lydia, please," said Vera. "Oh all right, I won't fuss. I've learned all about the industry. Cathy Vandamme and I had lunch together; I like her a lot."

"Can be a flaming cow," said Lydia lordly, "but then I'm one myself."

"And has Monsieur Dampierre made unacademic advances?" asked Castang.

"Only to say he has books at home one doesn't find in the public library. *Les Fleurs du Mal* illustrated by Félicien Rops, boy oh boy I can hardly wait, big fat women with black hair growing round their nipples, very Third Republic."

"Lydia, do stop trying to provoke me with these indecencies, do you mind?"

Castang has to take hold of his courage, and go up against the Proc. He's an unknown quantity, says Maurice Revel, and might jump either way. He's idealistic, he says. Meaning sensitive, donchaknow, to a socialist government. But don't think him just a creep; he has genuine qualities both of heart and intellect.

'But he's a natural right-winger; old family, judicial for generations. Incidentally, a friend of the Academy. A fence-sitter? Most people are, and most are more complicated than that.'

He has asked for an appointment: he has let it be known that he is the bearer of confidences upon a delicate subject.

"Monsieur le Procureur, bonjour." To invert the everyday formula is slightly more stately.

"Monsieur le Commissaire." Smiling face. "What good wind? Not often we see you here." Castang has never been there at all. "A nice picture for me, have you, to hang in my office?"

This is only to show that he knows who Castang is. It is the usual panelled room, sombre even when high-ceilinged and well lit, and would be improved by a few Dutch dignitaries of the seventeenth century with red noses and large white collars. To show that he's a cheerful, friendly type, the magistrate is not wearing a suit but a tweed jacket and fawn trousers: he has loafer shoes with little tassels on his bony, prominent feet.

His brown hair is longish, a little rumpled as though his secretary had been running her hand through it. A large gingerish moustache completed this cavalier exterior, but there's a strong conservative palate behind it, had run Maurice Revel's warning; the liberal leanings are an impression he seeks to leave with the listener. The magistrates of this generation are strongly polarised. The leftwing ones are noisy and at times petulant; the tories are rigid in reaction.

The moustache is bristly and the coolish greenish eyes are expectant.

"Well now, Castang," a quick glance at the card on his desk to make sure of getting the name right, "some nice frauds for me?"

"Could it be confidential?"

"If that be your wish, certainly. Suzanne," pressing his voice key, "hold calls would you, and no interruptions. No, Castang, I'd prefer it if you didn't smoke."

"A morals charge, so I thought that the greatest discretion . . ."

"Quite right."

"Corruption of minors. Little countryhouse parties. Difficult, as always, to know how far it goes, because in the usual absence of complaint . . ."

"A ring, eh? 'Ballets roses'?"

"Just one man as far as is known, but a notable, and children of notables involved." The Procureur frowned.

"I've heard nothing of this. What do your colleagues of the Regional Service have to say?"

"One of my points. I came across this by accident and haven't uh, mentioned it elsewhere; felt it right to approach you, sir, before anything – "

"Quite right. No complaint, we can deal discreetly. But what d'you have that's evidential?"

"Not a great deal. A schoolchild – "

"We're hearing a lot of nonsense these days about lowering the age of consent."

"Thirteen–fourteen, coeval with my daughter who drew my attention to disturbed behaviour. I observed some signs of physical maltreatment and a doctor confirmed indications of sexual molestation, but there's no evidence that boys . . . However, the parents refused to proceed so there the matter rested. This is six months old; a banal occurrence and one had to be prudent." Castang's stilted police language shows embarrassment, but the Proc is nodding encouragement; continue.

"Observation shows a restless undercurrent among the early teenage group in the lycée classes. Rumour, but straws begin to show a pattern, and I've been thinking that a watch . . . But the Regional Service – I mean that if one were to get a press leak . . ."

"A good point and it could happen. Some parent, anonymously."

"I was thinking, perhaps the Gendarmerie . . ."

"And you a PJ man!" A smile which could be called unpleasant. He knows, thought Castang, that I got dropped from a criminal brigade, that I might quite like to stick an elbow in the colleagues' eye, and finds some malicious amusement in the fact. He kept his own eyes downcast, like a nun given audience with the Pope.

"I thought perhaps some surveillance, and if occasion presents then a quick raid to establish the delict – rather like a proof of adultery; but since no complaint has been laid, an officer once formally mandated," mumbling at the sticky point but the Proc lets this one go because he's seen another.

"You've grounds for a mandate but what I don't see is your personal involvement: professionally, your terrain . . ."

"I do have to declare an interest. My own daughter, I've some reason to believe in approaches; uh, children of that age are secretive." Castang, you are a sad hypocrite!

"It's understandable you don't want the matter bruited abroad. Hearings in camera, but the press once it scents scandal . . . You shall have your mandate. Remains for me to

know who this satyr is – a local notable you said, but regardless
of position or notoriety . . ."

"Yes, but the shoe pinches."

"Oh dear, in the public eye; what is it, a politician or
television?"

"Bit of both."

"Too bad for him." And if one thinks that Castang's hypocrisy
is filthy, which it is, one should pause before sending him to the
salt mine. He has been punished in the past, a long way past his
deserving, and one should recall that speaking of hypocrisy he
has been to a good school. There's a great deal of it around.

To take a smallish but apposite example, the Procureur
de la République has shown an indecent eagerness to get his
teeth into a nice sex scandal involving a celebrity, has rushed
his fences, and delivered himself into Castang's hands. He isn't
averse to a bit of notoriety of his own. The Press will make a
stir? – a useful way of being noticed by one's superiors. Who
in fact refuses to do a bit of politicking, in the good cause of
ambition? It is much like Castang, who sees a chance of getting
out of the hole of the Beaux Arts.

Or to take a wider view of the whole matter: – Use the
word 'Justice' and you utter, indivisibly, the word 'Cant'.

"Well, who is it?"

"Academy. Our resident literary prophet."

"Oh, dear Jesus, not Dampierre."

Castang is firm in the saddle even if the horse shies, tosses
its head, and would like to jam the rider's leg painfully against
the gatepost.

Now is this wise, Commissaire? Premature? Bearing in
mind the last time a scandal touched the Academy, how
the press did yelp, is that going to do your career any good?
And the personal involvement, uh, your daughter – of course
I know there's no axe to grind, but an advocate suggesting a
vengeful spirit . . . And if the evidence were inconclusive, horrible nightmares of suits for wrongful accusation, a show-cause
in disproof of legitimate suspicion.

But he had locked himself into an agreement to pursue, and been startled into the 'Good God, but Dampierre – I know him', an admission fatal to any notion entertained of tipping a fellow off, in private.

Some time after Castang had gone, Maurice Revel dropped in, or perhaps stopped by, just to see, as he put it to himself, how the man took it. Not so much perturbed as irritated, and that chiefly by not quite seeing how he could have been talked into this. No need for antibiotics, decided Monsieur Revel, applying soothing ointment.

"But you can disqualify yourself. Perfectly good grounds; personal acquaintance."

"There's bound to be a stink. The Procureur General . . ."

"Might well decide that on the general notoriety question alone it should revert to another jurisdiction. But it may not come to anything; mostly hearsay, from what you tell me."

"That'll be for you to decide – you're the senior judge of instruction; sorry but you'll have to bear the brunt of this."

"It's what instructing judges are for," placidly.

People in the 'industry' have a short attention span, but if interested by a technical problem they take trouble, and Cathy Vandamme had been at pains with the miniaturised electronics.

"It must attract no attention; mm, something she can wear even if she takes her clothes off – even in the water.

"We aren't the FBI, we don't use these things much. One can get very sensitive microphones but the trickier they are the more they distort and we can almost always find a means of – if it's outside the camera then you don't need to hide it." This simple truth had not occurred to Castang. "Easy to put one in a bracelet or a wristwatch but then you get too wide a variation." Finally a pendant on a short chain has been found and hung round her neck. The little relay was another pest. This would work comfortably over the distance from the house to the cottage – increase the power and you increase the distortion – and can simply be dumped in a shopping bag. Young girls carry all sorts of junk around and left by the side of a pool it attracts no attention. All this had been adjusted for Lydia's larynx or lung cavities or whatever they were, and the pool.

Castang is counting upon this pool, and getting anxious because one gets lovely sunset evenings in October, but the damned weather may break up at any moment. He still had to attract his tiger.

This shikari act is better when boasted about afterwards. A flash forward please, to me standing on my – tigerskin – hearthrug, in my starched evening shirt, drinking brandy. 'Here was the Russian infantry – guns, guns, guns. And here was I at the head of the old sixtyninth.' Of course, the PJ knows all about lying in wait for villains, generally in acute discomfort (known to the trade as pissing-in-the-jam-tin, and Commissaires don't do it much), but this is a bit special. Er, Colonel Sebastian Moran, late of the Indian Army. You got the servants to build a platform in a tree; bamboos. How high can a tiger jump, anyhow? Climb, with the aid of butlers, bearers, etcetera. You can't smoke or scratch and the yawning is agony. Bamboo squeaks and sways about and you hope the goddamn servants tied the string properly. Up amid all this foliage is a hostile insect population and nasty creepycrawlies like leeches. Mustn't swig at the silver hipflask or you'll shoot your own toe off. No wonder Colonel Moran started cheating at cards: small blame to him.

Brief, Castang has the galloping fidgets.

Maria fidgets too. I've a deadline to meet. Well I suppose I can leave you the key of the cottage. I do quite often lend it to people.

Because here Cathy has installed the amplifier, with instructions for tuning same. Remember? One can slip in and out from the road without being noticed.

Lydia fidgets too at the literary sessions in the Golden

Hart, and the tiger with eyes for no one but that tiresome Carmen Vannier. She overacts (spiteful rather than professional jealousy).

Lydia is also subject to the magic. 'We had all about Guillaume Apollinaire, and the poets killed in the war. I never thought that boring old *Grand Meaulnes* could be so good!' Oh yes, one had to keep reminding oneself that the man was no charlatan. She could not use her transmitter in the Golden Hart. As Cathy had warned him, you couldn't expect to get other voices to any useful degree, and it's anyhow way out of the receiver's range. A pity because in the café, reported Lydia, Dampierre used his television voice rather than the peculiar tangential mumble, pitched for an audience. 'And he wants us to talk as well as listen.'

So that Castang, in a simpler sort of 'planque', lasting half an hour and needing no jam-tin, sat in the car, parked in the little market square, Tuesday and Friday evenings between seven fifteen and fortyfive (Monsieur Dampierre does not expect his pupils to be clock-watchers) to see who gets offered a lift. Carmen Vannier! Has he a sixth sense for parents who make no fuss at their offspring being belated? If Lydia were not home by eight Vera would be wanting to know why.

The PJ cop has learned much, including never to be surprised; or be as surprised as you like, but never be Astonished.

So that when they came out and Lydia instead of walking homeward slipped in to the cream-coloured Mercedes, Castang could feel a slightly moth-eaten triumph: a vindication and a let-down. An anticlimax after the tense imaginings. Even a little frightened, for a cop is no more emotional than a nurse but it is still his daughter.

An evening in early October in the Ile de France. There was no moon tonight, nor stars. Cloudy and humid but warmer than June. Twilight was coming on, the owl time. Castang stopped on the outskirts of the town to call the gendarmerie. Okay, they said laconically, for Lieutenant Lawless knows about these Tuesday evenings. He'll pick you up out there.

The cottage was dark, shuttered. He could not be sure whether Maria were away or not. He fumbled with unfamiliar keys before realising that he was being feverish for nothing. The little house smelt lived-in, aired, and reassuringly of Maria's presence. She would be working late, at the studios.

He switched on the receiver. Cathy has filled his head with stuff about frequencies and carrier bands which he has never properly taken in: he had a moment of panic at getting nothing but the hum, before realising that Lydia has been told not to turn it on before need arises. Her voice yelled suddenly at him so that he turned the volume down in a frenzy; controlled the frenzy and helped himself to Maria's excellent port. Kopke, 1960 – what had she said? Something ending in 'hot and sticky'. There had been an answering mumble from Dampierre he hadn't caught. They had expected this and worked out simple codewords for Lydia to give them some notion of whatever was afoot. That pool, for instance – was it warmed? If the weather is chilly – if it should be raining . . . Certainly they were on the terrace there at the back. A nice brick surround, rough and soft to the feet, as Maria had reported it, a hornbeam hedge to keep the wind off . . .

The child's voice came more clearly now, recognisable, pitched higher than Lydia's real tones and with a tinny squeak to it; like the secretary on the phone from Hongkong, saying Mr Wu will make you an extra-special discount. Dampierre's answer, frustratingly blurry.

". . . . . Baron Empain." What the hell? The name seemed familiar but –

"I don't know; I don't get it that often." What? Until in the silence came the explosive pop, unmistakable, of a champagne cork. Not 'Baron Empain' but 'verre de champagne'.

It would take an older listener than Castang, and a clandestine listener to wartime broadcasts of the BBC. Though even if it were thought safe, few people in France could have understood the upside-down language of the ITMA programmes. Colonel Chinstrap was a Dampierre in reverse: one heard his fruity voice arrive from a distance – someone complaining of their cough bein' chronic . . .

'Scoff a gin 'n' tonic, sir? I don't mind if I do.'

Much of Maria's direction has gone to keeping Lydia neutral: children of fourteen, selfconscious roleplayers . . .

"I love the way the sparks climb in their little fountain." 'Tell the truth and it will sound convincing.' Good advice to any witness, agrees the police officer. Sitting on a hard chair in front of the radio receiver, Castang finds himself leaning forward, as though to get closer to it. As old people will grip the telephone and shout down it, in the wish to get closer to a grandchild.

He stares at the receiver; it is a 'professional' set, with a row of stupid meters waggling their silly needles, and idiotically he wishes to clutch it and shout "Remember, Lydia!"

"Mm . . . But I thought it wasn't supposed to be sweet." When the child, on someone's birthday, has had a glass of champagne it has been dry! Dampierre seems an oldfashioned sort of seducer, and the thought makes Castang grin, loosening his neck muscles.

". . . . . . pool." There was no mistaking the sibilants of the word *piscine*. Latin; a shell, he thought vaguely.

"Oh yes, I'd love to. But I'm afraid I haven't got a – " The answer blurred but easily guessed at: the old gag of Oh but in this pool nobody's got one, and it's not even allowed.

Now, Lydia, you can skip that equally banal line about it's getting late and my parents will be wondering –

"Well-ll," hesitancy nicely timed, "I suppose in my slip I could, if you don't mind . . ." Damn, damn; sudden irruption of annoying tango music, not very loud but definitely intrusive. Lydia coped competently.

"Could we have it off though, please? It's lovely and quiet here – I heard an owl." Merciful obliteration of bandoneon, though a disillusioned ditty of Jacques Brel's is sawing inside Castang's head. 'T'as voulu voir Vesoul et on a vu Vesoul . . .'

". . . other glass?"

"Oh yes please." He hopes Lydia's head stays clear. She has never had more than one glass – hm, officially. The boys ply them with cans of beer. Lord knows what they steal from supermarkets.

A loud splash, and loud water noises so that ludicrously he reaches to turn the sound down, for fear of somebody hearing . . .

At a guess, Lydia has jumped in feet first, with the sound idea that an ordinary dive might risk peeling her knickers off; elastic of the waistband mostly a bit shaky.

"Hush," said Castang amidst thrashing noises. The door had opened and there was a heavy-breathing gendarme just behind him. Lieutenant Lawless raised an eyebrow, stretched a hand to the tuner; the sound instantly got clearer: why couldn't Castang have thought of that? Porpoise-noises, and a "Not cold a bit."

"Exhilarating to watch you. A nereid." Clear. She had come to rest close by, but a classical exposition of nereids and their affinities was obscured by sploshes as prudent Lydia sculled backward. Sealsounds originating in her chest, wurrawurra, she had done a surface dive and was under water. 'Wouldn't it bugger the mike?' had asked prudent-Castang, but no no, had said Cathy Vandamme, it was made specially. 'We found it in stock, left over from somebody's beach scene.' It was a little bronze sea-horse and quite suitable as a pendant for a young girl. Lydia disliked it but had been told to shut up. Swoosh, it now said, and panted.

"But why don't you take that thing off? It must feel horrid." A reasonable and paternal tone. Castang might have said the same. Wet underpants are anyhow more indecent if anything than being naked and Lydia has rehearsed this with Erich. But instinct is now telling her to keep a determined grip upon the drenched rag.

Maria had thought about these details.

'Look, Lydia, in a situation which embarrasses you, some clumsy behaviour will only irritate and provoke trouble.

Recall, the moment you're at any real risk, we'll know, and act accordingly.'

"Hush," said Lawless to his big-booted Sergeant Jonas.

". . . . ." Words obliterated, but sidling, wheedling cadences allowed a fairly accurate guess. It was getting darker. Castang wondered whether there were floodlamps on that terrace.

"Not hesitating over long, are we?" he asked. A breath on Castang's neck smells of whisky. He turns and there is Maria, who has as usual kicked her shoes off.

"It works," she whispered. It is comic that they all behave as though frightened of being overheard. Castang badly wanted to get up and pace about, like a little boy who needs to do pipi.

"I don't want her pinned in a corner."

"Shut up then," said Lawless placidly. The PJ being premature again . . .

"Lydia . . ." The voice had come suddenly close. "You have a beautiful name." Maria did something sensibly feminine, putting her hands on his neck and pressing her thumbs into his spine.

"Here's a towel, for your wet hair."

"Thank you," pinched and breathless.

"The drops of water . . . on your skin . . . make a marvellous – stay still a second – composition." What had he got, a camera? But Lawless decided he had enough. The two pairs of gendarmerie boots crunched on the gravel outside, passed into silence on the overgrown path leading up to the house.

Lydia's voice unexpectedly adult said, "Don't touch me, please."

"Only giving you the – but tell you what I'll – like that you're unforgettable. Just stand and turn a little, lifting your arms to pin your hair – " Yes, a camera.

"I should be getting dressed."

"Lovely night – you won't be chilled once you're dry. You're much too tense, you need a drink." Hurry up – what was taking them so long? He could hear Lydia's teeth chattering; amplified by the microphone, a shocking noise. But Dampierre would be shrewd enough not to try to rush the girl. "Classical draperies, glass in your hand, hair in a knot – like Madame Récamier – oh, what is it?" in a voice gone thin and tetchy; interruption untimely, very.

"M'sieu, m'sieu." Castang had forgotten the old woman, an agitated mutter, as though behind a curtain, muffled by Lydia's quick-heaved breathing. "Police – police – I can't stop them."

A moment's pause over some confused background, and Lawless' voice, official tone but pitched to carry to the mike. Castang stood up, at attention, exactly as though physically present, his eyes fixed on the loudspeaker, the tape turning on the recorder.

"You are Monsieur Dampierre I believe, is that correct? I am an officer of Gendarmerie."

The reaction was instantaneous. The sidling voice was in a breath replaced by the public-speaking television voice. It was cool and academic, and pitched just right for microphones.

"What can . . . possibly . . . be the meaning of this? You are trespassing, officer. You intrude without permission upon private property. And may I beg to remind you, after the hour of sunset. A grave infraction of law, for which you will be held to answer."

Both voices came sharp and loud, magnified by the water of the pool, barely blurred by the scratchy scuffle, as though on an old gramophone-record, of Lydia dressing in a hurry, throwing her frock over her head, freezing-cold now and dragging on her woolly between little gasps, managing now unnoticed to snatch off her soaking pants and stuff them in the basket . . .

"I'm afraid that cannot be held to apply." Lawless saying don't-try-to-tell-me-the-law. "I establish a flagrant breach. I am here in pursuance of a complaint made regarding behaviour towards a child under age."

"You can have no conceivable evidence of any such thing."

"I have powers of search and arrest, Monsieur Dampierre."

Castang has stood this quite long enough – too long, for nervous reaction has got the better of Lydia, who is now crying hard, and trying gallantly to be quiet about it. He ran out of the house and up the path; the gate was open . . . Controlled his breath to walk on stage; the stage so vividly imagined and now so prosaic.

Dampierre was arguing, defiant and not a bit intimidated, a lean hairy body in shorts and a towel across the shoulders, which should have looked ridiculous and didn't.

"You will discover," shooting it at the indifferent Lawless, "that you have very gravely overstepped whatever juridical support you claim to find in this so-called mandate." Yes, there were floodlamps – an impossibly theatrical scene. Castang, paying no attention, went straight across to shivering Lydia.

"There you are, darling," with perfect banality. "I hope you haven't caught a chill."

Dampierre had broken off, to stare at him.

"Haven't I seen you before?"

"You have."

"A-ha. I detect a conspiracy."

"This is my daughter."

Naturally there was a noise: a very great deal of noise. Lawless, irritated by obstruction and abuse, in law termed 'rebellion', bade Dampierre dress, had him taken in by a secretly gleeful Sergeant Jonas, and held overnight, before being charged in the morning with 'détournement de mineur' and 'outrage to authority'. It was thought best to say nothing about the tape for the moment, which even if admissible would be the subject of endless legal arguments. The confiscated camera ought to do it, with Lydia's statement as dictated to the painstaking Sergeant Jonas. Castang signed his own deposition in his capacity as private citizen.

It falls, perhaps inexorably, into a bureaucratic style, for he remains the Officer of Judicial Police: upon dates previous to this matters have been brought to his notice. While insufficiently supported by evidence to warrant direct action, these have been circumstantial enough to attract a professionally trained eye. He had thus felt anxieties, which when brought to the notice of the Procureur . . .

The report from the Gendarmerie will be of this same wooden nature: confirming the delivery of a mandate, to be used with circumspection, if an occasion arose which, in the judgment of a prudent officer, should be deemed . . .

Mention is thus made of the supportive evidence, as brought to the attention of: bottle of champagne consumed, towelling bathrobe property of the inculpated, twilit scene of action, wet undergarment property of a female minor, a camera containing photographs of a suggestive nature; said female minor in state of near-nudity. In light of complaint made by guardian of said minor, it is felt that a prima facie case may be made out for a delict of seduction if not indecent assault upon person.

All this would of course be hammered out in the morning. Dampierre, held overnight for giving the Gendarmerie a lot of lip, was inculpated and set at liberty.

Lydia had been cross and sleepy. Hostile remarks, and 'pushing people away'; a form of mild shock, and nobody paid much attention. She is a child, though she sometimes forgets this.

"Want a cup of cocoa?" asked Maria.

"No!"

"Very well then, don't."

"Want to talk?" asked Lawless, indifferent whether she did or not.

"No!"

"All right. Better, in the morning. You can come and see me, with your father."

"No I won't." Lawless jerked his head at Castang, towards a come-and-talk-outside. Sergeant Jonas had gone off with Dampierre in the official car. The two sat and had a smoke.

"You won't push her," said Lawless. "But you know all that."

"I'd like to forget I'm a police officer. Creates confusion."

"Sure. One of us is enough. No need to tell you either? – this isn't very conclusive. I didn't want to wait longer, with you there chewing your fingers; hurried me, rather. We've no real flagrant delict, right? I hoped the surprise might push the bugger off balance but he's a cool one. Denies everything, what can we pin on him? No physical interference, she wasn't strictly molested, mm? I can make a charge of attempted corruption but no violence offered, so he'll claim willing cooperation. I've no means of pressing him. The judge might even throw it out. You're excluded as a witness, being her father, and the Russian lady won't appear – just as well in view of this tape, which we keep quiet about; a defence lawyer would make a lot of hay with that."

"The judge won't throw it out," said Castang. "But he'll have to build his case on the instruction. He may turn up another instance, once we've this much to go upon. Bound to be publicity."

"We'll look at it in the morning, and the tale your girl tells then."

"It's just the start," said Castang, wiser than he knew.

Lydia in the morning was rational but didn't want him with her, which he found understandable and Vera went instead. She found it a peculiar sensation, facing the same man in the office where she had had to describe an attempted rape on herself – but Lydia had suffered no violence, even in words. It had all been quite innocuous just as Maria had promised. But what does a girl of fourteen feel, within herself, to be innocuous? It does not have to correspond with what she says.

For Miss was being adult this morning, remembering her training. Lawless brought her to his own office.

"This is straightforward. I know from the listening post that you came to no harm, that we needed no doctor to look you over – you understand why we'd have wanted that, in any doubt?"

"Yes."

"The little radio was to ensure your safety, not to spy. But we're making no mention of it, since it wasn't strictly legal. Anyhow, what I heard is not what I saw; the law puts a lot of emphasis upon eye witness. You tell me what happened now, in your own words. The judge will want to hear it from your mouth, but for now you're the complainant, and without your statement I can't make my report."

"You let him go?"

"Yes. We don't hold people unless there's violence, and I don't think there was?"

"No."

"Just the one point really. In the course of these moves around the pool, he didn't try to lay hands on you?"

"He'd have liked to."

"Yes, but there's a legal distinction between that and touching your skin."

"Then no."

"See if you agree with this formula," typing professionally, not like her father with two fingers. " 'He expressed admiration for my physique and a wish to handle my body.' Don't say so unless you're sure of it. You don't have to recall exact words, but I want you quite clear on intention. Now do you remember actual terms used? Any direct reference in a sexual sense?"

"Yes."

"Which you recognised? The judge will want to know your reaction."

"Well, I've been trained to handle that."

"I must not put words in your mouth. Trained by your parents to recognise and avoid approaches?"

"Of course. Especially the slimy sort. Sweeties. Toffee or a glass of champagne."

"It was his suggestion that you swim in the pool? And take off your clothes? You agreed willingly? I want you to be careful about answering honestly."

"Look, it was a lovely evening. I was sticky and I wanted to swim. But I fucking well wasn't going to take my pants off."

"He asked you to? Sure of that?"

"Stuff about a fountain statue. Sort of aesthetic – it shouldn't be bronze but lead." Good convincing detail, thought Vera.

"All right. Read carefully the paragraph at the bottom, where it says you accept this as a true and faithful account. You sign. Now your mother signs this brief endorsement, that I have put questions to you fairly, haven't sought to influence you, add to or subtract from your account, spoken to you throughout in her presence . . . Fine, thank you, Mademoiselle, we're through." With no sign that he's ever seen me before, thought Vera gratefully.

The police may recommend, but it is the judge who decides; who holds a preliminary hearing, where whoever may have been charged with an offence is still a 'witness', until the judge chooses the grounds for eventual legal pursuit and pronounces inculpation; a formal process which gives the accused the right to legal representation and access to all the known facts. The Public, which knows nothing about law, concludes that 'inculpated' means guilty, giving rise to the myth that in France you must prove yourself innocent. Clever people, like Monsieur Dampierre, much prefer the formal charge, which the magistrate may at any moment annul or abandon, to the ambiguous situation of witness. It gives also an opening to snivel in public about persecutions by the magistrature, with impunity accused of bias and corruption.

Dampierre lost no time. His lawyer, an expert upon contracts, skilled negotiator with publishers, on occasion a dab hand at libel, knows nothing of criminal procedure and cares less; what's the point?

"My dear Jacques, I have been taken up upon a ridiculous presumption that I corrupt the morals of my pupils. Should we perhaps consult some eminent criminal pleader?"

"Waste of time and money. Inculpation is meaningless jargon but we can turn it to advantage. I'll be down to see you the moment I've popped in to sort this judge out." The luminary bade his secretary rearrange appointments, for the bone promises to be meaty. Maître Ayala of the Paris Bar also polishes his image.

He is anglophil; he likes to talk English. He doesn't go so far as to wear a wig, but isn't averse to claret, cigars, and twelve-cylinder Jaguar cars – he has thought of a Rolls but it really needs a driver, which would dilute his dynamism. It's only eleven o'clock, a nice time to be suffocated with indignation for the benefit of Monsieur Revel, this little judge.

What! Here is a man of the greatest eminence, since what higher honour – ?

Yes yes, Maître, but why don't you save all this for the press?

Possibly, Monsieur le Juge, but have you given adequate weight to the fact that in thus besmirching – denigrating – ?

"Maître, do by all means get it off your chest. Reflect, then, upon these points. I have time for any matter of fact you may wish to submit, but not for rhetoric. The charge is substantiated or it is not, and I alone decide that. If so – then the tribunal will give scope for your talents. But there isn't one person in a thousand within France who could name five members of the Academy, let alone forty, as you know perfectly: to the public it is a row of snuffy old gentlemen who fall asleep at banquets.

"What you're really talking about is television: let's get our frame of reference clear. Your client, exalted and virtuous gentleman, is recognisable because he is a well-known entertainer. You are going to try to intimidate me with a fluster of publicity. I'm aware of it, expect it. Your argument amounts to a claim that it becomes impossible to try a public figure for anything, because of the emotions aroused. I'm only the instructing magistrate; if we can get that much settled I'll expect you with your client tomorrow morning at nine o'clock. He doesn't have to be dragged in, handcuffed between two gendarmes, merely to give pleasure to the photographers. We're agreed?"

Midday, and if thus a little early for claret and cigars by no means for Monsieur Dampierre's champagne.

"We've the press lined up for three this afternoon, giving them plenty of time for lunch. Provisionally, I think this hotel in the village; where you give your evening classes."

"I don't want them here," Dampierre looking round the rows of leather-bound classics.

"Quite so, and one of our lines is the intolerable intrusion upon privacy. Gendarmerie, indeed; we'll make them eat that. What little sharper of a Procureur thought to promote himself some limelight with this show of zeal?"

"That's a slightly worrying aspect. I know him enough – a good family – to suspect that he was somehow manoeuvred into this. But I can't make contact. I'm told he's seedy, gone to some spa in the Pyrenees for the cure."

"Camouflage. Don't pursue that, you leave it all to me. Mustn't be seen tampering with mechanics of legal process. I've had a word with this judge, he's making the usual noises about probity and impartiality but we'll soon show him which way his bread is buttered. Now the press – d'you want me to handle them? Tactically quite a nice point. You might gain from the dignified withdrawal, the duty towards reserve. Or do we make the point of total transparency from the start? You are then better equipped to – "

"Yes. I don't think we should be defensive. Take a firm stance at the outset, nip it in the bud. Private life – no nibbling at that. But public life open to all comers – this is owed to the reader, the listener, the – "

"Exactly. You welcome enquiry. Don't lay it on too thick but malicious tongues etcetera, these are the hostages to fame, say nothing about fortune, dignified confidence. I'll whip down to the village and lay that on."

The Golden Hart was pleased to cooperate. We'll use the room he always has, and about how many chairs? – but Maître Ayala was already on the phone to the television station.

"Mesdames, Messieurs. A pleasure to see you. I have been called upon to make explanations, and what more natural than that I should make them to you here, where I am accustomed to simple and informal efforts without publicity, to the furtherance of a subject close to my heart. The defence of our language, the purity and riches of our tradition, the enlivenment and enjoyment of an incomparable literary history" – the French will be rhetorical even at a press conference.

Very nice, thought Maître Ayala; the chair he always uses and the microphone the right height. Nice low-key sound; they sit at his feet like the children and with that we have it made.

National press. The audience for Academy writers outside France is small, and the international press won't bother unless the scandal grows beyond the tattle stage. These journalists are used to keeping a respectful silence; none of the heckling you'd expect of an English crowd. The professor 'confers' magisterially and they sit like mice. Rhetoric is second nature to them all.

Dampierre did it well: a soft, slightly hesitant manner, a small deprecating smile, a faint hint of self-mockery. Adroit

balance of an idealist's vision with acceptance of sordid realities. No wonder, thought Ayala, that his client – valued client
– has become a sought-after television performer: that's good!
Just the right amount of peering over the reading glasses and
making a lip at an unworthy concept. Mannerisms become dear
to the viewer; fast little jokes clearcut – no wonder the girls love
him. Doubtless the story is true – but the public will not feel
censorious towards frailties.

"Some legalistic minds appear to believe that enthusiasm
has led me into familiarity, that my affections become personal,
that reason may be betrayed by emotion. I could dismiss such
notions as ridiculous, and instead I will come to the defence of
sentiment; am I not defending sincerity against cynicism, ideals
against materialism, Chateaubriand against Talleyrand?"

Speak up then, thought Castang, hidden at the back; don't
just sit there writing it all down on your slates. He greatly
prefers Talleyrand!

"Monsieur Dampierre, with your permission. We've a convention in the written press, of using the word *explain* as a
warning to the alert reader to expect the opposite, and the
word *confide* to suggest that the confidences might be a scrap
disingenuous: d'you have any comment upon these usages?"

"Ah, I think I recognise the speaker. Our friends, to
adopt another polite usage, of the leftwing press. I also
recognise the technique, which is that of insinuation, knowing
well that a suggestion unsupported by fact would result in an
action for defamation and an award of heavy damages. We are
accustomed to these obliquities; next question."

"Since you raise the point by yourself using the phrase –
is the suggestion supported by fact?"

"Facts, to the best of my knowledge and belief, under the
democratic system we enjoy and support, are subject to the
interpretation of courts of law . . . Yes?"

"Oh I'm sorry, I thought you weren't finished." Not going
to get it all his own way, thought Castang.

"If I have correctly understood you," snappish, "since we

are concerned here with alleged facts, shortly to be examined
for what they are worth, as I sincerely hope by more judicial
heads than is perhaps your own, we will have some light shed
upon what is fact and what is merely prurient rumour."

Not very well fielded, thought Maître. Allowed himself to be
drawn. Still, this is only the chat-show.

Castang has met Monsieur Maurice Revel upon social occasions, and informally in his office. There, a softspoken man,
in middle age and beginning to be rotund. A diffident and
unassuming manner. Able to see a joke – make one now and
then. But 'in his robe' a very different person.

An examining magistrate does not wear a robe, and nowadays
is quite likely to be in jeans and a check shirt. Not Monsieur
Revel, who is more, today, than in the office. He is aware of
the power of his office, a different question; a believer more-
over in dignity and, yes – majesty. At work he wears a dark
business suit, a white shirt of that heavyish poplin that looks to
be slightly starched, a subfusc tie. And has never seen Castang
before. Monsieur le Commissaire recognises the flowers and
the coffee machine, but nothing else. In fact Castang sees
nothing funny about his own present situation: he is under
interrogation.

And to paraphrase a remark of Monsieur Revel's, it is
certainly immoral, if not actively illegal, to record an exchange
(by interposition of shorthand writer if not magnetic tape) with
half of it missing. Castang's answers will read word for word,
but the questions won't. The clerk will have replaced them by
the notorious abbreviation 's.i.' This stands for 'sur intervention' or 'in reply to'. By thus effacing his side of the record
the judge has his ass covered. Castang's phrase? – judges use
it too. Henri has heard Maurice call the practice tendentious,
pusillanimous; and now he is hiding behind it. Decidedly, this
is not the Revel Castang knows.

"Now, as I understand it, there's a recording of these happenings: where is it?"

"Held in the custody of the lieutenant of gendarmerie."

"They haven't said a word about it. Am I to conclude it's been suppressed?"

"Held at the disposal of authority, M'sieu le Juge."

"It's not clear that such would be admissible as evidence. It was not made upon the authority of a magistrate; the law is explicit. Now be careful with your answer; for what purpose was this recording made?"

"Prudence. Protection of a minor, to enable – correct that – to facilitate intervention should that minor be deemed at risk."

"That's your claim. It can be argued that a mechanism was constructed and concealed to entice and entrap."

"I'd repudiate the suggestion."

"You would, would you? Come, Monsieur Castang, this is your daughter. Guessing that suggestions or advances might be made to her, are you seriously denying a malicious purpose?"

"I would deny malice."

"But you'd admit to vindictive feelings?"

"I would not."

"Will you then define the feelings with which you prepared this snare?"

"The word 'feelings' is tendentious and 'snare' inadmissible. My opinions were and are those of a responsible man and father of small children."

"You would agree that a contrary opinion is tenable?"

"Not my job to evaluate opinion, Monsieur le Juge."

"Put to you, that your action was a provocation, prompted by vengeful emotion?"

"You're calling for a conclusion of the witness, in an area outside my competence."

"This competence is that of an experienced police officer?"

"That is certainly my function."

"You have thus notions of the rules governing evidence?"

"Generalised guidelines."

"Reply to me: what guideline do you adopt, to the suggestion that a recording be made of this meeting?"

"I know the approximate legal position."

"To wit?"

"That a court would be unlikely to accept a recorded exchange without strong supportive evidence."

"What conclusion do you draw?"

"I would submit that the evidence exists, needs no support from any recording, and thus that a recording was prepared with no design of entrapment but for the protective purpose mentioned."

"Very well, Monsieur Castang. You are not thus urging that this recording should be taken into account? I wish to understand you clearly."

"That will be for Monsieur le Juge to evaluate. I urge nothing."

"I have one further question for you. You have stated that your emotions were those of a responsible citizen, head of a family?"

"That is so."

"Likewise, these guide the actions of an experienced police officer. My question is this: which of these functions was predominant in your mind?"

"Choosing my words, those to be expected from the father of young girls."

"I'll examine you a little further, with your permission. You'd describe yourself as a modern parent? Tolerant? Adaptable?"

"The question is polarised. I'd regard a fourteen-year-old girl as vulnerable and inexperienced."

"You allow your daughter to mix freely with people of less restrictive views?"

"I won't agree that these are restrictive views."

"Expand upon that a little."

"I would hold the view that a child of this age must learn experience, in a society where views vary."

"Thus, if she finds herself in liberal company, you'd see nothing untoward?"

"Nothing at all, with an important exception."

"Which is?"

"That anyone holding a position as teacher, educator, accepts responsibilities. It's in loco parentis. I'd expect that principle to be upheld by any court."

"That is all, Monsieur Castang, for the present."

Castang was chagrined, not to have seen it coming. It was so obvious! And like many things of the sort, it had never even crossed his mind. Now his daughter was having to pay for his shortsightedness, and he should have been the last person to underestimate neighbourhood gossip.

Lydia had taken a day off 'with a chill' and gone back to school the next day quite ready to behave as though nothing had happened. But meantime Maître Ayala and the Press had been busy. Certainly, she was not named in any of the reports, but schoolchildren are quick to put two and two together. She had been seen getting into the cream-coloured Mercedes, and that was enough.

Among grown-up people the balance of opinion would be firm on the side of approval for Castang's viewpoint. Even today it is likely that this would be the same in any country. For one who jeered at a fuss made over nothing, who shrugged that a girl of fourteen is nubile and may as well get used to the idea, there would be two who would disagree sharply. One has to draw the line, they would be saying, the older men in pubs and the housewives at the greengrocer: let that go and you'll have types who wouldn't stop at a girl of twelve or eleven. It needs no sophisticated instruction to see that physiological precocity bears no relation to psychological readiness. In every café and supermarket there'll be somebody loud in their knowledge of the exceptions, and as surely someone to retort that exceptions prove the rule.

Children all think they know better, of course. Lydia came home feeling battered. She'd had a sour day.

"I'm not going back to that stinking school." It wasn't the moment to play the heavy father.

A child is vulnerable to the brutalities of her age-group, but Lydia whose tongue is quick can defend herself. Patronising sniggers from an older group are more painful: a truism but some of the sneers were nasty. 'Caroline Cunnilingue' could be expected to be voluble. But there had also been dirty remarks made by teachers . . . The dignity of a fourteenyearold is fragile. Castang, himself surrounded by the carapace of indifference which grows around any working cop (what nurse notices the pisspots?), is vulnerable to meanness of mind shown towards his daughter.

"After a horse throws you," he said to Vera, "you get straight back up. I don't think the parallel applies. Think about it, shall we? There are other schools. It'll blow over no doubt but I see no point in forcing her. I'll have a word with the school. They're defensive of course about their precious Academician."

The mail brought a letter, begging him to be so extremely obliging as to spare a moment to see the Headmaster. Hm, their writing-paper is too cheap for their French. Business firms in this country will still thank you for your esteemed favours, and everyone from the President down implores you to accept the expression of his distinguished sentiments. Like that missive of astonishment that your phone bill is overdue, this got a lot of servility and menace into three lines.

"So good of you to come." A baldish man, with a little grey beard and an aggressively stripy bow-tie.

"Monsieur Castang . . . to come straight to the point," like everyone who says this, not doing so. "Can't be called a discreet occurrence, can it? Newspapers, television. I've had to issue an instruction, anyone connected with the establishment saying anything to a reporter will risk disciplinary action.

"Er, stricto senso Lydia cannot be said to have broken rules. My own unwavering conviction is that it is inconceivable that Monsieur Dampierre – I have been besieged, literally swamped by parents demanding clarification – to wit that there is no foundation whatsoever in these uh – " Delicate, while addressing the Author of These Allegations.

"Not literally swamped," said Castang pleasantly. "At least, I see no tidemark on the wall."

"It hardly seems the moment to make jokes."

"Come to the point then, shall we?"

"Monsieur le Surveillant informs me that Lydia is absent from class – a diplomatic chill, no doubt?"

"I've no intention of allowing her to be exposed to insinuation and abuse."

"I do understand that you should be led to use er, immoderate language. In the interests of all it would be as well perhaps if the absence were prolonged until uh, justice pronounces. Please do understand, no suspension; no punitory measure; but there exists an obligation to be discreet . . ."

"I quite agree," said Castang, getting up. "This obligation exists for examining magistrates. Also for officers of police. It is a pity that it does not also apply to parents and especially teachers."

"Believe me I deplore – alas, not all heads are as cool as ours, Monsieur er, le Commissaire, good morning."

"Good appetite," said Castang since it was getting on for lunch time.

He stopped in the village on the way home. If Lydia has measles what are suitable distractions?

One or two people were giving him odd looks. That's the way of it, even when you haven't been further into television than No Comment. Nice that the wine man was into Commerce and telling him he'd have twelve for the price of eleven.

There'd been more letters. He'd put them in his pocket unread: one gets a feel for them from the envelopes.

The first was on standard writing-paper and neatly typed by someone used to office paperwork.

Monsieur,
   You are hereby informed that a group of parents, representative of the generalised sentiment within the Lycée, have adopted the resolution to address a jointly signed letter to the Minister, urging that you be removed forthwith from any office that you hold, and prevented from causing further malicious damage to the moral climate of the establishment attended by our children.
   (Signed) The Secretary to the Protest Committee

Very French in form. One supposes that the sentiment would be similar just about anywhere.

The second was the you-won't-catch-me format of the illiterate; words cut out of newspaper and glued to a sheet. The exception was the word 'fuck' which occurs in print quite often these days, but which the author had not found immediately available and had had to supply with heavy pressure from a ballpoint.

If your daughter wants to get Fukked then you can have faith we will see to it.

Castang went to see-to the lock on the front gate, and meditated upon the letterbox. It might be as well to have a word with the post-office, in case of parcels with shit or amateur explosive devices. And there were also two letters for Lydia, which he opened, read, and put back in his pocket. Censored. You should, you know, Castang, have thought about all this earlier.

"Lydia, would you like a glass of champagne?"

"Oh yes, please."

"You won't be going back to that school, incidentally."

"No loss. This a celebration?"

"Yes, it's known as putting out more flags."

The 'pub' is a bistrot, that anachronism mourned by everyone nostalgic for the old-Paris. There are hardly any left because they were the haunt of the poor, and the poor of Paris are mostly now too poor to sit in the pub and play cards. Gone, mostly to the cemetery, are les petits vieux, the old men with pensions from the railways or the post-office who used to potter about in berets and espadrilles, items of antique clothing now worn only by tourists. But Chez Léon is still there because Léon himself is seventyeight and an obstinate old bastard.

It is near the Canal Saint Martin, round the corner from the Hôtel du Nord which nobody has quite dared knock down because the French are sentimental about it. This too is the last pallid remnant of the Simenon country, where Maigret wopped back all that white wine. Léon shuffles about with his braces holding up the shapeless trousers, smelly as an old dog, seeing and hearing nothing; perhaps Arletty's celebrated slummy screech of 'Has my face got Atmosphere?' It is quiet here. A few Arabs from the building sites come in for lemonade to rinse out the cement dust.

"D'you think the old bugger has anything drinkable? Hey Léon, deux canons. Deaf as a post . . . God, what rotgut." The stuff the clochards drink, and just what they both need.

The Sous-chef is not much older than Castang, but two steps higher and a world grander. It would be selfpity to talk about luck: one is what one is, and Castang is not jealous of his friend with the big office who can pick up his phone and get a chef de cabinet in any ministry; the Elysée if he wants it. Fast Eddie.

"Well Henri, you're in a scrape. I put you in a place where nothing is easier than to keep quiet – I tell you to keep quiet – and who d'you choose to cook your dinner but the Académie, and a television star into the bargain. How do you do it? As a sounding board it couldn't be bettered. You've three ministers I know of asking who the hell is Castang. You're after my job, maybe? Jesus, Saint Cloud or Versailles are brimming over with dirty old men, and you have to pick this one! I won't complain when the louse doesn't get his contract renewed, but why d'you have to have him feel up your daughter, aren't there enough about?"

Madame Saulnier has told it him all already; he just shrugs. Good ol' Jacques, sleeps with half the wives in Neuilly, much too cute to have one of his own. What is one to tell him? About Vera? About Carlotta?

"Any time you want my resignation, you can have it."

"Oh don't be so bloody wet! Why do I bring you here, to talk? They – I won't say the Elysée but not a hundred kilometres off – are not in fact all that displeased.

"Politically, it's not thought inept. It's going to drive another wedge between the Christian Democrats and the National Front, a splinter under the fingernail. Léon here will be infinitely the wiser when I tell you the Minister is going to give you your moment of immortality, next Question Time in the Assembly."

Politics, thought Castang dully. I'm as wise as old Léon, talking to himself behind the zinc.

"So the Patron is not even having his expected nervous fit. His wife gave him this new kind of electric razor because of his shadow problem, and he was trying it out when I came in with some paper. Singing so please you, prancing about like a fucking ballerina, am I going to be the white swan or the black one today?" This domestic view of the Director being Odette–Odile in a wired tulle skirt is not without charm.

"But if this business of the tape comes out, you could be in trouble." Yes, and how did it come out? The lieutenant of gendarmerie no doubt, covering his ass. Everybody's fireproof but me. "So what you do," said Jacques, swigging the cheap blue wine with every appearance of enjoyment, "you find a few more girls who've been fondled by the Academy, and get them to put the boot in."

These are the people who hold the 'less restrictive views'. A modern couple, under forty. Respectably married, since in the livingroom, visible if not prominent, is a framed wedding photo with the bride in a long white frock and the groom in morning dress. Maybe they kept it thinking it a big laugh, but at least they are married, and perhaps it means something more to them than convenience.

Both are university-trained and have jobs called creative. They fit well together. Quite likely they married to satisfy bourgeois conventions in the families: Castang hasn't done any police work, and has now only to use his eyes.

It's a good apartment, airy, large, high; plenty of balcony. Living this far out they, and probably the firm they work for, avoid the high rents, cramped quarters and endless traffic snarls of the city. They would both run quite expensive cars, hers smaller only because easier to park. They've separate bank accounts and a loose agreement over the allotting of expenses. They've a good understanding with one another, a lot of affection and even respect. If there were a serious divergence they'd divorce, amicably and without breaking the china. Ringing up, Castang had had no more reluctance to overcome than a fear of being bored. By all means come round for a drink; we're both at home. Marc and Sophie – they sound like the title of a television sit-com but they're Carmen Vannier's parents.

The flat was as predicted, comfortably furnished in modern taste; plenty of gadgets. In advertising – that's an expanding industry and they'd have plenty of money. Both were smartly dressed, there was a wood fire for the chilly evening and a polite welcome. Marc was expansive, offering whisky; Sophie smiles in a way called sexy and secretive even when it's neither. He shows some brawny forearm, she a lot of pretty depilated leg, and both could be advertising deodorants with a little more light for the camera. Not fair, surely – snide remark? But be honest; they're both rather dull. They convey that bland instant-food feel as though all their thoughts and ideas came out of weekly magazines.

"You can interview us," with gusts of laughter, "but not Carmen."

"Very well, I'll come straight to the point. Would you sign a complaint, on behalf of Carmen?"

"No." They have plainly discussed it, since his phonecall alerted them to his business, and as plainly they agree. "Not getting into squalid controversy with press or lawyers. She'd be interrogated by the magistrate who'd be offering us a lot of nosy impertinence. No way."

"I might put it perhaps, you weren't all that happy with Carmen being fumbled by the literary guru."

"No indeed, the old pig," said Marc. "Private opinion, I'd have gone round to sort him out if he'd done her any harm. Kick them in, assuming he's got any. But in public, not getting dragged into this business, does more harm than good."

"She's very pretty," said Sophie who is pretty herself, "and hell, she's only fourteen. Look, Mr Castang, personally I sympathise with your viewpoint. But one must be careful not to get pushed into the wrong position."

He understands. Don't lose face, the message says; never look like a loser. Gravy is only for winners, and we're winners and staying that way.

"Carmen protected herself," with some pity for whoever doesn't. "He's quite a soft old thing really. No photos, she said, and kindly drive me home. 'Course if I'd known I'd never – don't get the idea I'm indifferent to her welfare. She may as well learn what's what, though. 'Nother time, don't play with fire, 'less you like the flavour." Cock-teaser, thought Castang.

"Okay. Just establishing where we stand."

"Have another," said Marc hospitably.

"Right to peg him," thought Sophie. "He'd have finished by going too far."

And what was the name of the other, right at the start? Sabine –

and that was serious. Not just taking pictures. Did those people realise what had happened? Had the child managed to keep up the secrecy? He had been to see the mother, after hearing the news from Denis Manuel. She'd been very hostile indeed. It hadn't happened at all and was in any case no business of his. But he'd handled it badly, going at the wrong time. People in the restaurant business are tense and nervous in the evenings. Perhaps now he'd hear different music. And they had had time to think things over.

Castang chose his moment, next morning, just before midday, when a restaurant is calm: the 'mise-en-place' is complete. The cooks are having a smoke outside by the dustbins, and the waiters a bite to eat. And instead of going in through the salle, Madame's domain, he went to the service entrance. Nice place – riverside restaurants are always attractive. Now that the weather had gone cold the waterfront terrace was closed; the chairs piled and dead leaves drifting down. A casual cook waved him through the kitchen to the office where the owner sat, surrounded by telephones and paperwork but relaxed with a pre-prandial beer, in chef's whites, his hat off, thin fair hair over a bald spot and a long anxious nose. He looked up when Castang came in. They'd never seen each other before, but recognition came into his eyes.

"Sit down," pouring himself more beer, to give himself a countenance. "I can guess your errand . . . This is going to be hard to explain . . . I've been pretty worried. Not knowing exactly what happened. Not happy about it. The girl's been acting dodgy ever since. Withdrawn, uh, sullen, won't talk . . . Damn it, I've enough on my mind. This business is sixteen hours a day, eats one up totally. I just haven't the time. The phone never stops; if it isn't the staff it's the customers, if it isn't a supplier it's some goddamn health inspector."

Castang knew he wasn't going to get anywhere. The man would go on bombarding him with anger and guilt, genuine feelings and childish excuses. Aware and ashamed of his own cowardice. The man looked nervously at his watch.

"We've at best seven minutes. Look, let me try and explain. Will you try to understand? . . . This is a very demanding business. It's tough permanently to get and keep good people, to jockey the competition, to bullshit the guide books and the tourist board and the Préfecture and all the rest; okay, that's my job, I chose it, I'm good at it, allright, no complaint. But my wife – she's totally involved, wrapped up, obsessed, I don't know what word to use . . . Anything, get me right, *anything* that goes wrong, that's a challenge – an insult you'd almost think, an outrage. Takes it all so personally. I had to put in new equipment here last year, I'm over three hundred thousand into the bank, no way will she admit anything which could – her nightmare is something which could . . . Jesus, the girl is her mother's affair, I can't go running after to ask have you done your homework and have you remembered to take your pill? Up to eleven I'm up to both eyes, I'm bloody lucky if I can get to bed before two, with the marketing for the next day.

"Look, be a good chap, forget it. This academy fellow, this Dampierre, he's a big shot. Customer, brings in other customers. You'd maybe not realise how insidious word of mouth can be, get on the wrong side a fellow like that, cause a pack of damage. But above all my wife . . . look, fuck off will you, she'll be in here any moment and if there's one thing I want to avoid it's a row." Sure. Castang understands. Got a wife of his own.

Vera is not alone in the house, but she is screwed into a tight airless solitude of selfhatred. The racket in the children's room is doubly distanced by the thick-walled old house and by her silent shouting. She is sitting in a big chair, feet under her and knees in her face. She has cramps in her belly; her bowels are turned to water: Castang would say simply squitters. She is smoking furiously, a thing she seldom does; and drinking fiercely too, Czechly, even Polishly punishing a cognac bottle: Henri makes jokes about 'that elegant turn of the wrist'.

All this is her doing – she is being guilty, forever being guilty, tied up in the tangles of family and in a moment she'll start crying because of the cognac and then the string will be wet and the knots will be more difficult than ever and then what will happen if she has to sit in a hurry on the lavy?

Families are terribly important to me. Look at my own father, a life-long Party Member and so proud of it, and what I did to him. Daughters are important – look at me, he never forgave me and I don't wonder.

I am the lousiest imaginable wife. First I was a Communist refugee, blackest mark there could possibly be for a police career and never once has Henri complained. Then I fell off the ladder while pretending to be good at gym and all these years I've wondered whether I fell off on purpose wanting to be punished. I did hurt my spine. But I sat there enjoying it. I transferred all that guilt about my former family and used it to cling to my man and my own children and I'm so tight and puritanical about them it simply is not to believe.

And on top of all this I'm a weirdy. Who the hell needs artists (least of all Czech artists, they're four a penny)?

Least of all does a working cop need cattle like that tied to his feet. He is trying all the time to understand and to accommodate: he goes along with notions he doesn't want and doesn't need out of simple loyalty, and then he gets into trouble with a thing like this, and it's my fault. Me with my peasant upbringing. I've crippled him and I've ruined his career.

Interlude, while she had to go and sit on the . . . Coming back she felt better. Had another drink. This was doing her good. Henri was teaching Lydia how to drink champagne and she stood by with her long disapproving face, and she has drunk half a bottle of cognac and he won't know whether to laugh or be furious.

She summons artists to her aid. Not dotties; she doesn't

want any Gauguins or van Goghs today, thanks, much though she loves them. She wants the ones who paid no attention to Kings, to Ministers, to Financiers, to friends or to enemies, but who went imperturbably on with their work. Summon Vermeer and Velasquez. Summon the Deaf Man, my beloved Goya. Summon the other Deaf Man, the Chinese one, Chu Ta, who has been such a tower of strength to me over these last six months. Was he really deaf? Or did he just stop talking, because that was such a waste of time, and listening gets in the way of looking?

The painter of one thing at a time. Stone. Bird. Bamboo. Fish. Duck.

One thing at a time. Hold on to that because that, at least, you have understood. Reeds. Wild cherry trees.

Helped by that I was not raped. I killed a man but for that I feel no guilt. Henri learns too how to be deaf, to disregard the noise and clatter of the world. Dickens wrote a fine ending, to Dorrit, about that. Henri's admired Stendhal is about that. It is the lesson learned by Fabrice, and by Madame de Sanseverina. To stand, against the baseness.

Vera's head is a lot better, thank you. So are her bowels.

"Come round for a drink," said Denis Manuel's voice in Castang's ear.

He was sitting on the edge of his desk, dangling a foot, politely waiting before pouring out the stiff-one allowed after a rough consulting-hour.

"Mm . . . I've known two or three doctors who popped off with cirrhosis in the midst of a flourishing career."

"I've known more cops than that do the same," the policeman gloomily. "This is the country where the police is permanently pissed carrying big pistols. Hence the prevalence of cops saying Sorry, I didn't mean to kill him but you see, I thought he made a threatening move."

"Also the country where you can consult three doctors for the same attack of indigestion, be repaid by the Social Security, and then spend the proceeds on a witchdoctor because you didn't believe in the first three."

"Funny country!" said Castang who was depressed.

"Never mind. We're sharp on the individual liberties. I had dinner with Maurice Revel, so I'm a pipeline. He doesn't want to see you socially awhile, because that would be improper. The word is to keep that tape from getting known: no way can that be countenanced."

"Article three-sixty-eight, first paragraph," impatiently. "Upon private property and without consent of the subject. When not duly authorised by a magistrate. Fuck Maurice Revel, it was he talked me into this."

"Yes, well, he thinks he has a case. Thin ice, and scruples to struggle with, but he'll get there, Dampierre and all his friends notwithstanding. 'The bringing of charges'," in a quote voice, " 'which are then refuted by chicanery and influence, even if only thought by the public to be so' – all the magistrates are furious at known crimes being amnestied for so-called reasons of state."

"Yes yes," said Castang crossly. "I don't give a damn about economic crimes; the state's always the worst offender. But it's not the moment for Maurice to start getting scruples. The figures for crimes against children – "

"Gently – I'm as worried as you are."

"You aren't quite as likely to lose your job."

Carlotta appeared in the doorway looking serious; looking indeed worried. He stared at her dully; more meaningless paper? It could not be said that he'd really had his mind on his work, these last days.

"Come in my office a sec." He got up mechanically and got a sudden broad flashing smile. "Are you thinking that every cop in Paris is shaking his head over you and thinking Poor Imbecile? Well, I'm not. Here," bending over her desk which was littered with photographs, "Brun's made a positive identification on these." He remembered, then.

"Oh. Yes, that's serious. We'll have to go in there."

It dated back some weeks. Castang had been dashing to the lavatory. His phone was ringing, there was much on his mind, Frau Morandière catching him in the passage has just thrust papers into his hand with injunctions to verify something, when a man wondering which way to go wavered and Castang bumped into him.

He knows this man. It is a buried memory but it had had importance at the time. The man senses his recognition and the search for identity.

"Commissaire Castang, isn't it? I'm not likely to forget you. You spent a morning interrogating me."

Stamps! The man from the Place d'Armes – and instantly that northern town flashes back; the gothic and baroque buildings, the special smell . . .

There is a mnemonic which goes with this man's name – a colour. Noir, Blanc . . .

"Brun," smiling a little, helping him.

Of course! Irritation at forgetting, and guilt too: those stamps had been an infernal bore. They had cropped up afresh after months and he had tried to shuffle them off on to Carlotta, pleading a rush of work. As obstinately she had pushed them back; stamps were of no interest to anyone. But somebody (doubtless Frau Morandière) had written to Monsieur Brun saying they had a possible trace and could he perhaps identify . . . and here he was. He showed no sign of surprise at finding Castang here in Paris. Every victim of crime is convinced that his affairs must be as prominent in the police mind as in his own.

"I'm sorry, a lot on my mind . . . let's see. Those dias – Madame Salès must have them. Look, come into my office and I'll have a search – excuse me a moment."

What has happened? Well, nothing much; the enquiry into Monsieur Brun's adventures has ground to a halt for lack of evidence, and been replaced by the vaguer process of thinking that if valuable goods have been stolen they may surface eventually and be recognised.

This might now be the case: a Swiss gentleman in Lausanne rather thought he might – that's to say he found the offer dodgy. Couldn't verify without keeping, couldn't keep without paying – worried about being out of pocket and wanting to know about the insurance . . . He had been persuaded to send some photos. Cautious, tiresome. Brun has been asked to see whether he recognises . . . Wouldn't it have been simpler to send the rubbish to Lille? Yes, but the police like other people to take the trouble.

"Where has that projection machine got to, bonjour? Madame Morandière!" Bloody Carlotta is out and Castang stuck with it. She hates cases to go out of her hands, except into his . . .

The wretched Brun can't be sure and seeing Castang's irritation takes refuge in a welter of technicalities. If they were in poor condition there'd be any number of things recognisable. A scratch or area of thinning, fading; a pulled perforation, but you see these are good, and from photographs – he'd need to look at the real thing, with a glass.

"Well then," exasperated, "you'll have to go to Switzerland." And people wonder why criminal enquiries should be slow.

And thereafter more slowly still. The unhappy Brun ('I'm beginning to dread the very sound of his name') had made positive identifications, the man in Lausanne was persuaded; with much labour a trace had been made to lead back to a dealer in the Palais Royal. That's right: on our doorstep, here in Paris.

Castang had tried to get rid of the dossier then by turning it over to the criminal brigade. He wasn't going to sit outside no fucking antique shop waiting for signs of suspect characters.

The criminal brigade, equally stubborn that this was Fine Arts, didn't want to know. After learning to some surprise what a lot of money was involved they'd agreed grudgingly to lend Castang a trainee.

This boy had spent many hours in observation and had taken many photos. It doesn't do to imagine fancy work with microphones or whatever (this period had coincided with Maria's 'training' of Lydia). The PJ doesn't have this sophisticated equipment. Much too expensive! The best it can or will do is a lot of plodding and gazing (trainees are expendable) and maybe a camera with a long lens.

Until today. The criminal brigade had sent a batch of photos to Lille and Brun had got excited. He had after all seen his bandits; they hadn't been masked all the time. And true; among all the chalky old characters who frequent dingy little shops in the Palais Royal (rather an area for specialists in old weapons, antique uniforms, toy soldiers, things that chalky old gentlemen like to collect) a few of these chaps did look out of place.

Certainties, with photos taken at a distance, are less certain even than stamps; which at least stay still. It is not easy to get a recognisable close-up of someone walking in the street. Castang, sceptical about wishful-thinking, took a lot of persuading. Maybe they had something here. But what? Someone here today, gone tomorrow, hasn't been seen since. And then maybe some stamps. Which are locked up in a safe, and how to get a look at that?

"If I can once get a look," promised Brun, "I will be able to say with total certainty" – and at last the instructing judge had been persuaded to add a search warrant to his rogatory commission. Jesus, it had been easier with Dampierre.

But now the clinch had come – they hope. A small thin man, with a trace of Vietnamese blood, has been observed entering the shop a second (recorded) time. And Brun says he's certain. Now is this or isn't it the same man as one thought to be concerned in a robbery long on the books of PJ Orléans, carried out by the same method (tying people up with lots of sticky tape)?

"Get Brun up to Paris," Castang now tells Carlotta. "We'll have to go in to see." She is aghast. Not accustomed to this tough stuff.

Probably Castang would not have thus precipitated events. But he is fed up too with the hanging about, the caution, the inaction. He is in the mood for risk.

"If Brun has this chap rightly tagged," Castang was studying the photos on the desk, "he's a cobra. Carries a big gun, stuck it in Brun's face, jabbed him with it. I don't like him and I don't like his friends. Even around a tea table. We go in there together and you need a gun too."

"A gun!" said Carlotta appalled.

"I don't like them either but this is one time I do. Now don't be silly, you're a policewoman, you've been taught."

"I had to fire the stupid thing at school but I've never touched it since – I don't even have one."

"Jean-Marie will get you one." This is the trainee. He's solemn about it, brings it with enthusiasm, borrowed from a female colleague and guaranteed suitable to the hand and forearm of Madame le Commissaire. Utter bullshit, says Castang, it's a standard FN automatic, all he means is it isn't a magnum. Adequate weapon, though; he's dissolving with laughter at Carlotta wearing it, ruthless with her feeble protests: the female behind and this great Thing back of the hip. "Shiny-seated gabardine straining at the leash. Israeli settler in the disputed territories, standing no nonsense. Now d'you remember what you were taught about firing it?"

"No."

But at home Castang is serious, locks himself in the bathroom so that Vera won't see, to clean, oil and pull through his own long buried gun; an absolutely ordinary police-positive revolver. This is quite dangerous enough, automatics are too much so. As simple and reliable as you can get; Smith & Wesson. Thirtyeight calibre which is nine millimetre and quite enough too for his slight build. The thing is worn and shiny; he'd carried it a lot in the days when he had to. He isn't laughing at all while remembering a moment long ago in the Rue d'Aboukir, when he and a Paris colleague had had to winkle out a man hidden in the garment district and it had not been funny. Sharp and sudden and real bullets and no Western movie.

He can remember more times being shot at. Including the worst moment he has ever gone through, of being shot by another police officer. He has his jacket off and his sleeves rolled, and without wanting to think about it the fingers of his right hand are massaging the 'tennis elbow' of his left arm; shot to pieces by a three-fiftyseven magnum, reconstructed by plastic – very – surgery, and half crippled to this day; gives him a lot of pain in humid weather. Oh yes, he has the right to dislike guns. Not to underestimate them either.

"What on earth were you doing?" asks Lydia, as nosy as she is cheeky.

"Good God, can't a man even cut his toenails in peace?"

"Not so much the gun," he lectures Carlotta, "as the excess nervousness. A jeweller or these little toy-soldier shops, they feel vulnerable and one can understand it: they've valuable stocks and they're frightened, no matter how many electronic devices they have. What gets up my nose is they've all got guns – remember the baker's wife, up in Reims? So frightened she shot an Arab boy just for stealing a croissant."

They have arrived. The Palais Royal isn't far, and they've walked. Calming effect.

"Very well, we'll run over it again. Jean-Marie, your job is the door and the street, nobody in or out, not that there's going to be a crowd, stamp-shop isn't the supermarket but just in case of a customer you block them off, very quiet and tactful. Monsieur Brun stays out too until we give him the word to come and look at any stamps he might put his name to. Man, don't look so embarrassed. Carlotta, you're my back-up, you add authority to my timid and hesitant mien, because I play this as soft as I possibly can."

The Palais Royal is a quiet backwater between the Rue de Rivoli and the Opera boulevards; a quadrangle of classical colonnades. The interior courtyard, where children used to play, is nowadays bedizened with sticks of peppermint rock in varying heights. These are the notorious 'colonnes Buren', supposed to animate the dreary surroundings. The black-and-white colours have gone dingy and they can be seen as a sad fiasco. Neither Castang nor Carlotta would call them art. The upper stories are light and dignified, and might contain talent and imagination instead of government bureaux. The arcaded street level mingles obscure agencies and quiet, dark little shops. During the Regency this was the hot quarter, all bordels and gambling dens, but you are looking at it now and it's dullness personified. Without trees or children it is fossilised.

Castang pushed the door open looking intimidated, and the old man answering the bell's tinkle beamed upon them. What a nice couple. Plainly, not collectors. Looking for an investment no doubt, or perhaps just a present for Dad and Mum's wedding anniversary.

"Like to see some stamps," says Castang smiling. "But perhaps I ought to say first that we are police officers," unbuttoning his coat slowly: phony cops have been known to try this trick and he doesn't want the old man, now stiffened in a glare, to grab at any guns. So that the unbuttoning is very deliberate; papers are hauled out but he lets the old boy take a good look at his gunbelt too. "We have authority," showing his card, " – signed by a magistrate – to demand that you open your safe. We think it possible that you are holding certain items thought to have been acquired illegally. So we've brought along an expert, to check. This may take some time but we're in no hurry." And no doubt it would all have been a nice dull morning's work. But unbeknownst, melodrama comes to take a hand. It so often does.

There were protests, of course.

"In the case of immediate compliance," bland, "it will certainly be noted favourably that you made no obstruction. Just in case of a conceivable charge of harbouring." Carlotta is feeling reassured. No need of any guns. But Mama, there's a man coming. Line from a Brel poem; he makes it sound pretty sinister.

Light, quick footsteps on the pavement, swinging along quite uncaring. That almighty ass Jean-Marie – but he's only a boy and he loses his nerve: he has seen western movies but this is the slant-eyed-little-yellow-bastard in person and said to be very quick with his big gun. The other side of the doorway, Brun is making frightful grimaces. Luckily for himself Jean-Marie makes no move but the cop-smell is strong. The Vietnamese might have thought Brun's face familiar to him. He slipped into the shop, quick and noiseless, and said, "Freeze the door." The old man did too, remarkably quick but it is a commonplace electronic precaution.

Castang recognised him too.

"Hallo there," turning sideways to present a smaller target, "come to join the party?" Rustily, he is pulling his gun, but Castang isn't streetwise any more; far too slow. The little man – he is smaller than Castang – has the delicate, fragile-seeming Vietnamese hands but they are far quicker. Certainly he would have shot Castang then and there but for his being exactly in line with the old stampdealer. And a calibre that size goes right on through. He needs a moment to take it all in. Jean-Marie outside in a panic has his gun out like one o'clock struck, but the door is frozen. There is not much time, before the lunatic is ringing the fire brigade.

The professional takes in the scene while thinking ahead. There is a cop outside, and maybe two. The chief is this one here; a pro but oldish, a deskwatcher, no great problem. But a pro, so that is where you keep the eye. The woman is nothing; one of these females they have along to show they aren't racist. Perfectly true in the sense that Carlotta has never had the slightest interest in the muscular stuff. She did pass her exams in Lyon; oh dear, those hearty commando-instructors with fitness-obsessions. But any idiot can pass exams. She hadn't enjoyed leaping about obstacle courses. You do it, though. Concentrate, that's all. They'd been continually astonished that 'the intellectual' could also swarm walls. She concentrated now. Automatic pistols are dangerous things: remember the safety mechanisms.

Carlotta is dressed for economic crime; a Spanish trouser suit, dashing but rather tight. On account of the gun, a ridiculous raincoat. It has a fur collar! Castang had been sarcastic about this. 'And suppose it were to rain?' But there'd been more. One always listened carefully to instructors, looking bright and ready to give them feedback, because they liked that.

'Don't aim it. Just point it, loose as though it were your finger. If it ever comes to shooting, shoot as you point. Recall that it kicks up. Do it instinctive and keeping low; knee height is about right.'

"Now you can bring the gun out," smiling. "Hand open. Sugar for the horse. We'll take a walk now. You first. Lady next. Lady got a gun?"

"Yes," said Carlotta, shooting him.

She'd taken it all very literally and her reaction times are fast. She pointed it at his foot and near as possible missed him altogether, frightening herself badly when the thing went off twice because of pressing too hard. It was later established that she just touched the back of a knee ligament.

The results with high-velocity ninemillimetre ammunition are spectacular. Almost as good as casting the lasso round the shoulders of a nasty in a western, and jerking him clear off his feet. The gun skidded with a bang against the counter. Carlotta pointed hers at the old man's face, endangering the ceiling, and said, "No more guns, all right?"

"And unfreeze the door," said Castang climbing up with two guns. They looked at each other.

"Rest. Very good," exactly like the physical-training instructor after they'd done thirty stride jumps without getting out of breath. He didn't say anything sentimental like 'You probably saved my life'. You would never have guessed they'd ever been in bed together either. She uttered a high nervous giggle and handed him the gun. He looked silly holding three.

However, a reader familiar with Charles Dickens would have pounced on the ensuing scene. Wemmick and Mr Jaggers have been betrayed into a most unusual moment of softheartedness, and they take it out on the unfortunate Mike (whose sister has been picked up for shoplifting).

'What do you mean by coming in here snivelling like that?' bellows Wemmick. Mike protests that a man has his feelings.

'Get out of this office,' says Mr Jaggers. 'I'll have no feelings here.' In the event, it is the unhappy Jean-Marie.

"You're in the wrong fucking trade, boy, and I'll have a word to say to your commissaire about sending you out wet behind the ears."

"You great nin," said Carlotta.

"Good catch. Wanted by PJ Orléans. When the ambulance comes whip him off to Hôtel-Dieu." The Cusco ward; it's where they park the wounded villains. "Now how about opening this safe?"

Some parliamentary sessions are televised, in France, and a regular feature is Question Time on Wednesday afternoons, when Deputies get up to launch a barbed attack, and the responsible Minister is called upon to reply. Not a very edifying spectacle; a lot of catcalling. Quite amusing to watch, and Castang, having been tipped off did so. Those two lights of the right wing, Monsieur Piquemal and Monsieur Mauvoisin, divinely-appointed scourges of the Government, were in excellent voice.

Their favourite target is the Keeper of the Seals; title of the minister responsible for the administration of justice; lawcourts, also prisons, which bore him greatly, because he is a jurist, brought in to work at the aggiornamento of the legal codes. He is not a professional politician. He has not the languid manner, the debating skills, the expertise in sarcasms tinged with insult. He is lucid, earnest, honest; things no real Minister would ever dream of. He can be tart when pressed, and knows how to land an uppercut, but he hates the lions-den atmosphere of the Chamber, and the malevolent fiends snigger, because his hands tremble, holding the papers to which he will punctiliously refer, and it shows on camera, and Mauvoisin, that demagogue and noisy lout, loves that.

The lout conveys, in stinging tones, anxieties concerning a threatened miscarriage of justice; for a distinguished public figure, eminent this and that, is being persecuted and putatively framed by a socialist rabble of corrupt officials.

This suggestion was repudiated, quietly and with dignity. Piquemal leapt up with a supplementary. Were there or were there not improper methods employed by the police, for whom the Minister of the Interior is answerable?

That tough, lounging and sniggering three places along the front bench, scarcely bothers getting up. In a voice of extreme fatigue, fails to see anything which needs to be added to his colleague's vigorous reply. An unparliamentary gesture added; that of glee in pulling the plug upon Piquemal. Uproar. The incident was closed, by the President of the Assembly ringing his little bell.

But it was noticed, and commented upon, that whereas the Keeper had gone to bat for his subordinate, a judge unable to defend himself against injurious imputations because of the obligation-towards-reserve, the Minister of the Interior had not put himself to any trouble to exculpate a police officer.

Castang keeps the piece of cake with the cherry on it till last. This also holds good for the post; open the horrible ones first. He was in the office, reducing the stamps muddle to police prose, when the messenger brought him two envelopes.

The first was the standard small-brown with which the

administration of the French Republic defends itself against charges of wastefulness. We may have overspent by ten million francs upon cosmetic changes of ill-conceived nature, but we use recycled paper. He grimaced at a closely-typed page with the letterhead of the PJ's central hierarchy, and flipped to the second, because one always starts with the end of officialese: the content, if any, is expressed in the last two lines before the Distinguished Salutations.

This was brief and to the point.

> In accordance with the above findings you are hereby repri-
> manded. Together with the motivation for same the fact will
> be noted upon your dossier.

This civil-service euphemism conveys the end of a career. The signature was the usual squiggle over the official tampon identifying the Chef de Service, Section of Economic Affairs. Castang cannot remember ever having laid eyes upon him.

Oh well, that's that. He has been half-expecting something of the sort. A glance through the first page, bristly little paragraphs beginning 'Whereas . . .' showed that they hadn't pinned anything illegal on him. No suspension followed by a court of enquiry. This was purely an administrative measure based on the usual truck about good order and discipline, and would be meaningless but for being, to a middle-rank commissaire, the garage. There would be another note tomorrow transferring him to Archives, unless it was felt that the present corner was dusty enough to finish his days in.

Carlotta came in, possibly upon stamps business: he turned the letter towards her, making some flippant remark.

"Ditching you, are they? Sodomites." Through her job she has learned a lot about politics but like the Minister of Justice she does not sit easy with the politicians. "I still haven't made out what you did that was so awful."

"Made them conspicuous. That's the sin."

"You mean if there hadn't been all that fuss about – "

"That's right. They closed ranks around him, but can't afford to do that again, so soon after."

The reference is to that fast young commissaire, pride of the criminal brigades, chief of a sensitive territory in central Paris. It had been alleged that he was too friendly with known gangsters, though the implications of corruption were unsupported save by the evidence of prostitutes. Still, an austere judge of instruction had incriminated him on charges of malfeasance.

The defence was eloquent. The entire PJ apparatus was mobilised in solidarity with this brilliant subject: first in his class, at school, a born winner rapidly promoted. The judge, under heavy fire, refused to abandon the charges, and the ensuing trial had deliberately been turned into an acrimonious confrontation between magistrates, painted as amiable theorists knowing nothing of police realities, and the Syndicate of Commissaires, outraged at criticism of their time-honoured usage of informers.

The prostitutes, in plain fear for their skin, retracted their accusations before the tribunal. The Court acquitted him, distancing itself with some difficulty from any suggestion that the examining magistrate might have exceeded his brief.

A victory for the PJ? Yes; rather pyrrhic. The brilliant young commissaire would be unheard of for a number of years. The public was left with its already firm conviction that the police are a pack of crooks, thick-as-thieves with the real crooks who have more skill and less hypocrisy.

Pyrrhic especially for Castang, who has no close pals in the brigades, and perhaps too many among judges of instruction. Who has been told a few times already to keep his mouth shut. We don't like publicity. Especially not tales about television personalities who happen to be in the Academy. So a lot of commissaires of the grade just above him are finding him tarnished.

Is he even French, this chap? Germanophil, anglophil; does he really Belong? It's to be doubted. We're all very european nowadays and this means we've no time for anyone who doesn't grasp that our national territory has to be defended.

Has he strong supporters? Not a true Parisien, not one of Us; an obscure performer in the provinces, and a Czech wife, fuck That. Yes – the present Sous-chef for criminal affairs. That one is good at politics. Perhaps even over-supple; friends with absolutely everyone. We can bypass him, it is felt. For the Syndicate of Commissaires is a fairly powerful lobby in ministry corridors, and very rightwing indeed. We may have a leftwing Minister, but he is highly supple himself. Has a sensitive nose too. The other day, on television, did he stand up to defend his boy? Did he hell!

They looked at his book. Born in Paris, 'fortythree, obscure parentage, hum. School, bright boy, baccalaureat in 'sixtyone with a mention Good – bright, beuh. No money. Into the police as a street agent, detached and sent to the university as officer material. Degree, modern languages, law, police-school. Inspector – Paris, 'sixtyeight – Oh! Promoted to PJ 'seventy, detached PJ Regional-service, while on frontier work picked up this Czech – oh hell, who needs to read further?

Castang looked at his second envelope. A small one, white, containing a card. Printed invitation no doubt, artist's preview, cocktail, name filled in by secretary, generally miss-spelt.

Wrong! An engraved heading, and prim female handwriting.

Monsieur Castang is prayed to present himself at the office of the Director of Police Judiciaire, this morning at eleven precisely.

An honour! Having been officially reprimanded by some three-farthing rat in Economic Affairs, one is going to be guillotined by the Chief.

So we'd better go to that in style. He changed his shirt, looked at the tie he kept for previews, didn't like it, stopped in the Rue de Rivoli to buy a new one. "Blood colour, I think," to a frozenfaced counterman.

The Administration hates new offices, but likes spending a lot upon pomps. Thus Finance, unstuck from palatial apartments in the Louvre, moved upriver to new quarters where interior decorators excelled themselves. Finance recks not of a telling-off in next year's report from the Cour des Comptes: every piddling section chef has a table of polished granite full of gadgets to do his work. But the Quai des Orfèvres is a monument in French history, and no architect has done more than facelift the riverfront suites occupied by the biggest of the police biggies. They've done what they can with soundproofing and airfiltering, but a few microns of the smelly lower classes do keep sidling in.

The secretary is in her late forties, will never grow a day older, and looks as though just about to read the Six o'clock News on the BBC. She gave him a small smile, keyed her intercom, whispered "Monsieur Castang is here", and clicked her electronic doorlatch with a gracious little nod, like royalty through the window of the gold coach. All the historic clocks in the Ile de la Cité whirred and clashed and chimed and tinkled eleven, and Castang went to be guillotined.

A man got up, politely, from his desk by the big south window, and held out his hand. Polite yes, but completely impersonal. The hangman doesn't ask either how you feel this morning. The desk was of no polished stone nor rare wood intricately inlaid but was just a desk and the man was just a man: the suit looked Galeries Lafayette rather than Lanvin. Intelligent eyes but that is not a rare feature; good hair and teeth, which in France is. Commissaires of police come all shapes and sizes, and so do the graduates of the National School of Administration.

"Sit down." He sat himself, put his hands behind his neck to stretch his back, like any deskbound official. He looked at Castang for some time and now he looked like a cop. He smiled suddenly.

"You've got yourself in a scrape." Undramatic. "Like a cup of coffee? I'm having one. 'Coffee for two, Sara, please.' And so Paris is ringing with your exploits? You're a Baron Noir?" The Black Baron had been the pilot of a small private plane, whose night-time aerobatics over central Paris – a thing naturally most strictly forbidden – had caused consternation among security services. Rows of cops on high rooftops caught colds waiting for him to reappear.

"You made people look foolish. That'll never do."

A pretty young girl brought in the coffee. The service was Limoges, the only sign of luxury Castang saw. The electronics, the intelligence systems, the instant retrievals, were all in the outer office. The young girl poured out the coffee and brought Castang his cup.

"Smoke if you like." High heels showed off her excellent legs.

"Memories are short and Paris is provincial. In Madrid, this would have made three lines at the bottom of page seven.

"I'll put a question to you. In your view, which would be the more troublesome to me? The enticement of a well-known public figure, by a supposedly able and experienced PJ commissaire?

"Or a municipal agent of police in Montpellier? An oaf of two-three years' standing, who has been given a uniform and a big gun. And doubtless befuddled by apéritifs shoots an unarmed boy in the course of an identity check. Take an impersonal view." He is resting his elbow on the table, the coffeecup cradled in a well-shaped hand.

"Plainly, the first is the more troublesome. But the second is the more grave."

"Indeed. Why?"

"Because of the public. They may be stirred up about the literary gent, since the press and the television made much of it. But it doesn't touch them. The boy in Montpellier is one of themselves, and more to the point so is the oaf."

"Yes? Go on."

"I suppose it will be said that proves my political naïveté. I don't agree," getting warmer. "What is called politically expedient is always short-term. Your first case looks bad, but less superficially it's the second which is bad, because the people take it instinctively to heart."

"Unfortunately for yourself, it's the first that carries the immediate political consequences."

"I'll have to live with them, won't I."

"I'll have to live with them too," mildly.

"But you're telling me, in a civilised way, that I'll have to bear the blame." The Director put down the coffeecup with a clink and showed an unexpected grin.

"You are fortunate. A man in a high position, himself contemptuous of what you term short-sighted politics, has urged that you be penalised no further." He knows about the reprimand, thought Castang.

"I came to this post from the Directorate of Criminal Affairs. In that capacity, I wouldn't want to employ you. I wouldn't sleep well at night, wondering when you'd bring a charge of corruption against the Prefect.

"Nor can you be continued in an active role in the Paris area. Even in your present obscurity which – as I gather – was merited by a run-in with the political branch. There are too many people about with rancorous memories.

"Fortunately – and I now apply this word to myself – I have discovered a bolthole. Politics – we're alone here; there's no tape" – ah, he knows too about the tape – "is finding space enough to manoeuvre.

"It's not a hole one pushes bolts into," illustrating with his hands. "I wouldn't be sure the bolt would stay pushed," stinging. "Nor is it a hole with no air or light. Cupboards, we've plenty of cupboards. You're in one now. I don't believe you rate a cupboard. That is why I asked to see you; it was to make up my mind.

"Mm, the Minister; he's keen to bring to completion this project for reform of the penal codes. Parallel to various enactments of our partners in the Community.

"These of course are in practice what they always are, compromises achieved, laboriously, by committees.

"To put an end to speculation there's a slot in Bruxelles. We've a professor of jurisprudence there. And any number of people with a lot to say about international law. What's lacking, right now, is someone with pragmatic experience of penal affairs. This is a relatively minor advisory post. It's in my gift. After listening to you, I don't think I want you buried in la Corrèze. I'll offer it to you. I'd advise you to take it."

Castang lit a little cigar, and watched as the air-conditioning took hold of the smoke and suppressed it.

"I'll take it."

The Director's face did not change.

"Your character interests me." An indifferent tone. "You don't accuse me of castrating you."

"Are you?"

"I rather think not. Temperamentally you might be quite a good candidate. You have other qualifications too, for a post which might be less silly than it sounds. For myself, I won't be wondering what the hell you're getting up to. Bluntly, I'll be happy to be rid of you. But I think you might make something of it. You haven't so much as asked what it pays.

"Might suit your wife, too." Well! thought Castang; there seems not to be much you haven't enquired into. "So since you haven't asked, this post carries the rank of divisional commissaire. We must maintain a certain prestige. It is as you realise a symbolic status, since the authority is more nominal than real.

"Still, it's money, isn't it. And you may be departmentally disqualified, but they won't know that in Bonn. There are also," wooden, "a number of perks and privileges. All right, Monsieur le Divisionnaire?" standing up; holding out his hand. "Let me be the first to congratulate you upon your promotion."

"So you are losing me," he said to Carlotta. She was sitting at her desk being the forceful executive, with two piles divided into Ins and Outs, initialling 'CLS' on the never-ending paper: firm pretty hand, Sheaffer pen, strong black handwriting. More than ever, he is grateful to her. "I'm only conscious that they'll give you some other bum, that the Director wants disgraced.

"I'm not getting shot this time, even if they knocked off the leg irons and brought me out in the courtyard. I'm getting slightly castrated, it's true." Her eyes grew enormous, looking at him, but she said nothing.

"I was hauled up before the big chief. So I'll not – ever – have a criminal brigade of my own. But to sweeten the pill while firing me, there's a bureaucrat job in Belgium. When we want to extradite a terrorist, I'll be the one filling in forms in Danish. I've also had a reprimand put on the book. The Chef likes a sense of balance in his estimates. Little touch of politics here, little moral scruple there."

"I had decided not to mention it," said Carlotta. "A rocket came down from the Inspectorate, inviting me to comment upon your competence and personal morals. So I marked E for Excellent and apposed my initials," doing so as she spoke.

"Very good of you," said Castang gravely. "In view of that, and considering that this post carries the rank of divisional commissaire, I'll take you to lunch, shall I, and we'll have some champagne?"

"Since you are now my superior officer," getting up, "your offer is an order. Any other orders? – I'll obey mechanically."

"Flowers on the table," she said in the restaurant. "Cocktails. I do believe, in Brussel a lot of whisky flows. You can have a Mercedes car. And a pretty secretary."

"Want the job?" asked Castang.

"But don't forget," said Carlotta over coffee, "the things you learned here. About pictures, you know. You know, I'd like to ask you back to the flat. Am I a bit too drunk, d'you think?"

"I am though," he said.

Vera took the news well. Her paler, narrower, northern eyes grew as big as Carlotta's. Thinking of Bruxelles anyone's mind turns to a Brel poem, and hers to the one which has been in the back of his mind for some time now.

> Look well out, child, look well out.
> Across the plain, over there
> At the height of the reeds. . .
> There's a man who is coming
> Whom I do not know.

Just as he might have found the answer in the second verse:

> Not at all; only the wind
> Lifting a little the sand.

But Lydia, delighted at the prospect of champagne which she is now old enough to share, bursts out singing: the one with the whisky voice and the dotty accordeon accompaniment . . .

> "T'as voulu voir Vierzon
> Et on a vu Vierzon."

I went to see Vesoul/And now I've seen Vesoul.

> "I wished to see your sister,
> Instead I saw your mother.
> It's always the same."

Oh yes, definitely.

While Lydia insists that it's going to be her, miss bossyboots, who opens the bottle, Castang is wondering whether really his career is finished.

While Vera, watching the child's fingers untwisting the wire, wonders whether perhaps his and hers have just barely started.

But it was weeks later. It had stretched into months and